Lover
and Thief

Books by Arthur Maling

Lover and Thief
A Taste of Treason
From Thunder Bay
The Koberg Link
The Rheingold Route
Lucky Devil
When Last Seen *(Editor)*
Shroeder's Game
Ripoff
Bent Man
Dingdong
The Snowman
Loophole
Go-Between
Decoy

Lover
and Thief

Arthur Maling

1817

HARPER & ROW, PUBLISHERS, New York
Cambridge, Philadelphia, San Francisco, Washington
London, Mexico City, São Paulo, Singapore, Sydney

FIRST EDITION

Copyeditor: Marjorie Horvitz
Designer: Erich Hobbing

Library of Congress Cataloging-in-Publication Data

Maling, Arthur.
  Lover and thief.

  I. Title.
PS3563.A4313L68   1988   813'.54   87-45645
ISBN 0-06-015857-3

---

88 89 90 91 92 RRD 10 9 8 7 6 5 4 3 2 1

Lover
and Thief

1

"This is Calvin Bix," I said, "returning your call."

"Thank God," said Anita Danton. She sounded as if she'd had a rough night.

I frowned at the coffee percolator, which was taking a long time. My own night hadn't been so great, either. I'd spent six cold hours in my car, parked outside the house of the foolish daughter-in-law of a very dangerous man, waiting for her to sneak out and make a dash for her boyfriend's apartment. Waiting in vain.

"You said it's important," I reminded Anita Danton. According to my answering service, she'd left three messages. The first said, "Please call as soon as possible"; the second, "Urgent"; and the third, "Must speak with you at once."

"It is," she said now, with fervor. "It is indeed. I need your help, Mr. Bix. I'm simply beside myself. I've been robbed."

The coffee finally began to perk. I cradled the telephone between shoulder and ear, poured, and said, "Who gave you my name, Mrs. Danton?"

"My lawyer. Gordon Lockhart. Lockhart, Fratern, Ney and Wright. You've done work for them, he said. You're the premier private investigator in Chicago."

I took a sip of coffee. I'd been classified in many ways, but "premier" was a new one.

"He said you should call him if there's any question," she added.

Lockhart, Fratern, Ney and Wright represented some of Chicago's top companies and richest citizens. Although I'd never met Lockhart, I'd had dealings with a couple of his partners. They'd recommended me to corporate clients. In one case I'd discovered which engineer was selling company secrets to the Japanese; in another I'd checked out candidates for a division vice-presidency.

"Robbed of what?"

"Some of my jewelry. Three valuable pieces. I know who took them. What I want is for you to find him and make him give them back. Please, Mr. Bix. I'm just crushed."

"Have you notified the police?"

A pause was followed by, "Not yet. I'll explain when I see you. You will help me, won't you? I don't know where else to turn."

I tried to draw conclusions from the voice, but couldn't. It was like too many others I'd listened to over the years, the voices of people who were suddenly faced with ugly situations and were overwhelmed. Anxiety was what these voices conveyed. Come quickly. Do something. Solve my problem.

"Is the jewelry insured? Have you reported the loss?"

"It is, but I haven't, because I don't want anyone to know. Really, it's so hard to explain on the phone. If you'll come over . . ."

The situation was always one that couldn't be discussed by telephone, that required a personal meeting.

"Where do you live, Mrs. Danton?"

She gave me the address. It was eighteen-karat Gold Coast.

I thought about the foolish daughter-in-law, whose name was Babette Mantino. I wondered whether I could turn that surveillance over to Frank Norris.

"All right," I said to Anita Danton. "I'll be there in about an hour."

She groaned with relief. "Oh, thank you, Mr. Bix! Thank you *so* much!"

I put down the telephone, finished my coffee, and called Gordon Lockhart.

Danton, I thought as I waited for the lawyer to finish the conversation he was having with somebody else. The name was familiar, and yet I couldn't place it. Socialite? Businesswoman? Who?

At last Lockhart came on the line. "Yes, Bix," he said in the flat, matter-of-fact tone that a lot of lawyers use when they want to keep their distance. Those lawyers who don't like having to resort to private investigators.

"I've just finished talking to Anita Danton," I said. "You referred her?"

"I did. She's both client and friend."

"What, exactly, is the problem?"

"Didn't she tell you?"

"Only in a general way."

"I can't help you with the details, I'm afraid. As I understand it, some of her jewelry is missing. She believes it was stolen by an acquaintance of hers."

"She says she hasn't called the police or her insurance company."

"Because of the personal factor. She isn't eager to press charges. All she wants is to get the jewelry back."

"I see." The situation wasn't unusual. I'd dealt with others like it, including one in which the thief was the victim's son. "And Mrs. Danton is someone who owns a lot of jewelry?"

"Mrs. Danton is the widow of Howard Danton," Lockhart said irritably. Being the widow of Howard Danton, I gathered, was like being the Big Dipper or the Southern Cross—everybody is supposed to have heard of you. "Danton Realty. And her father was Stanford Wales. Wales Stores."

3

Suddenly it came to me. I'd seen Anita Danton's name recently in the newspapers. In connection with a fund-raising event. "Isn't she on committees?"

"Many." Lockhart's irritation vanished. "With you, I feel, she's in safe hands."

"Thanks." I didn't tell him that she wasn't in my hands yet, that I intended merely to listen to her story, that one of the reasons for my success was I knew which cases to turn down.

"Good luck." Lockhart paused. "Live up to your reputation."

And that was that. A moment later he was no longer on the line.

I drank one more cup of coffee and went into the bathroom to shower and shave. I was beginning to feel reasonably cheerful.

The premier private investigator in Chicago, I thought as I went out onto the balcony to check the weather. Well, maybe I am.

Even by November standards, the weather was bad. A gusty wind was blowing in from the northeast at perhaps twenty miles an hour, the sky was slate-colored, and the temperature was in the high teens.

Nevertheless I stood there for a couple of minutes, hands on the iron railing, surveying from twenty stories up my sector of the city. It took in a lot of territory—park, lagoon, zoo, lake, and the back of the high-rises that faced Lake Shore Drive. I'd bought the condo, after my marriage broke up, mainly because of the view. The apartment itself was nothing special—living room, bedroom, kitchen; no frills—but the panorama was grand.

From where I stood I could see the street on which Anita Danton lived. Also the streets that paralleled and crossed it. I knew this area of the city better than any other, not just because I lived in it but also because many of my former clients did too. Much of my work consisted of gathering evidence to be used in contested divorce cases, and while the divorce rate is no higher on Chicago's Near North Side than anywhere else in the city, it's more profitable. I'd spent an awful lot of hours tracking husbands and wives from their apartments on Lake Shore Drive and the nearby side streets to wherever they met their lovers. Adultery isn't the awful sin it once was, but it still means big bucks in certain divorce settlements and custody fights.

As in the Mantino case, which involved an eight-year-old boy as well as money.

Chilled, I went inside. I slipped the Leica into my pocket so that I could give it to Frank Norris if I decided to use him. Then I dismissed the Mantino family from my mind, put on my topcoat, and got ready to meet the woman who claimed her friend had stolen her jewelry.

Her house was an authentic-looking Venetian palazzo that, instead of fronting on the Grand Canal, faced two leafless locust trees and a string of cars parked bumper to bumper. Unlike other houses on the block, it wasn't a consulate, hadn't been converted into apartments, didn't enjoy landmark status. Where a gondola should have been tied to a pole there was a little tin sign that said the property was protected by the Tremaine Security Service.

The front door opened so soon after I rang the bell that I guessed Anita Danton had been standing with one hand on the knob, waiting for me to show up.

"Mr. Bix!" she exclaimed. "Come in. Oh, do come in."

Three excited Yorkshire terriers rushed about, barking.

I crossed the threshold, which, I noted, was monitored by an electric eye. The dogs sniffed my shoes from all angles. A maid appeared from a Gothic-shaped doorway at the far end of the foyer. She was elderly and walked with a slight limp. Her gray hair was braided around her head into a sort of halo. She took my coat.

"We'll go upstairs to the library," Anita Danton said. She was wearing lots of eye makeup, three gold bracelets, and a blue wool housecoat with a mink collar.

I followed her across the black and white marble floor to the curved staircase, admiring the art pieces. I guessed that they were expensive, but didn't really know; two years with the U.S. Army in Germany hadn't turned me into a connoisseur. Still, as, accompanied by the dogs, we walked along the balcony at the top of the stairs, I saw enough jade, ivory, and silver knickknacks to make me admire the thief's restraint. He could have got away with much more than three pieces of jewelry.

We entered the library, a walnut-paneled room with two leaded windows in one wall and bookshelves in the others.

"Now then," Anita Danton said, "sit down and listen to the story of a sadly deceived woman."

I settled into a wing chair. One of the dogs settled on my foot.

"Sadly deceived," I thought. Like "premier." I wondered whether Anita Danton talked that way all the time or only when she was upset.

That she was upset was beyond doubt. The makeup didn't mask the shadows under her eyes. Nor did the forced brightness disguise the tremor in her voice. This lady was distressed.

But on the other hand, there was something actressy about her. She didn't find it easy, I suspected, to be herself under any circumstances.

"You live here alone?" I asked.

She seated herself on a cane-backed chair with spindly legs, but immediately got up to take a cigarette from a silver box on the desk. "I hope you don't mind if I smoke."

I shook my head.

She lit the cigarette and sat down again. "Except for the help, I do. Since last summer, that is. Until then my daughter lived with me, but she has her own apartment now."

"And the help consists of?"

"Helga and Sonia. Helga's the one you saw. Sonia's the cook. They're sisters. They've been with me for eons."

"And the jewelry that's missing? Three pieces, you said."

"My diamond and sapphire necklace and the matching earrings."

"Valued at how much?"

"I don't know for sure. My insurance man has the appraisal. Between seventy-five and a hundred thousand dollars, I'd say. At least."

"And nothing else is gone?"

"I was wearing my ring. He couldn't get that."

"He being who, Mrs. Danton?"

Her expression became tragic. "His name is Peter Ives. I should have known better. I thought . . . I thought . . . I'm a fool, but I thought . . ." She shook her head.

I waited for her to go on.

Presently she said, "I'm going to tell you the worst first, Mr. Bix. Think what you will. Peter's younger than I. Considerably younger. I closed my eyes to that. I was fond of him. I still am. One doesn't get over being fond of people right away, does one? Even when they've betrayed you."

"How old is this Ives, then?"

She concentrated on stubbing out her cigarette. "Thirty."

I marveled in silence. Anita Danton was brushing fifty.

"I know what you're thinking," she went on, "and you're right. It was one of those things, though. I became . . . fond of him."

"You saw a lot of each other?"

She nodded.

"What does he do for a living?"

"He's an actor."

"Professional? Member of Equity and all?"

"Oh, yes!" She seemed pleased to have found something positive to say about him. "He's been in several commercials, including the one for Barley Bran in which the man's mowing the lawn. You might have seen it. Anyway, yes, he works when he can. You know how it is with actors."

"How did the two of you meet?"

"At a party. I don't suppose you're acquainted with Laura McKay? She's an interior decorator. We're friends, and she gives the most interesting parties of anyone I know. Peter was there with Janet Fleming, the agent. Those are the kind of people you meet at Laura's. People who do unusual things. Fun people."

I said nothing. I knew Laura McKay from way back, however. She'd been one of my early clients. I'd tracked down a couple that had skipped town owing her a bundle.

"Just before he moved here," Anita Danton continued, "Peter almost got the part of the intern on *Family World*. The only reason he didn't is because the woman who writes it insisted that the intern should have a square jaw and Peter's is more oval. Ridiculous, isn't it, but that's fate. If Peter's jaw had been squarer, he'd have stayed in New York and we never would have met."

"What makes you think he's the one who stole your necklace and earrings?"

Her expression had become sunnier, but now the clouds closed in again. "Because he's the only one who knew where I put them."

"Oh?"

She went to the desk for another cigarette.

"Why don't I begin at the beginning," she said when she returned.

The beginning had to do with the Orchestral Ball, which had taken place the preceding Saturday night and had been, as she put it, gala. Also with the bank. She kept her jewelry in a safe-deposit box, and the bank was closed on weekends, so she'd taken the jewelry out on Friday and had planned to put it back on Monday.

Peter had been her escort at the ball. He'd brought her home and had spent the night with her. He'd seen her hide the jewelry in her shoe.

"Your *shoe?* Shoes are the first place thieves look."

"It's not like you think," Anita Danton assured me. "Let me show you."

The sadly deceived woman, her three Yorkshire terriers, and I went from the library to the bedroom. On the way we

8

passed some more nice paintings and art objects.

The bedroom was on the third floor and extended across the entire front of the house. Its color scheme was lilac, silver, and white. Everything harmonized. Even the cabinet that housed the television set had a silver-leaf finish.

"Nice," I said, taking it all in.

"Laura did it for me," Anita Danton said. "After my husband died." With a sweeping gesture she indicated a long wall of sliding doors. "That's what I mean. And there are more closets around the corner in the dressing room." She slid open two of the doors. "My shoes."

Both closets had floor-to-ceiling shelving designed specifically for footwear. I made a quick estimate. Seventy pairs.

She pointed. "I put my necklace and earrings in the black oxford there. The left one."

"Your usual place?"

"I don't have a 'usual' place, Mr. Bix. A precaution my husband taught me to take. Sometimes I don't put my jewelry in a shoe at all; I roll it up in a pair of panty hose or fold it into one of my slips."

"But you're positive that this time . . . ?"

"Absolutely. And Peter saw me do it."

"Occasionally people get absentminded, Mrs. Danton. I've had cases like that. What someone thought was missing—"

"I'm not forgetful, Mr. Bix. And I turned this room upside down. Every drawer. Every shelf. Until I was ready to drop. If you're not going to believe me . . ."

She didn't say what she would do if I didn't believe her. It didn't matter, though. I was getting convinced. She hadn't forgotten where she'd put her necklace and earrings; she'd merely brought the wrong elements into contact—sapphires, diamonds, and a struggling actor young enough to be her son.

"When did Peter leave?"

"Sunday. After brunch. He must have had the jewelry in his pocket."

"And when did you miss it?"

"Yesterday. I went to get it to take it to the bank, and it wasn't there."

"It was a mistake not to call for help right away."

Anita Danton gazed into my eyes. "Do you believe in temporary insanity, Mr. Bix?"

I didn't answer.

"Well, I do," she went on. "And yesterday that's what I was: temporarily insane. If only you'd seen me! Every shelf. Every drawer. Places I hadn't looked in years. On the floor, on a ladder, and on the telephone. Oh, God, was I on the telephone! I don't know how many times I dialed Peter's number. Forty, fifty, eighty. Twice I went to his apartment. Nobody was home. In between, I kept calling. I was utterly manic. Utterly. In the closet one minute, on the telephone the next, then back to the closet. Until finally I pulled myself together enough to get in touch with Gordon. Which was what I should have done in the first place, but I was simply too distraught. I mean—Peter! After all we'd done together, all we'd shared. To have stolen from me, to have robbed me. I was—take my word for it, Mr. Bix—temporarily insane."

It was a good performance. I enjoyed it. And it was too hammy not to be true.

"Where does Peter live, Mrs. Danton?"

She gave me his address. He lived a couple of miles north, in the Lincoln Park area.

"Do you have a picture of him?"

She went to an antique white commode and took some photographs from the top drawer.

I studied them. They were artistic shots, dramatically lighted; the kind of photographs actors and models carry with them to auditions and job interviews. In one, Ives was wearing a toreador outfit. In another, he was a cowboy. In a third, he had on a leather vest that revealed his bare chest. In all of the pictures he was a handsome man with a lean face, dark hair, and high cheekbones. The toreador outfit seemed to suit him best—he really did look Spanish in it—

but all three getups appeared to be right for him. I had the odd feeling that Peter Ives was not one individual but several.

"May I keep these?" I asked.

"If they'll help," Anita Danton replied.

We went down to the ground floor. I checked the front and back doors for evidence of forced entry. As I'd expected, there wasn't any. I also spent a few minutes talking with Helga and Sonia. Had they noticed anything out of place? Anything missing?

They hadn't, they said. All the silver was accounted for. All the everything.

Neither woman was a fan of her employer's boyfriend. When I mentioned his name, Helga pursed her lips and Sonia gave a disapproving snort.

I didn't throw a lot of effort into the I'm-a-detective routine. I didn't think it was called for. What with the electric eye, the security service, and the yappy dogs, I believed it unlikely that a burglar could have got into the house and up to the third floor without being caught, even with Ives's assistance.

Anita Danton was right, in my opinion. Ives had walked out of the house Sunday afternoon with her necklace and earrings in his pocket. Essentially, this was a simple case.

Joining her in the library, where she'd waited while I was in the kitchen, I said, "I want to be honest with you. I'm expensive, Mrs. Danton, and I don't think you need me."

Her shoulders sagged. "Oh, don't say that! I do need you. The cost doesn't matter."

"You'd be better off going to the police. They've got computers; they're hooked up to the entire world."

"I can't go to the police, Mr. Bix. What would people say?"

And there it was, the core of her problem. Fear of publicity, of gossip, of ridicule. Middle-aged woman, younger man. Socialite robbed by youthful escort. Serves her right.

"It wouldn't necessarily be picked up by the press," I said.

"People wouldn't necessarily find out."

"But they might. My daughter. My brother. All my friends."

I wanted to say, "You're the victim, lady, not the criminal. What's to be ashamed of?" I knew she wouldn't see it that way, though, so I said, "The problem is, forty-eight hours have gone by since Ives left here. By now he could be in Brazil, in Hong Kong, anywhere. With your jewelry."

Her shoulders sagged even more. "There's no hope, then?"

"I didn't say that, Mrs. Danton. I said he could be. I've dealt with other situations like this. I've been successful with them. It isn't easy for an amateur to dispose of expensive, identifiable jewelry. He needs contacts and generally doesn't have them."

Her eyes lit up. She nearly smiled. "You *will* help me?"

I hesitated. I'd told her the truth. Pro and con. If she still wanted to hire me . . .

"Yes," I said. "I'll see what I can do."

Anita Danton clasped her hands. "You're a dear, dear man! You really are. How much of a retainer would you like?"

Ten minutes later, her check in my pocket, I was on the way to my office to arrange for Frank Norris to take over the Mantino surveillance.

2

Frank arrived shortly before noon, eyebrows and all. He was a big, jowly man with thick, shaggy eyebrows that, like the hair on his head, were turning white. They gave him a look of fierceness. He reminded me somehow of an angry Saint Peter.

"O.K.," he declared as he took off his plaid wool jacket and hunter's cap. "I'm here. What's the big deal?"

His question, I guessed, was prompted by the fact that over the telephone I'd said I had a job for him but hadn't specified what it was. Usually I laid everything out right away.

He hung his jacket and cap on the coat tree and deposited himself on the visitor's chair. Noticing the camera on my desk, he said, "Holy shit! The Leica?"

I nodded. "For you. On loan."

He shook his head. "I don't think I want this job."

"You'll love it," I assured him.

Picking up the little camera, he examined it with interest. I'd described it to him, but this was the first time he'd ever seen it. "James Bond," he said, "move over; make room for Frank Norris."

I watched him sight through the lens. "There's film in it," I said.

The Leica was one of the few extraordinary tools I allowed myself. It did, literally, have an espionage history. I'd bought it from a former CIA agent I'd got acquainted with in Fort Lauderdale. I'd gone there for a short vacation, and he'd gone there to die, done in not by the KGB but by advanced cancer of the bone marrow. When he learned that I was a private investigator, he decided that we had something in common and told me about himself. He also sold me the camera, which he said he wouldn't be needing any longer. It had been altered by an expert he knew in Singapore. Although not exactly miniature, it was small enough to fit easily into the palm of your hand, and it turned out marvelous photographs.

"What am I supposed to take pictures of?" Frank asked.

"Adultery," I replied.

"Whose?"

"A woman named Babette Mantino. The wife of Allen Mantino."

"Isn't he related to . . . ?"

"The youngest son."

Frank put the camera down. "How do you *find* these cases, Cal?"

"I don't find them," I said. "They find me. The guy's lawyer called me, told me the story. I went to see the guy, I liked him, I said O.K. I've been working on it a week. But this morning I got another case I want to spend time on, and I need someone to spell me on Mantino. Besides, I think the woman might have spotted me—she's been cagey the past couple of days. You she's never seen."

"Contested divorce?"

"Right. And she has no grounds. He's the one with grounds. Unless he can prove it, though . . ."

"But his old man . . ."

"That's why he's using me, Frank. He's afraid of what his old man might do to the woman if she wins."

14

"An unexpected face-lift with a razor," Frank speculated. "A hysterectomy with a switchblade."

"Possibilities," I agreed. "Bear Mantino is a proud man. Family honor is important to him. And he's crazy about his grandchildren. It's bad enough that a son and daughter-in-law of his are separated. If he finds out that the reason they're separated is because his daughter-in-law is cheating on his son, and if she gets away with it—gets custody of the kid and the two-million-dollar settlement she's asking for—a nasty crime is liable to be committed."

"And the son wants to *protect* the woman who's cheating on him?"

"Yes, that's part of it. He's a decent guy, Frank. He *does* want to keep his wife from being hurt, although there's more to it than that. He also wants custody of his son. He doesn't want the boy to be raised by his wife and whoever she happens to shack up with. And of course he isn't eager to part with two million bucks, either."

Frank nodded thoughtfully. He'd spent several years on the police department's organized-crime squad and knew a lot about individual members of the Syndicate. He knew that Sal Mantino, nicknamed Bear because of his size and strength, could be a deadly enemy. Also that Bear was at the top of Chicago's loan-shark and extortionist hierarchy, with links to criminals throughout the country. But at the same time he knew that men like Bear Mantino were capable of producing law-abiding offspring and often did just that.

"What's with the wife?" he asked. "She have a death wish? A zero IQ? What?"

"May queen, cheerleader, president of her sorority . . . you name it. The trouble is, she's won too many elections. She thinks she's so desirable that the rules don't apply to her. Reading between the lines, I'd say she married Allen to spite her parents, who didn't think she should. Now she's tired of him and she's got it into her head that any judge, any jury, will side with her because of her father-in-law's reputation. In which she's right; a lot of them would; any son of Bear

Mantino's has got to be a creep. Want some lunch?"

"If you're buying. But what about the other guy, the guy who's laying her?"

I smiled. "Cellist in a string quartet."

Frank's eyebrows rose. The effect was dramatic.

"Honest to God," I said. "A cellist. I don't think he has the slightest idea who she really is or what he's fooling around with."

"Someone ought to call him up, tell him if he's not careful he's liable to wind up with his balls in his coat pocket."

"I've thought of that. But it wouldn't help Allen's case. Come on, let's go to lunch."

We went to the coffee shop in the building where my office is. The food wasn't great—it never is—but Frank seemed to enjoy his hot roast beef sandwich with mashed potatoes and gravy. As the meal progressed, he mellowed. He told me about his older daughter, who was due to give birth in a few weeks. The doctor had decided to do a caesarean, and Frank was worried. They don't decide to do caesareans when everything is going all right, he said. And it wasn't as if this was her first child—she'd already had two in, as he put it, the normal way. Why couldn't she have this one in the normal way too?

Nor was his daughter's condition his only concern. He'd just received an asshole letter, he told me, from the owners' association of the complex in Florida where he had his condo. In the interest of economy, the letter said, the association had voted not to heat the community swimming pool during the months of December, January, and February.

"The coldest fucking months of the year," Frank complained bemusedly as he jabbed his fork into a slice of cherry pie, "and no heat in the pool. A bunch of idiots is what they are. Morons."

"Sounds like it," I agreed. "When are you going down there?"

"Soon as Maureen has the baby."

For a moment I felt envy. Frank was leading a good life.

16

What with his pension from the police department, his Social Security, and the money he picked up free-lancing with me and others like me, he was able to winter in Florida and keep a small sailboat in Wisconsin for summer weekends. He'd been contentedly married for thirty-five years and had raised four nice children. Now he was cashing in. Being rewarded. He was a lucky man.

I also felt affection. Despite his outward gruffness, he was good-hearted. He'd seen the worst that people could be and do, and it hadn't soured him. He wasn't a burned-out case like so many policemen and ex-policemen. What's more, he was perfectly suited for jobs like the one I was giving him. He had patience. Brains help, but what you really need as a detective is the ability to stand on a sidewalk for hours, regardless of weather, with your eyes focused on a particular doorway, or to spend an entire day in a government office, looking through old records, without going bonkers.

"About this Mantino woman," he said presently. "The cello player—is he the only one?"

"No," I said. "There've been others, and maybe still are. But right now he's the main one. I've followed her to his apartment twice, but I haven't been able to get the sort of evidence that would stand up in court. It's just a matter of time, I think, of the right moment. Anyway, he doesn't go to her place, she goes to his. It's in an old-fashioned three-story walk-up, the kind with the back staircase on the outside of the building. The back stairs lead to an open porch on each floor, and each porch has a door to the kitchen and a window. You can see into the kitchen through the window, but you can't see into the bedroom, and that's the problem."

Frank wiped his mouth and dropped the napkin onto the table with a flourish. "O.K. I understand. Leave it to me."

We returned to my office. I gave him the addresses of Babette Mantino and the cellist. Then I showed him how the camera worked, and he lumbered off.

I continued to sit at my desk for a few minutes, wondering how things would have turned out if I'd stayed in the police department instead of quitting after three years to start my own business. Would I have become another Frank Norris? Probably not, I decided. I still would have been me. But I wouldn't be divorced. Phyllis had been happy as the wife of a policeman, miserable as the wife of a self-employed private investigator who was doing well. Even now she socialized mainly with the wives of men I'd known on the force. I would never be able to understand it. Most women want their husbands to get ahead, but Phyllis had wanted hers to stay behind. Upward mobility scared her.

After a while I shook off those thoughts. Leaving the office, I got my car out of the garage and headed north to pick up the trail of Peter Ives.

The Lincoln Park district is a little bit of everything. The eastern edge of it, which borders the park, the marinas, and Lake Michigan, is lined with high-rise apartment buildings that are almost as classy now as they were a generation or two ago, when they were built. But west of them the demographics have changed. Buildings that used to house Rotarians and Elks with their PTA wives and home-before-dark children now house a mixed bag of singles and two-income couples from many walks of life. Young lawyers, X-ray technicians, hairstylists, and department store buyers live side by side with middle-level drug pushers, pimps, and other types who tend to get nervous whenever they see a squad car coming their way.

Ives's building was halfway down a very long block that was yuppie at one end and welfare at the other. Flanked by a pair of old walk-ups that had seen better days, it was a bare-bones structure, four stories tall, with a yellow brick facade, rows of exactly alike windows, and no trim of any kind. It looked like an institution.

A decal on the front door said: DELIVER ALL GOODS IN REAR. Another, on the glass panel beside the door, said: NO PETS. Except for a business card that an ambitious entrepreneur had attached to the wall above the mailboxes, the vestibule was as unadorned as the building's exterior. The card said "George Pappas, Expert Tailoring." Evidently Pappas wasn't a tenant, however; his name didn't appear on the directory.

The directory was arranged by apartment number. Each listing had a button next to it, and there was a speaking tube at the top. A quick glance at the names showed how the population mix of the city was changing. Under O'Boyle and Lindquist were Gupta and Hakim. Washington and Driscoll were separated by Chang.

Ives, I noted, occupied apartment 2-C. I pushed the button and waited. Nothing happened.

I peered into Ives's mailbox. It was hard to see through the narrow slits, but I spotted several envelopes.

The glass door between the vestibule and the inner lobby was locked. To get beyond the vestibule you had to be buzzed in by a tenant or use a key. I decided to wait a few minutes and see what turned up. Meanwhile, I would check the parking area.

It was L-shaped, with stalls along the west side of the building and across the back. The stalls had numbers that corresponded to the apartment numbers. A handmade sign said that the parking spaces were for tenants only; violators would be toed by the Zeus Towing Co. Whoever had done the lettering had left the *w* out of "towed."

I'd heard of Zeus Towing. A bad outfit, people said. Commando tactics.

The stall marked "2-C" was located behind the building and was vacant.

I returned to the vestibule and waited to get lucky.

It was a short wait. In less than five minutes I was in the automatic elevator, holding the grocery bag of a fluttery old lady who'd had trouble removing her keys from her pocketbook without dropping the groceries. I'd offered assistance, and we'd entered the inner lobby together. I was so kind, she'd said gratefully. It hadn't occurred to her to ask what I was doing there.

19

I volunteered the information anyway, though. I'd come to visit Peter Ives, I said; did she know him?

"Ives," she repeated. The name didn't seem to register with her.

"Actor," I said. "Apartment 2-C."

That made it easier. "No," she said, "I'm afraid not. I don't know any actors. Since my friend Ruby died, I don't go to the theater."

"Not stage," I said. "Television. The Barley Bran commercials."

But that didn't get me anywhere, either. She merely said that she always poached herself an egg for breakfast—a person needs protein.

She lived on the top floor, and I carried the groceries as far as her front door. She displayed no interest at all in who I was, and she had nothing further to say about Ives.

Scratch one, I thought. Fifteen to go.

I began to work my way down through the building, stopping at each apartment. I planned to get the stay-at-homes out of the way before five o'clock and then concentrate on the tenants who had nine-to-five jobs.

By the time I reached the second floor, I'd rung seven doorbells and had three responses. One of the three came from a woman who refused to open the door, yelling through it that she never spoke to strangers. Another came from a woman who opened her door on its safety chain, hastily said that she'd never heard of anyone named Peter Ives, and then slammed the door in my face. But at apartment 3-A I met with success. The door was opened by a young man whose hair reached his shoulders and whose pupils were dilated to the size of dimes.

He invited me in. I accepted the invitation.

The apartment reeked of marijuana smoke and incense. Its occupant, whose name was Edgar, was wearing a pair of cutoff jeans and nothing else. He was so stoned that he believed I was someone named Wendell, whom he'd met before. He did admit to knowing Peter Ives, however. He even mentioned Ives's apartment number. And when I showed him the photographs Anita Danton had given me, he said, "Yeah, that's him. Lotsa clothes."

He couldn't remember the last time he'd seen Ives. A week or two, he guessed. And he had no idea where Ives might be if he wasn't in the building.

"Try the woman with the kid," he suggested. "She might know. She'n him're thick, Wendell. What've you got to lose?"

"What woman is that?" I asked.

Edgar pointed toward the floor. "Apartment under this. Has a little baby."

"She's a friend of Peter Ives?"

Edgar nodded solemnly. "Thick."

I thanked him and went down to the apartment below his. As I approached the front door, I heard an infant crying.

Before ringing the doorbell, I checked the apartment across the corridor. It was Ives's.

The infant continued to cry.

I pushed the doorbell.

A moment later the door was thrown open and I found myself facing a beautiful but harried-looking young woman in a white terry-cloth bathrobe and pink house slippers that had rabbit faces on them.

"I'm *sorry* about the goddamn noise," she said, "but I can't get him to stop." Then she frowned. "Who *are* you?"

"My name is Calvin Bix," I said. "May I come in?"

She hesitated.

"I'm very good with babies." I smiled. "Really."

"In that case," she said, "sure. The kid's driving me nuts."

I entered the apartment.

Ten minutes later the infant was asleep.

3

"I can't get over it," Jill said.

That was her name: Jill Cranmer. And the baby's name was Andrew.

I shrugged. The truth was, I was as surprised as she. "Lucky you had a bottle of wine."

I'd filled a wineglass, dipped a finger into it, put the finger to the baby's lips, and hoped for the best. The best had happened; the little guy had sucked my finger greedily. So I'd given him a refill, and he'd guzzled that too, and presently, his head on my shoulder, he'd zonked out.

This was his birthday, his mother told me. He was a hundred days old.

"It won't make him sick?" she asked as we put him in his crib.

I grinned. "He might have a slight hangover when he wakes up."

"You're not being serious."

"Everyone's entitled to get drunk on their birthday."

"Come on now, Cal."

I'd become Cal to her as soon as I'd introduced myself.

"He won't be sick and he won't have a hangover, either. But I wouldn't recommend your giving him wine whenever he cries." I was making it up as I went along. I'd seen the wine thing done at a circumcision ceremony. It had worked then, and I'd figured it might work now. "Of course," I added, "some babies don't like wine. They prefer beer."

"You're awful," Jill said. She looked at the wineglass, which was still almost full. "Why don't you finish it?"

"If you'll join me."

She went into the kitchen for another glass. I poked about, noting details. It was your basic one-bedroom apartment, and small. The view from the living room, like that from the bedroom, was of the parking lot at the rear of the building. Even on a bright day, I thought, the place would be dreary. But Jill had livened it up with a Navajo rug, some pictures, a modular wall unit with white shelves that held an assortment of books and ceramic cats as well as a television set.

What I didn't see was any evidence of male occupancy. Everything, from the box of disposable diapers on the floor beside the crib to the hairnet on the end table, was for mother or child. The only indication I could find that somewhere Andrew had a father was a framed photograph I'd glimpsed in the bedroom. The photograph was of a nice-looking, dark-haired man in a sport shirt who, at the instant the shutter clicked, was grinning and squinting into the sun.

Jill put the second glass on the coffee table, and I filled it. She seated herself on the sofa and by way of invitation patted the cushion beside her.

"This is all so weird," she said after I'd joined her. "You come barging in, you say you want to ask me some questions, you put my baby to sleep, I don't know a thing about you, and here we are drinking wine together. I must be nuts."

I didn't remind her that I hadn't barged in—she'd stood aside, holding the door open with her foot.

"You must think I'm a pushover," she added.

Impressions were beginning to take shape. Her blue eyes registered doubt. Her robe had egg stains on the pocket and other stains elsewhere. She was wearing no wedding ring.

An exceptionally pretty young woman, I decided, but

adrift. She'd come loose from whatever mooring she'd once had, and now was lost.

"Those questions you wanted to ask me," she said. "You're taking a poll?"

"No," I said. "I'm trying to locate your across-the-hall neighbor, Peter Ives."

She managed to keep smiling, but she stiffened. "Oh?"

"You know him?"

It took her a moment to make up her mind. "Yes. A little. Why?"

"Any idea where he is? No one seems to know."

"You're what? A detective?"

"Of a sort. I work for law firms. One of them is trying to find Ives for a client, a big New York ad agency."

"Which agency?"

"They don't tell me things like that. All I know is it has to do with a cereal. Ives was in a commercial for this cereal, and now the company wants to do a follow-up commercial with the same cast, but the agency can't locate Ives. All anybody knows is, he's supposed to be at this address. When's the last time you saw him?"

Jill frowned. "I have to stop and think. Last week sometime. Thursday or Friday."

"You and he are friends?"

"Yes, but not close friends. I mean, we don't see each other every day or anything like that."

"Who else around here might be a friend of his?"

"I'm not sure."

"What can you tell me about him?"

Jill made a big deal out of taking a sip of wine. "Like what do you want to know, Cal?"

"Anything that'll help me find him."

"He's very nice, but as I say, we're not close."

I got up, strolled about the room, and paused to look at one of the pictures. It was a large watercolor of a sentinel-like saguaro cactus, its branches extending out and up at right angles. There was something exaggerated and spiky about it.

Moving on to the modular unit, I took a book from one of the shelves. It was a paperback copy of *A Streetcar Named Desire*. About half of the books were plays, I observed, and the other half were romances.

I brought the copy of *A Streetcar Named Desire* back to the sofa with me. "You an actress?" I asked as I sat down. I put the book on the coffee table.

"A little," Jill replied.

"What does that mean?"

"Amateur. I've never had a chance to do it full-time, like Peter."

"Where does Peter come from, Jill?"

She frowned at her the wineglass.

"Where?" I repeated.

She drew her robe more tightly around her legs. "How should I know?"

"Your neighbors say you and he see a lot of each other."

"If you think—"

"Where does he come from, Jill?"

"California, I believe. Around Los Angeles."

"Who in Los Angeles would he go back to if he was in trouble?"

"I have no idea. Listen, Cal—"

"When's the last time you saw him?"

"I already told you. Last week. Thursday or Friday. Thursday, I think. I'm not sure. Listen, Cal, now that Andy's asleep, I'd like to do what I've been trying to do all day— wash my hair. So if you don't mind . . ."

Don't crowd her, I thought. You may need her again. "O.K.," I said. "I guess I'm finished. You've been very helpful." I stood up. "And that's one swell baby you've got."

She walked me to the door, and I left. From the corridor I heard her attach the safety chain.

There were two other apartments on the second floor. No one was at home in either of them. I went downstairs to the first floor and rang the bell of apartment 1-D.

"Who's there?" a deep voice called.

"I'd like to ask some questions," I said.

The door opened, and I found myself face to face with a dark-skinned man in tuxedo pants, an open tuxedo shirt, and a turban.

"I am Panjit Gupta," he said gravely. "What may I do for you?"

It took me a moment to adjust. "My name is Calvin Bix," I said. "I'm an investigator. May I come in?"

"Of course," he said, with a willingness I seldom encountered. "I don't have much time, I'm afraid—I have to be at work—but if you have questions . . ."

He stood aside, and I walked into the living room.

"I hope you don't object if I finish dressing," he said. "Judal is very angry when I'm late."

"Judal?"

"My employer. I work at his restaurant, the Ganges Palace. You've been there, perhaps?"

"I'm afraid not."

"You must try it. The food is most tasty."

He went into the bedroom and returned with his studs. Inserting them into the slots, he said, "A terrible occurrence, I must say. Life in these United States is becoming quite lawless. At times I think Western civilization is collapsing before our very eyes. Especially when things like this happen."

"Things like what?"

He gave me a puzzled frown. "You're an investigator, you said."

"Yes."

"Aren't you investigating the shooting, then?"

I put everything else out of my mind. "Describe it in your own words."

Reassured, he got the front of his shirt closed. "I didn't see it happen," he said. "I didn't go downstairs until I heard the

26

police sirens. But then, when I heard the sirens and looked out the window and saw the crowd gathering, I was overwhelmed by curiosity."

"This was when, exactly?"

"Last Thursday. My day off. Judal is not generous with days off."

"What time?"

"Seven o'clock less perhaps ten minutes. I was preparing to go to a movie film that started at seven-thirty. But because of the shooting I missed the seven-thirty performance."

"And where did this shooting take place?"

"One moment," said Gupta.

He went into the bedroom. When he reappeared, he was wearing a black satin bow tie, a cummerbund, and the jacket of his tuxedo. He looked every inch a headwaiter.

"You were saying," I prompted.

The shooting had occurred in the parking lot behind the building, he told me. The intended victim had been the driver of one of the trucks that towed unauthorized vehicles from stalls reserved for tenants. No one had been hurt, but the headlights of the tow truck had been shot out and the truck's windshield had been shattered and the driver had been very upset—he'd seen the would-be killer and believed him to be a vengeful car owner.

"No one was hurt, though?" I said.

"Most fortunately not. But when you think what might have happened . . ."

"And the man who did the shooting got away?"

"That is the sad, the tragically sad, outcome," Gupta said. "Criminals should not commit crimes and escape."

"There's one individual in particular I want to ask you about," I said. "He lives on the floor above you. His name is Peter Ives. You know him?"

Gupta's eyes, big to begin with, got bigger. "He is innocent, I'm sure."

"You do know him, then?"

"We meet occasionally in the laundry room. He does not at all resemble the criminal who tried to shoot the driver."

"You know what the criminal looks like?"

"Indeed. I was present in the crowd when the driver described him to the police. He said he was small, but with a large head and light hair. Ives is tall, with dark hair."

"What else did the driver say?"

Gupta consulted his wristwatch. "My goodness, it is twenty minutes after four. I must go quickly, Mr. Bix, or Judal will impose a fine on me. Judal is a good businessman, but harsh. I hope soon to find another position. Excuse me."

He got his raincoat from the closet and put it on. "I suggest you question Mr. Lindquist," he said. "He's our maintenance man and he's the one who summoned the police."

The two of us left the apartment together. In the corridor, Gupta pointed out Lindquist's apartment, which was down the hall. I thanked him.

He inclined his head solemnly and said, "I am happy to have been able to assist you in your investigation." He glanced at his wristwatch again, decided not to wait for the elevator and loped down the stairs two at a time.

I rang the bell at the maintenance man's apartment, and he answered.

We hit it off immediately. Slender, with horn-rimmed glasses and a reddish beard, he was younger, brighter, and friendlier than most of the building-maintenance types I'd had dealings with over the years. When I told him I was an investigator and wanted to ask about the shooting in the parking lot, he didn't develop a paranoid scowl and say that it wasn't his fault; he simply nodded.

He'd only had this job since the first of the year, he explained, and he considered it to be temporary. He was taking one of his periodic breaks from the University of Chicago. He was doing graduate work in physics there, but dropped out from time to time to earn money.

The company that managed this building managed others

like it, he went on to say. Zeus had the towing contract for all of them. Zeus might be a crummy outfit, but on the other hand, some of the people who freeloaded in other people's parking stalls were crummy too. He described the driver of the tow truck who had shot at him as a Godzilla sort of guy named Martin. He'd had dealings with him before.

"After the thing happened," he recalled, "Martin ran into the building and near busted my bell. I buzzed him in, and he came charging up the stairs, his eyes all bugged out, white as a sheet. He was hyperventilating so I could hardly understand him. 'Call the cops, call the cops!' was all he could say. And when I wanted to know why, instead of explaining he began to jump up and down." Lindquist smiled. "He could have used the radio in the truck, but he was too scared."

"Don't those tow-ers usually work in teams?" I said.

"Most of the time, but not always. From now on this guy'll have a partner, though. I guarantee you." He paused. "If it'll help, we can go outside and I'll show you exactly where it happened."

"Great," I said.

It was almost dark, and the lights in the parking area were on. The bulbs were small, though, and didn't provide much illumination. It was the sort of setup that invited crime. Hundreds of muggings, rapes, and assaults took place each year in unguarded, underlit parking areas like this one.

I pictured the tow truck entering the driveway, moving slowly past the cars that were parked facing the side of the building. I pictured it beginning a right turn into the larger space at the rear of the building, where additional cars were parked.

"And here's the spot," Lindquist said. "The guy with the gun popped out from between two parked cars over there, was caught in the beam of the headlights, fired at them and knocked them out, ran forward, still firing, and then disappeared."

"Disappeared?"

"According to Martin."

"But he got a good look at the man?"

"Yes. According to him, the guy was real little. Five feet, at the most. Big head, blond hair, skinny legs. Like a kid with a grownup's face."

"Too bad there wasn't another witness," I said.

"There might have been one," Lindquist replied.

I looked at him.

"Martin thought he'd seen someone else, a man who was walking along the side of the building as he came up the driveway. He wasn't positive, though. And anyway, if a man really was there—whoever he was, he disappeared too."

Back in his apartment, I mentioned Peter Ives. I didn't say that he was my main concern; merely that I'd been to his apartment and he was out.

Lindquist's only response was, "Around here people are out more than they're in."

I asked a few general questions about Ives, but learned nothing. I didn't think Lindquist was being evasive; he simply wasn't interested in his fellow tenants. He made whatever repairs were necessary in their apartments, but had little contact with them otherwise. After a while I gave up trying to get additional information from him.

It was seven o'clock when I finally left the building. By then I'd talked with occupants of nine of its sixteen apartments, but I'd acquired no new facts about the man who'd stolen Anita Danton's necklace and earrings. No one I spoke with had seen him in the last few days or had any idea where he might be. One, a woman, suggested, as Edgar had done, that Jill Cranmer could help me. She didn't know Jill's name, however; she referred to her simply as "the lady on the second floor with the baby."

On the way home I stopped for dinner at a Chinese restaurant on Clark Street. Sitting in the booth, waiting to be served, I evaluated the afternoon's work.

I gave it a C—. Hunches but no facts. Questions but no answers.

Had Jill Cranmer heard the shots? Who had painted the picture of the cactus? Should I have started my investigation somewhere else?

Perhaps I should have, I decided. And from the restaurant I telephoned Laura McKay.

4

"Dear duck," Laura greeted me. "Dear, dear duck." And with that, she presented herself, chin up, arms out, for kissing.

I put my lips to hers. She clung to me. It was a more emotional embrace than I'd expected, and when it was over, I felt shaken.

"How long it's been," Laura said. "How much too long."

Time sped in reverse. Once again I was twenty-nine, with one year as a private investigator behind me, still getting used to being with people who were well-to-do and talked seriously about things like opera, still trying to overcome my wrong-side-of-the-tracks hang-up; eager to show how good I was, how smart, how cool. Once again I was a young Calvin Bix dealing with one of Chicago's best-known interior decorators and party givers, trying to remember not to call her "ma'm."

Now, as then, I was finding that I was susceptible to a certain type of woman. The Laura McKay type.

"Much too long," I agreed.

"I kept hoping I'd need a private investigator again," Laura said with a teasing smile, "or that you'd need a decorator, but it's taken all this while. You look absolutely, totally marvelous, duck dear. But you shouldn't wear brown. I thought I had you convinced of that. Brown is not your color."

I grinned. I'd forgotten the thing about brown. "You look great too, Laura."

She led me by the hand from the foyer into the living room. The living room had a wall of windows that faced Lake Michigan, and Laura had done the room in Lake Michigan colors—greens, blues, and grays.

"Would you like a drink?" she said. "I think I would. A little Dubonnet." She waved toward a wall panel that, when you tapped it, opened to reveal a wet bar.

I'd forgotten about the wet bar too, but suddenly it all came back, along with much more. I tapped the panel, took glasses from the shelf, poured the Dubonnet for Laura and a sociable Scotch for myself.

My affair with her had lasted no longer than the case she'd asked me to handle: two weeks. But there had been some strong feelings involved, and I'd been filled with remorse afterwards. I'd only been married for four years, and my son was just two years old. I'd never cheated on Phyllis before, and I hated myself. Those two weeks taught me a lot about irresistible forces.

Laura and I clinked glasses and sipped.

"Are you still married?" she asked.

"No," I replied.

Infidelity hadn't played a part in the breakup of my marriage. Phyllis had never suspected I was unfaithful to her. Our marriage had foundered on an altogether different shoal. I'd wanted us to move to the suburbs and hire a cleaning woman and begin living up to my income, but Phyllis hadn't wanted to leave her mother, her sisters, her old friends.

"And your son?" Laura asked. "Eddie, I believe his name was."

"Eddie's nearly fifteen," I said. "He comes to see me occasionally. Not very often, though."

"Poor duck."

"Yep." I grinned. "Poor duck."

"I hear your name occasionally. You seem to have clients in the right places."

"Yep. I do."

"I'm glad. You were destined to do well. I could spot it. I'm rarely wrong about things like that."

She was rarely wrong about most things, I'd learned. Although she came across as flighty, scatterbrained, and frivolous, she was none of those things. Behind all the chatter and the habit of calling everyone "duck" lurked an extraordinary intelligence, superb taste, and the greatest talent for self-promotion I'd ever run across. Compared to her, the careerists I'd met in the police department, men whose every move was determined by how it would affect their chances for promotion, were shrinking violets. Laura knew whom to cultivate, whom to entertain, and how to use her reputation as a hostess to further her interior decorating business. Born rich, she'd become richer through her own abilities and had had fun doing it.

But there was more to her than ambition. She was to many people a loyal, generous friend. During our brief relationship I'd had a chance to see that side of her too.

"You're not here because of sentiment, though, are you?" she continued. "You said on the telephone you need background information."

"That's true," I admitted. "But still . . ."

"Never mind. I understand. In a way, you're like I am. The head is always working, even when you don't want it to."

"Laura!"

"Anyway, you've aged well. You haven't lost that gangly, boyish look."

She'd aged well too, I thought. I'd never known, or cared, exactly how much older than I she was. Six or seven years, I guessed. But even now the skin, the body, the proud posture were those of a young woman—and I was as attracted as I'd been before.

"Background information," she reminded me.

"Right." I became businesslike. "This is confidential, Laura."

"Understood."

"I need to know about a client of yours. Anita Danton."

Laura raised an eyebrow.

"And a man she says she met at a party you gave. Peter Ives. What can you tell me about them? Start with her."

Laura put her glass on the coffee table and tucked her legs under her. "Am I permitted to ask who your client is?"

"Mrs. Danton."

"It's over between them?"

I didn't answer.

"In a way I'm sorry," Laura said. "He's been good for her. For the first time in her life she's been happy. People have been terrible about it, of course—some people. But those of us who are really fond of her have felt it was a blessing. She actually began to bloom, and it was so nice to see. What difference that he was twenty years younger? He was therapy for her, and I don't regret at all that I inadvertently introduced them." She paused. "Should I?"

I didn't answer that one, either.

"It *was* inadvertent," Laura continued. "I'd invited Janet Fleming to this party I was giving. She's a theatrical agent, in case you don't know, although you probably do. Anyway, she called me at the last minute and said there was a young man she'd been interviewing and would it be all right if she brought him along? It wasn't a sit-down dinner and one more didn't make any difference, so I said, 'By all means.' Well, it was Peter and he's really a most attractive creature, and when he and Anita met . . . What can I tell you; it simply happened. And I don't think the attraction was entirely one-sided. It's only my private opinion, but I believe he cares. Or at least he did."

"Mother-son?"

"Who knows?" Laura gazed toward the windows. The lights of the room were reflected in them, but she seemed to be seeing other things. "I've known Anita almost as long as I can remember, and let me tell you something. Her life can be summed up in just one word: pathetic. I'm not talking about her childhood particularly, although that wasn't great—her brother was the family favorite; she was just something extra. I'm talking about her marriage to Howard Danton, which must have been just plain hell. One of those perfect matches, money marrying money with both families' approval, except that Howard, for all his credentials, was a lush and a boor and he treated Anita like dirt. I don't know how she put up with it. In the long run she probably wouldn't have. Anyway, by the grace of a merciful Providence, Howard dropped dead of a heart attack at the age of forty-one, halfway through a tennis match. The children, a son and daughter, were just entering their teens. Anita did a noble job of raising them and seemed to have found herself. But then, two weeks after his high school graduation, the boy was out in the car Anita had given him as a graduation present and another teenager, who was high on God knows what, hit him head-on, going about eighty miles an hour, and killed him. Anita almost went out of her mind."

"Lord!"

"She deserved better, Cal. She's a good woman and she's always done her best. She may not be the brightest person in the world, but she's a good mother and a faithful friend and she gives to more charities than I can name. If she finally found in Peter someone who could make her forget some of the bad things that had happened to her, I, for one, couldn't care less that he was basically unsuitable. Whatever he was costing her, in my opinion, he was worth it." She sighed. "I just hope it didn't cost her *too* much."

I finished my Scotch. "What can you tell me about him?" I asked.

Laura drank some Dubonnet. "I'm in a difficult position," she said. "I want to help Anita, but I don't want to hurt Ellen."

"Ellen?"

"Anita's daughter. She and her mother aren't on speaking terms at the moment on account of Peter. Ellen absolutely can't stand him. His hanging about the house, spending the night in her mother's bedroom—to her it's like a desecration. The poor child was utterly miserable at home. Every time she turned around, there was Peter with poor, besotted Anita fawning over him. Anyway, to make a long story short, things came to a head a few months ago, and Ellen moved out of the house. She took an apartment of her own. I'm helping her fix it up."

I couldn't keep from smiling. Laura was right: The head was always working, even when she didn't want it to.

"I'm not doing anything behind Anita's back," she added quickly. "I told her about it, and she approves. Ellen is twenty-three, after all. She *should* be out on her own." She drank the rest of her Dubonnet and held the glass out to me. "Just a half."

I poured the wine.

"How serious *is* Anita's problem, Cal?"

"A fair amount of money is involved."

Laura gave the matter some thought. "In that case, I suppose I *should* tell you a bit about Peter. Not as much as Ellen could, but a bit. What she told me. What I persuaded her, after much effort, not to tell her mother. Ellen had him investigated, you see."

"By whom?" I was genuinely startled.

"By someone like yourself."

"You mean I'm covering ground that's already been covered by another private detective?"

"I'm afraid so, darling."

I burst out laughing. "This is great. Give me the guy's name. Maybe I can buy his notes."

Laura looked alarmed. "I will not. And I want you to promise me on your word of honor you won't let Ellen know I told you. I had a terrible time keeping her from running to her mother with the man's report. It would hurt Anita, I thought, and instead of making things better it would make them worse."

"So tell me," I said. "What did the report say?"

"Perhaps I did the wrong thing," she said thoughtfully, "but what's done is done. The report said that Peter was born in Los Angeles, had a terrible childhood, and ran away from home when he was fourteen."

"Go on."

"His parents separated when he was very young. There were stepfathers, one after another, foster homes—no stability, no kindness, nothing. Like those poor, sad children you see on television, Peter became a runaway. A fourteen-year-old street person. He's never been back to see his mother, but later he got together with his father—his real father. Years later.

"What amazes me is that he survived. He did, though. Not only survived but succeeded; came up in the world. Evidently he got in with some people who were on the fringe of show business and through them he got a few bit parts, and he learned. You wouldn't believe for a minute, if you met him today, that he's hardly had any schooling. You'd think he was a college graduate. You have to hand it to him, Cal. . . . You aren't impressed?"

"Not particularly. My childhood was no bed of roses, either. Go on."

Laura's eyes seemed to get darker. "I'll never understand you," she said. One minute you're sensitive and understanding, the next you're like nails. But maybe you're right. Peter *did* go astray. A little. But each time he was arrested he was released."

"*Arrested?*"

"But released."

"How many times?"

"Ellen didn't say, and I didn't ask. More than once, though. And in the end he had to leave the city in a hurry—

the police were looking for him again, and that time it was more serious."

"More serious how?"

Laura shifted her position on the couch. "It had to do with some jewelry he was accused of stealing from someone he was going with. Don't look at me like that. I'm not defending him. I'm merely saying that in spite of all odds, he became educated and acquired good manners. I think he deserves credit for that."

"When he left Los Angeles, where did he go?"

"To Tucson. That's where his father was living, and by then they were in touch. He settled down in Tucson and lived there for several years. Then, about a year ago, he moved to New York, and from New York he came here."

"The Los Angeles jewel theft . . . ?"

"Nothing came of that, according to the report. I suspect that the jewelry wasn't worth a great deal."

"No criminal record in Tucson?"

Laura shook her head "So you see, it really isn't so awful, is it?" She ran a playful finger up the back of my neck.

"In Tucson he did what?"

"Worked in a hotel and belonged to a little-theater group and was a very nice young man. Smile."

I closed my mental notebook, moved her finger from the back of my neck to my lap, and said, "I don't feel like smiling, Laura. I feel like asking you to go to bed with me."

Laura looked astonished.

"Will you?"

She pursed her lips and frowned.

"You're as direct as ever, aren't you, duck?"

"Yes. Will you, Laura?"

"Let me think it over. Meanwhile, why don't you try kissing me? The way you did when you came in, only longer."

I took her up on the suggestion.

5

I woke once. Laura was sleeping on her side, with one arm across my chest and the other under the pillow. It was too dark for me to see her face, but I could feel her breath against my shoulder. She was breathing slowly and evenly.

For a while I lay perfectly still, contented. I wished that the night would last indefinitely, that there would be no daybreak. But presently my left leg began to cramp, and I shifted position, turning toward Laura, drawing her closer. Our thighs touched. I ran my hand along her back. She murmured but didn't wake. I kissed the side of her neck and began to stroke her, throwing one leg over her ankles. She sighed, and her arms tensed. Her hand moved down to my waist, and her fingers spread. They made little kneading movements. I eased more of my weight onto her and ran my tongue between her lips. Her hands locked across the small of my back.

"Yes," she whispered. "Yes, yes."

We didn't hurry. When it was over, we fell asleep in a tangle of legs and sheets, and the next time I opened my eyes, the bedroom was light and the sound of running water was coming from the bathroom.

After a few minutes, the bathroom door opened and Laura emerged, wrapped in a big turquoise towel. Clutching the towel, she sat down on the edge of the bed, kissed me, and said, "Good morning. We must do this more often."

"Suits me," I replied.

Later, my hair still damp from the shower, my face sore from shaving with a miniature razor that wasn't meant for a masculine face, I was dressed and sitting at a glass-topped table in the kitchen with Laura, drinking coffee and munching toast. We'd started to talk, but had been interrupted by a telephone call. The call, I gathered, was from a cabinet-maker who was in doubt about dimensions. Laura brought a sketch from her office, and together they went over the numbers. Then someone else called, about carpeting. By the time the second call ended, my hair was dry and I was beginning to get restless.

"Sorry," Laura apologized. "Couldn't avoid. More toast?"

I shook my head. Professional matters were on my mind too. "I have a couple of questions," I said. "One, was Anita Danton ever particularly interested in the theater? Two, did you have anything to do with choosing her paintings?"

"Back to Anita, are we?"

"Can't help it," I said. "She's my cabinets and carpets."

Laura nodded. "I suppose. Well, in answer to question number one, not the theater but movies. She loves them. Always has. She used to have tons of old fan magazines. Probably still does. As for question number two, no, but I wish I had had. Some of those paintings are hideous."

"Thank you," I said, and got up. "For everything."

She rose and planted herself in front of me. "This is it, then? At least may I ask: Was I useful?"

I put my hands on her shoulders. "You were lovely, Laura. And if you invite me, I'll come back. But I've got to warn you: My hours are irregular, and I can't plan much in advance. Women seem to get tired of that, after a while."

"Thanks for the warning." She tilted her head back. "A kiss?"

I kissed her. Then I got my coat, kissed her again, and went home.

Everything in my apartment was as I'd left it. The coffee percolator was in the sink, the mug was on the table, the bed was unmade, and my shirt from two days ago was on the chair in the bedroom. That was one of the things about living alone I didn't like: nothing ever got moved while you were out.

There was only one message, my answering service reported. Frank Norris wanted me to call him at home.

I pushed buttons on the base of the telephone. Soon Frank answered.

"Bingo!" he said. "It happened!"

There was a slight tremor in his voice. This, to anyone who knew him well, meant he was in a state of high excitement. "What's 'it'?" I asked.

"Photographs. The answer to a prayer. That camera of yours is amazing."

"You've got them *already?*"

"And all X-rated." He chuckled, another good sign.

"I'll be damned."

Everything had broken just right, he explained. After leaving me, he'd gone straight to Babette Mantino's house. He'd been there less than fifteen minutes, parked up the block, when he'd seen a woman coming out of the house. The woman matched the description I'd given him. She'd got into a car and driven straight to the address where I'd said the musician lived.

Frank had followed her. Had watched her enter the building. Had found the back stairs, climbed to the porch, and waited. An hour and a half later, he had thirty-six marvelous shots. And neither the woman nor the man suspected a thing. How soon could he show me?

"The pictures are already developed?"

"The little-sized ones. I took the film to one of those one-hour places. Now I'm having a friend of mine make enlargements—I figured you'd be wanting eight-by-ten glossies for the lawyers. But the little-sized ones will give you something to work with. When can we get together?"

"Be at my office by eleven-thirty," I said.

"Bingo," Frank said again, and added, "For an old man, I still get around pretty good."

I hung up. Then I called Anita Danton and said I had to see her.

She had less of the blue stuff around her eyes and in general looked better than she had the day before. But there was still plenty of anxiety on her face.

"I hope you're the bearer of good news," she said as we shook hands.

"Too soon for that," I said. "I need more information."

The Yorkshire terriers sniffed my shoes. Helga plodded across the foyer to take my coat.

"What a frightful experience this is turning out to be," Anita Danton said woefully. "I feel totally drained."

I thought of movie magazines, of fantasies. And wondered who she was being at the moment. A middle-aged Joan Crawford? A late-in-life Bette Davis? I couldn't tell; I'd never been good at movie stars.

We went up the wide staircase to the library. All the art objects, all the expensive ornaments were where I remembered their being.

In the library, I perched on the desk and said, "I have some questions for you, Mrs. Danton."

She lit a cigarette and sat down.

"Let's talk about the day before the ball," I said, "and the day before that. Last Thursday and Friday. Did you see Ives either day?"

"I saw him on Friday. We had lunch together. After my beauty shop appointment."

"Did you tell him you were going to the bank to get your jewelry?"

She frowned. "I might have. I can't recall. Why?"

"Did you at any time tell him what jewelry you were going to wear to the ball?"

"I don't know. Probably not."

"Did you tell him you were going to wear *any* jewelry?"

"I don't really remember, Mr. Bix. Why are you asking?"

"Would he *assume* that you were going to wear jewelry?"

"I suppose so. He'd been to affairs like that with me before. I always wore some of my nice things. What are you getting at?"

"At motive, Mrs. Danton. Bear with me. What was his mood when you were with him on Friday? Was he different from usual? And on Saturday—how was he then? Nervous? Upset? Irritable? Edgy?"

"Edgy?" Anita Danton stubbed out her cigarette and looked at the dying glow. "How strange that you should use that word—it so exactly describes how he was on Friday. *Everything* seemed to bother him."

"And Saturday? How was he then?"

"Oh, he was wonderful on Saturday. He'd got over it, whatever it was. He was in *such* good spirits. Almost elated."

"Oh?"

"Is that important?"

"I believe so, Mrs. Danton. Because I believe that the theft of your necklace and earrings was premeditated—but not by much. I don't think the idea occurred to him until Friday, and what you call his elation on Saturday was the kind of nervous high that people often have before they do something dangerous."

She was all alertness now, leaning forward in her chair. "I've heard of that. I know what you mean."

"Peter was in a panic, Mrs. Danton. He was scared. His stealing your jewels was an act of desperation. He needed money to get out of town and make a new start."

"Scared? Of what? I can't imagine anything that would scare him into *stealing.*"

"My guess is that he had the best reason in the world for being scared. Someone was trying to kill him."

Anita Danton paled, and her eye shadow suddenly seemed a much deeper shade of blue. "Oh, dear God!"

"Which leads to my next question. Why would anyone *want* to kill him?"

Anita Danton clasped one hand tightly in the other. "I don't know. I can't imagine."

"Someone tried to shoot him Thursday night. Only a freak circumstance saved his life."

"But who would *do* a thing like that?"

"That's what I'd like *you* to tell *me.*"

She wilted visibly. "Impossible," she murmured. "Simply impossible."

"Did he ever mention a neighbor of his named Jill Cranmer?"

"No, I don't think so."

"Did he ever mention *any* of his neighbors?"

"No. Not to me."

"Have you ever been to his apartment?"

"Aside from Monday, you mean? Once. I'd bought him a fur parka as a surprise and I couldn't wait to give it to him. But otherwise, it's so much nicer here."

"Do you have a key to it?"

"To his apartment? What would I need one for?"

"Do you?"

"No. I do not."

"Too bad," I said. "I'd like to get into the place. Did he ever talk to you about Tucson, Arizona?"

"The Cholla Players, you mean?"

"What are the Cholla Players?"

"A little-theater group he belonged to when he lived there. They put on some very nice productions, he said. Ibsen. Shaw. Everything."

"What else did he tell you about Tucson?"

"Not much. It was just a phase for him."

"That picture you have in the upstairs hall—did he give it to you?"

"Which picture?"

"I only got a glimpse of it yesterday, but somehow it registered. It's different from your other pictures. It's a cactus, I think. Mind if I take another look?"

"Not at all."

We went from the second floor to the third. In the hall near the door to Anita Danton's bedroom was the painting I remembered, a large watercolor of a thorny shrub I couldn't identify. The strong, spiky lines, the exaggeration—I was almost certain it was the work of the same artist who had done the painting of the saguaro in Jill Cranmer's apartment.

"That's the one," I said. "Did Ives give it to you?"

"He didn't *give* it to me," Anita Danton replied. "He persuaded me to buy it. Why do you ask?"

"I have a hunch. Who's the artist?"

"A friend of his named Dennis Close. It's an ocotillo. The desert is full of them, I understand."

"This Dennis Close—he lives in Tucson?"

"Winters. Summers he lives here. He sells at the art fairs."

"You've met him?"

"Peter took me to his studio to buy the painting. As a favor, he said. Dennis had a big dental bill."

I saw a ray of hope. "Can I have his address and phone number?"

"I'm not sure I wrote it down. Let me look."

I studied the picture a moment longer. The man who had painted it, I thought, saw the world as a dangerous place. A place filled with barbs, jabs, and slashes, with the constant possibility of pain.

We returned to the library. Anita Danton couldn't find Close's name in her address book, and I couldn't find it in the telephone directory. But she remembered that she'd kept the receipt he'd given her for the picture, and after burrowing through an entire drawer of receipts, she located it. The address was at the top. I jotted it down.

She reached for a cigarette, but decided she didn't want one and let her hand fall to the desktop. "Peter running away. If only he'd told me. I would have given him money."

"How much would you have given him?"

She considered. "Not enough, I suppose."

"There's your answer," I said. "Not enough."

6

Frank had got there early. He was standing in the corridor outside my office. Same plaid jacket. Same hunter's cap. Different expression, though. Today the trace of a smile hovered between nose and chin.

"Wait till you see!" he said happily, and as soon as we were in the office he handed me an envelope. "Enjoy."

I hung my coat on the coat tree, sat down at my desk, and took a magnifying glass from the top drawer. Frank shed jacket and cap and stationed himself behind me, so that he could look over my shoulder. I opened the envelope and for the next few minutes peered through the magnifying glass at a miniature world that consisted of one room and two people.

The room was a spacious, old-fashioned kitchen. Not all of it was visible. I could see only a refrigerator on the far side, a stove and part of a counter on the left, the corner of a table and a bit of chair on the right. The man and woman occupied different places in the room in different photographs. Both were naked, but the man had a small towel draped around his neck.

On several occasions I'd viewed the kitchen from the same

perspective as Frank. I knew that the window was above the sink, that anyone near the sink could be seen only from the waist up, but as the person moved toward the refrigerator more body was revealed.

Frank had arranged the photographs in chronological order. The arrangement and his commentary gave me the feeling I was at a slide show.

"The guy comes into the kitchen first, see. They'd been doing it in the bedroom for a while, I guess, but he'd got thirsty, so he comes to get himself a glass of water. He's so horny, so hot to trot, he doesn't even think to pull down the shade, and there I am, less than three feet away, at the edge of the window. O.K., so he turns around, away from the window, because she's come into the kitchen too—she's followed him. He drinks some water. Then, see, she's drinking out of his glass. Look at how he's got his hand on her tit. One of them must have said something funny, because they both start to laugh.

"There, he's put the glass down and now he's getting even hornier, and so's she. He's got his hand on one tit and his mouth on the other—honest to God, how about that, Cal! Could it have been any better? Now look how she's got her head back, her eyes closed, will ya. But keep going, keep going . . .

"See, in that one they've moved over by the refrigerator and she's leaning against it, and he's down on his knees. Now it's later and he's the one against the fridge while she's kneeling. Look at that . . . But wait, you haven't seen the best yet. There. That's what I mean. With him sitting on the countertop. Could anybody have got better pictures than that? Could *anybody?*"

"No," I said. "Nobody. You make a wonderful dirty old man, Frank."

He guffawed. "Don't I? It's great to peep and get paid for it." He leaned over my shoulder and placed the Leica on my desk. "That camera is a real gem, Cal."

I thought of the CIA agent, no doubt long dead by now. I wished I could have put his Leica to use in a nobler cause. Frank dropped into the visitor's chair. "I'll have the eight-by-tens tomorrow morning. Want me to bring them here?"

"I'll let you know." I put the photographs and the magnifying glass in a desk drawer.

"Will I have to testify?"

"Not a chance."

The case, I knew, would be easily settled. Jerry Zabin, Allen Mantino's lawyer, would show the photographs to Babette Mantino's lawyer, and her suit would be dropped. Allen would get the divorce on his own terms.

"Good," said Frank. "I'll give you my time and expenses when I bring the eight-by-tens. Do you feel like lunch, maybe? I wouldn't mind another of those beef sandwiches."

We went to the same coffee shop where we'd eaten the day before. As we were waiting for the food to arrive, Frank let me know that he was available for additional assignments—some extra money would come in handy in Florida. I said I didn't have anything for him at the moment.

"What about this other case you're working on?" he suggested.

"Don't remind me," I said. "I'm sorry I took it."

"Bad?" Frank seemed surprised.

"More complicated than I expected." I thought about the afternoon ahead. Suppose Dennis Close had moved. Suppose he wasn't cooperative. Would I be better off talking to Ellen Danton instead? "I'm running into a bunch of stage-struck people."

"That what's making it complicated?"

"No, but I wish I could figure out what it means."

Frank changed the subject. As soon as he got to Florida, he said, he was going to start raising hell about them not heating the swimming pool.

Dennis first, I decided suddenly. He actually knew Ives.

*   *   *

After Frank left, I called Jerry Zabin.

"You just caught me," he said. "I'm on my way to lunch. Any progress?"

"Yep. Some of the best material I've ever got. It's the kind of material, though, that's liable to upset our client when he sees it, so I'd like you to be there when I show it to him. And I think you ought to get him ready in advance."

More often than not, I worked directly with the client. The lawyers preferred it that way, and so did I. But in this case I wanted the lawyer to be present. As a calming influence.

"Am I really necessary?" Zabin asked. He obviously wasn't thrilled by the prospect.

I told him what the photographs showed. "That's not easy for a husband to look at," I added.

Zabin gave in. "Would tomorrow afternoon be all right with you if it's all right with him?" he asked. "Two o'clock, say, at my office?"

We agreed tentatively on that time. Zabin promised to confirm the appointment through my answering service. I hung up and once again put the Mantino case out of my mind.

It was a four-story wooden house with a steep, gabled roof. The ground floor was occupied by a store that sold coffee and tea by the pound and by the cup. The name of the store was Grinds and Bumps. A sign on the window informed passersby that the special of the day was Kenya Dark Roast.

Beside the store was the entrance to a narrow hall and stairway. There were four mailboxes in the hall. The card in the slot of the one nearest the stairway said "Close, D."

Instead of ringing the bell, I returned to the sidewalk and looked about. I hadn't been on North Halsted Street in a long while.

The neighborhood had had a rebirth. It had become, for the first time in its history, "in." Houses such as the one in which Dennis Close lived had once been tenanted by turn-of-the-century immigrants who were coming up in the world. One of the longest thoroughfares in the city, Halsted was also one of the most ethnic. Depending on which part of it you were in, it was Italian, Irish, Greek, Polish, German, Swedish, or Ukrainian. This particular strip had been German, but after years of decline was now Third-Generation-American Artsy. Rents had gone up, and ground-floor spaces had been converted into trendy restaurants and boutiques.

Gazing up, I bet myself that Ives's friend lived just below the roof in what had been the attic, and that he was asleep— a dark-green shade was drawn across the dormer window.

I went into the building again and rang his bell. A staticky question came through the speaking tube. I stated my name, heard a comment I couldn't understand, climbed the stairs, and won half my bet: Dennis lived on the top floor, but he hadn't been asleep; he'd been working.

A slight, willowy young man, with a face that could almost be called pretty and raven-black hair, he was wearing white jeans, a black turtleneck sweater, white wool socks, and no shoes.

"I didn't get your name," he said with an uncertain smile.

"Bix," I said. "I'm a friend of Anita Danton's. May I come in?"

He stepped back from the doorway. "I wasn't expecting anyone."

The only light in the room came from a lamp that was clipped to a drawing board and from a slide projector. Reflected on a screen across the room was the image of a flowering plant with dozens of bayonet-like leaves. The picture on the drawing board was a half-finished watercolor of the plant.

"So this is how you do it," I said.

"Usually," he replied.

"What are you painting?"

"A yucca."

"Who took the photograph?"

"I did."

My eyes adjusted to the gloom. The apartment consisted of a single large room with a Pullman kitchen at one side. The kitchen could be closed off by a curtain, but the curtain wasn't drawn. Dishes were stacked on the drainboard of the sink. There wasn't much furniture—two sagging daybeds, three tables, two chairs, a chest of drawers. Several canvas suitcases were lined up end to end along one wall, and there was a tall cardboard carton near the window.

"Mrs. Danton said you might be able to help me," I said. "I'm trying to locate a friend of hers and yours. Peter Ives."

Dennis all but leaped away from me.

"Take it easy," I said. "I'm one of the good guys."

It didn't help, however. He looked like someone who'd just found a scorpion on his pillow.

"He's needed for a cereal commercial," I said.

The story didn't go over as well with him as it had with Jill Cranmer. When I moved toward him, he took another step backward.

"Let's turn off this projector," I suggested.

His confidence appeared to be seeping back. He turned off the projector and raised the window shade. I noticed things I hadn't seen before. Two round containers of slides on the floor. A portable television set. A stack of finished paintings beside the cardboard carton. The half-open door to a bathroom.

But he kept the drawing board between us. "I don't know anyone named Peter Ives," he said.

I shook my head.

"I don't! I swear I don't!"

"He brought Mrs. Danton here to buy one of your paintings. Of an ocotillo. And"—I took a chance—"you knew him in Tucson."

"I didn't! I swear!"

"Be honest."

"I don't know anyone named Peter Ives! Don't accuse me!"

"Accuse you of what?"

"Oh, Christ!" He swallowed. "Who are you? A policeman?"

"No."

"You're a policeman. I can tell."

I held out one of my business cards.

He hesitated, then took it. "Investigations, it says."

"Private," I pointed out.

He sat down on the nearer of the daybeds. Elbows on his knees, head in his hands, he was a forlorn, shoeless figure in black and white.

I looked at the picture on the drawing board. The plant's long, sharp leaves were exaggerated. To Dennis Close it was, for sure, a barbed-wire world.

"I don't have to talk to you," he said sullenly. "I don't have to tell you anything."

I decided to forget about the cereal commercial. "I'm going to lay it on the line," I said. "If Peter's done anything wrong, you could be named as accessory."

He said nothing.

"I'm not a policeman," I went on, "but I sure know how to call one. If Peter has stolen something, and if you helped him either before or after, you're in a tough spot, Dennis. People go to jail for helping other people steal or for covering up for them. Now, you can cooperate with me or with the police. Of the two, I'm your better bet."

He shook his head. "No."

"O.K. But the next detective who comes to see you won't be a private one." I moved toward the door.

He jumped up. "Hey, wait a minute!"

I stopped.

"I'd rather talk to you."

I turned back. "Then do it."

"You won't crucify me?"

"I promise."

We sat down at a table that evidently served a variety of

purposes. On it were a coffee jar partly filled with dirty water in which several brushes were soaking, a felt-tipped pen, a studded leather wristband, a plate with an apple and two still-green bananas, and a sprinkling of bread crumbs.

"I'm worried about Pete," Dennis began. "He didn't come back Sunday like he said he would."

"This past Sunday? Come back here?"

"Right."

"When's the last time you saw him?"

"Saturday."

"Where?"

"Here. He was going to take Mrs. Danton to this orchestra party and he was wearing his tux. He said he'd come back Sunday and get his other clothes."

"He has clothes here?"

"A whole suitcase of them." Dennis pointed to the largest of the canvas bags. "That one."

"How come?"

"You're not going to believe me, but it's the truth. He said someone was out to blow him away. Honest to God, those were his words: 'Blow me away.' "

"When?"

"Last Thursday."

I folded my arms on the table. "Go on."

At first Dennis told the story haltingly, in bursts. But he gained courage as he went along. Unexpectedly, Peter had rung the bell at about eight o'clock Thursday evening. He'd been wild-eyed, sweaty, and barely able to talk. He'd rambled incoherently about running for three blocks before finding a cab, about not knowing where to tell the driver to take him, about remembering Dennis and praying that Dennis would be home.

When he'd pulled himself together, he'd explained that he'd just had a terrible experience—someone had tried to blow him away. And the sequence of events he'd described corresponded with the one I imagined. A man with a gun temporarily blinded by headlights. Shots that missed. Miraculous escape.

He was afraid to go home, he'd said. Could he spend the night? Dennis had said yes. They'd talked for a little while, until Peter, exhausted, had fallen asleep in the middle of a sentence.

The next day, according to Dennis, Peter was more or less back to normal, but obviously worried. He was on somebody's hit list, he insisted, but didn't know why or what to do about it. He was afraid to stay in Chicago, though, or to return to his apartment, even to pack.

"He made me go there to get clothes for him and bring him his car," Dennis went on. "I didn't want to, but he made me. That's not being an accessory, is it?"

"Depends," I said. "How could he 'make' you?"

Dennis detoured onto a side road that took us through a landscape of career problems. It wasn't easy to make a living from painting, especially if none of the big galleries was interested in you. Peter, whom he'd met in Arizona, had sometimes lent him money, brought him clients, got him jobs.

"What kind of jobs?" I asked.

"Anything. Waiter, bartender, usher, bellboy. To tide me over until my check came."

The check, he explained, was from a small trust fund left him by one of his grandfathers. He received it quarterly. But it wasn't always enough.

He'd spent the past seven winters in the Southwest, he said, traveling in a van he owned, painting and photographing. He'd gone there originally for his health. There was something funny about his blood; it didn't have enough gamma globulin; he kept getting the flu. Summers, he lived in Chicago, where he'd grown up. When Peter had arrived in Chicago, he'd called Dennis, who was the only person in town he knew.

I steered us back to the main highway. "So Saturday was the last time you saw him?"

He nodded and described how, in a tailor-made tuxedo Mrs. Danton had bought for him, Peter had left to take her to the party, how he'd said he would be back the next day for his other clothes.

"Where did he intend to go from here?"

"He didn't say." Dennis toyed with the studded wristband. "Was he bullshitting me? Maybe *nothing* he said was true. With Peter you can't always be sure." He slapped himself across the palm of one hand with the wristband.

I changed the subject. "You know Jill Cranmer? She lives in the same building as Peter."

Dennis was startled. "You've met *Jill*?"

"Ran across her. Was she in the Cholla Players?"

"What *are* you, for Christ sake? What are you *after*?"

"I'm trying to find your friend Peter."

"Sure I know Jill. So does Pete. He's the one got her the apartment there. She came here from Tucson last spring. She'd been in some of the plays."

"You in them too?"

"No. I ushered and helped with scenery, though, a few times . . . I think I'd be better off with the real police."

"No, you wouldn't, Dennis. You wouldn't at all. You gave Peter a place to stay, got his car for him. If he stole anything, you're an accessory, and accessories don't make out very well with the real police . . . So if you know where Peter went, if you can give me any clue, you'd be doing yourself a big favor by telling me."

Dennis put down the wristband. "I don't know where he went. Honest to God I don't. He didn't tell me. But maybe there's something in his apartment that'll help you. If you want the key—"

"You have a key to Peter's apartment?"

"The one he gave me when I went to get his clothes. He never asked for it back." Dennis took a key ring from the pocket of his jeans and handed it to me. "The big key is for the downstairs door," he said. "The little one's for the door to his apartment."

"Thank you," I said. "Very much."

I left him staring dejectedly at the tabletop. I guessed he was trying to figure out what was true and what wasn't. Just as I was.

7

I paused for a moment outside Jill Cranmer's door. The television set was on. There were no other sounds.

Then, crossing the corridor, I put on my driving gloves and entered Ives's apartment. It was laid out like Gupta's, but seemed nicer. The furniture was new and attractive. There was no clutter. Everything was the right size and color for everything else. Laura was right; the teenaged runaway had become a man of taste.

Also, he'd spent a fair amount of money. The curved sofa, the brass coffee table, the rosewood and glass breakfront— these few items alone had cost thousands. Either Anita Danton had opened her purse wide or Ives was up to his ears in unpaid bills. Unless he had another source of income.

I worked my way through the place slowly and systematically, examining the contents of shelves and drawers, lifting cushions, reading labels.

Ives had a weakness for clothes. There were seven coats in the coat closet, all apparently his. He liked the fur parka Anita Danton had given him; he kept it on a special, padded hanger, apart from the other coats.

He was neat, health conscious, and vain. The bed was made, shirts and underwear were folded and stacked in their separate drawers, and shoes were in a compartmented bag. There was an alphabet of vitamin pills in the medicine cabinet; all the packaged foods on the kitchen shelves were of the sort that's supposed to be good for you; the linen closet had few linens in it but lots of stuff to make skin and hair look nice.

Cooking wasn't his thing. All I found in the refrigerator were some eggs and a carton of low-fat milk that had gone sour. And there were no kitchen appliances on the premises, not even a toaster.

Ives wasn't a drinker, either. The only bottle of liquor in the apartment was a fifth of vodka, and it was almost full.

But he probably did spend a big chunk of time watching television and listening to music. The television set had a videocassette recorder hooked up to it, and the lower part of the breakfront housed hi-fi equipment. One of the shelves of the breakfront had a couple of dozen tapes on it, including one labeled "The Voices of Peter Ives." And in the bedroom, on the bedside table, was a videocassette marked "Me, Myself and I."

Two watercolors by Dennis Close hung in the bedroom, and in the living room there was a large framed poster that advertised an exhibition of Matisse paintings that had been held in Paris in 1937. And there was an expensive tabletop book on the coffee table. Its subject was antique silver. Except for that book, all the reading matter in the apartment had to do with movies, rock music, and television.

I came across no playing cards, no games of any sort, no writing materials other than a ballpoint pen and a memo pad beside the telephone. What Ives did when he wasn't watching television, listening to music, or grooming himself, I didn't know. Perhaps nothing, I thought.

On the floor of the bedroom closet I found a box of photographs. In it were snapshots of Ives alone or with other people, and a stack of professionally made glossies, like the ones Anita Danton had, that showed him dressed for various roles. The glossies gave me the feeling I'd had when I'd seen them before: that Peter Ives somehow changed his identity with his clothes; that he was whatever he happened to be wearing.

In one of the snapshots I recognized Dennis. He was standing beside Ives at the edge of a swimming pool. A palm tree and a portion of an adobe bungalow were visible in the background. It was on the grounds of a hotel or country club, I guessed. In another snapshot Ives had his arms around Jill Cranmer and the man whose picture I'd seen in her apartment.

Putting the box of photographs aside, I considered what was missing. So far I hadn't seen a single letter, bill, receipt, canceled check, or personal document.

You're Peter Ives, I told myself. You receive money, you pay out money, you keep in touch with people. So where do you keep your bank statement, your mail, your address book? Why can't I find them?

I went back to the kitchen and gave it another sweep.

Nothing was concealed there.

The bedroom? Had I overlooked something in the dresser, the night table, the closet?

I gave the rest of the apartment a second going over too. With the same negative result.

Annoyed, I sat down on the sofa—and discovered the hiding place. Except that it wasn't a hiding place at all. Ives had put his personal papers in the handiest spot he could think of, a long, deep drawer in the coffee table. I simply hadn't noticed the drawer; to me, its two little handles had looked like parts of the table's legs.

The checkbook was there. So were bills, receipts, warranties for the television set and videocassette recorder, an order form for some body-building equipment that had been filled out but not mailed, and an address book. Along with a legal document that I read twice. A subpoena.

The subpoena had been issued by the United States District Court for the Northern District of Illinois. It commanded Peter Ives to appear at the office of the United

States Attorney in Chicago at ten-thirty in the morning of November twenty-first for the purpose of giving his deposition on behalf of the United States of America in the case of the United States of America versus Frederick W. Cahill Sharpe. It informed Ives that the deposition would be taken both stenographically and on videotape. It was dated November sixth.

The twenty-first was tomorrow.

Sharpe. I kept repeating the name to myself, running it through my mental sorter. Nothing dropped into the slot.

Why videotape? I wondered. The only answer I could come up with was that Ives wasn't expected to be present in person at the trial, because it was being held in a different jurisdiction. One that was far from Chicago.

I turned to the address book. Sharpe was listed among the *S*'s. No first name or initials, though. And although Ives had written down an address and telephone number, he hadn't included the zip code or area code.

The address was on Broadway. And Ives's apartment was less than two hundred yards from Chicago's Broadway.

But hundreds of cities have Broadways, and Sharpe's address was wrong for Chicago's Broadway. Besides, the first three digits of his telephone number weren't those of a Chicago exchange.

Did Tucson have a Broadway?

I picked up the telephone and called Tucson Directory Assistance.

Tucson had a Broadway, but no Sharpe at the address shown in Ives's book.

I put my feet up on the coffee table and did some more thinking. Then made another telephone call.

Gordon Lockhart was in conference, his secretary said. He couldn't be disturbed.

"Tell him this is Calvin Bix," I said. "I'm calling about Mrs. Danton, and it's important. I'll wait."

Almost immediately Lockhart was on the line.

"Yes, Bix."

"Mrs. Danton might have a bigger problem than she realizes," I said. "Her boyfriend Ives, who she thinks stole her jewelry, has been subpoenaed to appear in the U.S. Attorney's office tomorrow, to give a deposition. I don't know what it's about, but the case is the U.S. versus someone named Frederick W. Cahill Sharpe, who has an office on Broadway in a city I can't identify. Can you put one of your people on it? Mrs. Danton's reputation—"

"I understand. I'll have someone go to work on it right away."

I put the telephone back on its stand and leafed through the address book. Ives had the same habit as many other people: He jotted down street names but omitted zip codes, area codes, and, usually, the names of cities. And apparently he didn't know anyone whose last name began with X, Y, or Z. Those pages in the book were covered with a list I couldn't decipher. It consisted of letters and numerals.

Time to leave, I decided after a while. Slipping the address book into my pocket, I put everything else back into the drawer and closed it. Then I let myself out of the apartment—and almost knocked Jill Cranmer over. She'd been standing in the corridor, her ear to the door.

"Well, how about that?" I said.

"I—I—Cal! I thought I heard Peter come in."

A lie, I knew. I'd made virtually no noise as I'd moved about. Evidently Dennis had called her.

I took her by the arm. "Come in and talk to me."

"Andy," she said, resisting. "He's alone."

"He'll be all right for a few minutes."

"No. Really. I—"

I tugged. We crossed the threshold, and I closed the door. "Sit down," I said, nodding toward the sofa.

"Really, Cal, I—"

"Sit down, Jill!"

She seated herself reluctantly on the edge of the sofa. "You shouldn't be here," she said.

I wondered how much of my conversation with Lockhart she'd been able to hear. Not enough for me to worry about, I decided.

"Those gloves," she said. "You look like a burglar."

"Do I?" I held up the keys Dennis had given me. "I'm a friend of the family's. Let me show you something."

I brought the box of photographs from the bedroom closet and handed her the one of herself with Peter and the other man.

"Where was this taken?" I asked.

Her lips parted. Her nostrils flared. I'd seen people held at gunpoint who looked less alarmed.

"Where, Jill?"

"Ah . . . ah . . . at the Mountain Mirage."

"What's the Mountain Mirage?"

"A—a hotel."

"A hotel where?"

"In Arizona."

"Tucson?"

"Yes."

"Who's the other man in the picture? The one on your left."

"I don't know."

"Jill!"

"Honest."

"Who is he, Jill?"

"Honest to God, Cal."

"You also have a picture of him in your apartment. What's his name?"

She started to get up. "It's time for Andy's—"

I put my hand on her shoulder. "Sit still. What's the man's name?"

"I don't see why I—"

"You have a problem, Jill. I'm just the beginning of it. What's the man's name?"

Her eyes searched mine. Mine weren't helpful. "Chili," she said.

"Chili?"

She nodded.

"Chili what?"

She hesitated. "Solana."

"Chili Solana. O.K., what does he do?"

"He works at the hotel."

"The Mountain Mirage?"

Jill nodded again.

"That where Peter worked?"

"Yes. I don't see why—"

"And you? You worked at the Mountain Mirage too?"

She shook her head. "I worked in an office."

"But the three of you are friends. Were all of you in the Cholla Players?"

Again her nostrils flared. "I'm going to call the police. You have no right to be here. You lied to me. You're not part of any advertising agency with a commercial."

"Where were you last Thursday, Jill, when someone tried to shoot your friend Peter? It happened in the parking lot, right under your window. You must have been home. You must have heard the shots. What did you do? Has Peter called you? Where's he hiding?"

"I don't know, I don't know, I don't know, I don't know. Leave me alone. I'm going to scream."

"Answer my questions."

"I don't know anything about any shooting. I don't know where Peter is. I don't know where he went. Honest to God."

"Everyone in the building knows about the shooting. Where's Peter hiding, Jill? What's happened to him?"

"I don't know. You're asking questions you've no right to. All you are is a private detective."

"A private detective, am I?"

She realized that she'd made a mistake. And lowered her voice. "I think so. You must be."

"You figured that out, did you? With Dennis's help?"

"I've got to go, Cal. It's time for Andy's bottle." She started to get up again.

Again I put my hand on her shoulder. "Who's Frederick W. Cahill Sharpe?"

"I don't know. Take your hand off me."

"Who is he?"

"I don't *know*, I said. I've never heard of him, I swear on the Bible. I'm going home. You just try and stop me!"

She jumped to her feet. I didn't try to stop her. She opened the door, muttered, "Motherfucker," and left.

I returned the box of photographs to the closet, but kept the one of Ives with Jill and Solana.

Minutes later, as I was walking to my car, I saw Panjit Gupta coming toward me. He had a transparent cleaning bag over one arm.

With his free hand he waved.

I waved back. Presently the two of us were face to face. Through the plastic I saw his tuxedo.

"Mr. Bix!" He was all smiles. "Still pursuing your investigation?"

"Still at it," I said.

"Splendid, splendid. I hope you discover the guilty party. I will feel safer in my bed, knowing there is one less criminal on the streets."

"I'll do my best," I said.

We exchanged nods, and both of us walked on.

So far, I thought, Panjit Gupta had done more for me accidentally than anyone else had done on purpose.

8

"Messages?" I asked.

"Mr. Zabin," Veronica replied. Veronica worked the four-to-midnight shift at my answering service. "He confirms two o'clock tomorrow—his office."

"O.K. Anything else?" I was hoping for a message from Lockhart.

"No, sir."

I hung up and called Frank. His wife answered. Frank was in the basement, she said. Patching.

"Patching?"

"The linoleum. It's worn through. I'll call him."

Frank took his time but eventually picked up the telephone.

"Bring the pictures to my office in the morning," I said. "Nine-thirty all right?"

"If they're ready by then. I'll have to call the guy."

"Then call him. I've got to be at the U.S. Attorney's office at ten and I don't know how long I'll be there."

"You got business with the U.S. Attorney, Cal?"

"No. I just want to see if a certain party shows up."

"I could do that for you," Frank suggested. "Save you time."

I smiled. Frank the Hustler was emerging. "Thanks," I said, "but this is one I want to handle personally. I'll look for you at nine-thirty."

The next call took less than a minute. Mrs. Danton couldn't speak to me, Helga said; she had a migraine headache.

I thought about dinner. There were some frozen things in the refrigerator, but none of them appealed to me. In the end I decided to eat out. So I put on my coat, went down the block to Biffy's Buffet, had the tuna salad plate, and returned home with grievances. The tuna salad plate hadn't been good, and the busboy had accidentally knocked over my glass of water.

Images of Laura came and went. I felt restless. After a while I called her. But she too had an answering service, and the operator I spoke to said, in a wildly Appalachian accent, "Miz McKayyuh is aye-out?"—making it sound like a question. "Y'caya t'leave ya nay-um an' numbah?"

"Noah," I said, and hung up.

Taking Peter Ives's address book from my pocket, I went into the bedroom, made myself comfortable, and pretty soon was boring into another man's life.

Some of the addresses were almost certainly Arizonan; the streets had names like Gambel's Quail, Desertstar, Blackfoot Canyon. A few of the people in the book lived, I believed, in New York, but I wasn't sure; lots of cities had 72nd Sts., Broadways, and 3rd Aves. A few of the other people were obviously Chicagoans; they lived on Lake Shore Dr.—or as Ives abbreviated it in one instance, LSD—and other streets I was familiar with.

There was no entry for the Mountain Mirage, but Chili Solana was listed. Under C. No last name; just "Chili," on Eagle Drive. Jill was listed too, at an address I figured was in Tucson—Smokewood Mission Place.

Dennis's name was there, but his address and telephone number had been erased. A new telephone number had been penciled in, but not a new address. The new telephone number looked like a Chicago one. Anita Danton was also in the book. But the name I most wanted to find was missing. One of the reasons Ives had gone to Tucson, according to Laura, was that his father lived there. Yet this address book had only one *I* listed—Independence Motors.

When he'd been in trouble before, he'd run to his father, and it was possible, I reasoned, he'd done the same thing this time.

Or, if not his father, who else? Having been shot at, under whose roof would he seek shelter with his pocketful of diamonds and sapphires?

The little book offered no clue, and after a while I quit trying to find one. Instead I concentrated on the list at the back, on the *X, Y,* and *Z* pages.

I counted the entries. There were thirty. They were divided into three categories, headed *T, P,* and *F.* These, in turn, were divided into subcategories, which were also identified by letters. The subcategories under *T* were *VOS, FO, CC, WD,* and *RSL.* Some of these same letters, but not all of them, appeared under *P* as well, and *WD* was included under *F* too.

Each subcategory had one, two, or three entries listed under it. Those under *FO* in the *T* category were "Rose 219865," "Banl 557342," and "StVin 381123." Those under *CC* were "How 9176-B" and "Domin 5611-J."

Altogether, *T* had fourteen entries, *P* ten, and *F* six. There were various combinations of letters and numbers. They obviously weren't telephone numbers or addresses, but I checked them against the names in the front of the book anyway.

There was no "Rose," no "Banl," no "StVin." Nor was there any name that resembled "How" or "Domin." The list in the back seemed to have nothing to do with the names in the front.

I'd never dealt with codes. Decoding took muscles I didn't have. I felt like a pole vaulter who because of a screw-up finds himself entered in the hundred-yard dash.

Or was it a code? Perhaps it was merely a memo that Ives had written to himself and had nothing to do with messages sent or received.

I toyed with and discarded one theory after another. Time passed quickly. I was startled when I looked at the clock on the night table and saw the hands pointing to ten minutes after ten.

Lockhart, I thought. And called my answering service.

Yes, Veronica confirmed, a Mr. Gordon Lockhart had been trying to reach me. He'd left a number and wanted me to get back to him as soon as possible.

I dialed. A woman answered. But before I could tell her who I was, Lockhart picked up an extension telephone and said, "Bix?"

"Yes," I replied.

"Hang up, dear," he told the woman. "This is business." There was a click.

"I've been waiting for your call for hours," the lawyer said irritably.

I didn't tell him that I usually had my calls routed to the answering service even when I was home. I merely said, "Working."

"Anyway," he went on, "I've found out about the Sharpe trial. It hasn't started yet, but it's about to. In New York. And it's major. Money laundering."

I said nothing. Money laundering hadn't crossed my mind.

"Did you hear me?" Lockhart demanded.

"I heard. It's bad news, I think."

"I don't know the details," he said. "Trying to get information from the U.S. Attorney's office is very difficult. But I have someone in New York working on it and I'll know more tomorrow. Meanwhile, Bix, from what you've learned, how does this affect Mrs. Danton?"

"If I were Mrs. Danton," I said, "I'd forget about the jewelry and get on the first plane for Europe."

"Are you serious?"

"Does she know anyone in Europe she could stay with?"

"Vicky Scheyler is one of her best friends. But I don't see—"

"Who's Vicky Scheyler and where does she live?"

"In Germany. Her first husband was Sam Greene. After their divorce she married Otto Scheyler. *The* Otto Scheyler."

Judging by Lockhart's tone, I guessed that Otto Scheyler owned, at the very least, the entire Black Forest. "Well, you ought to advise our client to call her friend Vicky and invite herself over for a visit." I said. "At a hotel she'd be easy to locate, but at someone's house she wouldn't."

"Now wait a minute. Let's not overreact."

The voice of reason, I thought. Of conference rooms and "let's work it out." And maybe Lockhart was right. But he hadn't been in Ives's apartment, hadn't seen the subpoena, hadn't met Jill Cranmer or Dennis Close, whereas I had.

"The reason Mrs. Danton wanted to work with a private investigator instead of the police," I said, "is because she's afraid of publicity and gossip. Of being laughed at. She's afraid the word will get around that the good-looking young man she's been showing up at parties with stole her jewelry. I thought she was wrong to lose sleep over something like that, and told her so, but now the situation is different. If Ives is mixed up with someone who's about to go on trial for laundering money and it gets into the newspapers . . ."

"I see what you mean. But you're jumping to conclusions."

"True. I am. And I'm supposed to worry about her necklace and earrings, not her public image. But I'm beginning to think the necklace and earrings are the least of it. Someone tried to kill Ives last Thursday night. Took a couple of shots at him in the parking lot behind the building where he lives. Because of a freak circumstance the shots missed and he got away, but he was plenty scared. That, I think, was when he decided to steal whatever jewelry Mrs. Danton happened to be wearing on Saturday night. He needed getaway money."

"Someone doesn't want him to give that deposition," Lockhart speculated.

"Looks like it," I agreed.

"You believe he knows who fired the shots?"

"Most likely. Anyway, he's caught between a rock and a hard place—in trouble if he gives the testimony and in trouble if he doesn't. But as far as Mrs. Danton is concerned, it'll be worse if he doesn't. Say the prosecuting attorney in New York really needs the deposition and Ives doesn't show up tomorrow. Say the U.S. Attorney's office sends men out to find him and bring him in. At that point the story becomes bigger and the media are more liable to pick up on it. Even if Mrs. Danton's name isn't mentioned, the people whose opinions mean so much to her will make the connection, and everything she's afraid of will happen. Or if you want to go with an even worse scenario, picture Mrs. Danton on the witness stand, admitting that she knows Ives."

"You're looking at the darkest side possible," Lockhart said.

"One wrong friend can do a person a lot of harm."

"Let me sleep on it," he said. "You're not altogether wrong, I suppose. I have a full day tomorrow, but I'll work Anita in somehow. I'll tell her what you said."

"Do that," I urged.

"But," Lockhart added, "I'll also tell her I think you're being too pessimistic."

I sighed. "Suit yourself." I was glad that Gordon Lockhart was Anita Danton's lawyer and not mine.

It was still dark when I woke. The bedside clock said twenty minutes to six. I felt off schedule; usually I was sound asleep at that hour.

After a while I got up, made a pot of coffee, and took it into the living room. Sitting there, I watched the sky brighten. The lake slowly went from black to ash gray; buildings took on distinct shapes; trees, gnarled and bare, became recognizable. And one stubborn star lingered. I wondered which star it was.

A slap outside my front door announced the arrival of the newspaper. I took it in. The headline was MAYOR DENIES CONTRACT FRAUD. Chicago politics as usual, I thought, and turned to the sports pages. The big sports story wasn't about a team or a game, however, but about cocaine.

Graft. Drugs. Illegal profits. Thousands, millions, billions of dollars in need of laundering.

What did Peter Ives know about Frederick W. Cahill Sharpe that someone didn't want him to tell? Was he going to tell it anyway?

If he appeared at the U.S. Attorney's office, I would be able to corner him. And he would tell me what he'd done with the jewelry. I'd dealt with amateur thieves before; most of them were afraid of their own pasts. Ives would be no exception.

But somehow I didn't think he would appear. And if he didn't . . .

I considered my options. More pressure on Dennis Close? On Jill Cranmer? Telephone calls to other people listed in the address book?

Or how about a different approach? Pawnbrokers, for instance. I had good contacts among the big ones, and only a big one would handle a necklace and earrings worth a hundred thousand dollars. But it was more likely that Ives would take the jewelry to someone who made a business of fencing stolen merchandise.

I pictured Ives. Sunday afternoon. The jewelry in his pocket. Anxious to put as much distance between himself and Chicago, which way would he head? Or was he still in town?

He was wearing a tuxedo, I reminded myself. There weren't many places a man could go on a Sunday afternoon in a tuxedo without attracting attention. But suppose Dennis had lied about the tuxedo.

I decided to apply more pressure on Dennis, and to employ

Frank for that purpose. While I was in the U.S. Attorney's office, the retired policeman could play at being a policeman who wasn't retired.

I got to my office early. Chloe, the eight-to-four lady, said that there were no messages. I thanked her and said I'd take my own calls for a while.

"You mean it?" she asked.

Her disbelief was understandable. Early on, I'd learned that an answering service made a good screen. It kept me from having to take unwanted calls from salespeople, pollsters and, above all, hostiles. Every now and then I made an enemy, usually in connection with a divorce case. And sometimes one of the enemies tried to harass me over the telephone.

I took out the photographs of Babette Mantino and went through them again, planning what I would say to her husband and his lawyer. But before I got very far, the telephone rang.

"Mr. Bix?" It was a woman's voice, and unsteady.

"Yes."

"I need you. Right away. You may not remember me. I'm Clarice Bergen. I mean, I was when you knew me. My name is Rogers now. Something awful has happened."

"I remember you," I said. I'd helped her get a divorce.

"Arnie's disappeared, Mr. Bix. He's thirteen now, and I have him in boarding school in Connecticut. But I just got a call from the headmaster. He says Arnie's missing, and I'm afraid his father's kidnapped him. I need your help."

The details of the case came back to me, and I suspected that her fear was justified.

"I don't handle kidnapping cases," I said truthfully. I'd had several experiences with recovering children who'd been placed in the custody of one parent and then kidnapped by the other. I'd found that as often as not, the child wanted to stay with the kidnapper. After one particularly awful day, when I'd torn a screaming six-year-old girl from a father she loved so that I could return her to a mother she didn't, I'd said to myself, "No more."

"He might not have been kidnapped," my would-be client said quickly. "He might have run away."

There was a knock on my door. A moment later Frank appeared.

I said, "I'm sorry, Mrs. Rogers. Tell me where the school is, and I'll try to locate someone for you in that area. Otherwise let me suggest that you call your lawyer."

"Damn you!" the woman exploded, and slammed down the telephone.

I turned to Frank.

"Who was that?" he asked. "Your face is red."

"A satisfied client," I replied, and, putting the telephone back on its cradle, I took a deep breath.

Frank dropped a large envelope on my desk. "The guy charged me extra. Said he was up till midnight. Here's his bill. And here's mine."

I looked at the totals. They seemed fair enough. "Sit down," I said. "I've got something else for you."

Frank took off his coat. While he was hanging it up, the telephone rang again.

"I'm so glad to have caught you," Anita Danton said. "I was afraid I'd have to leave one of those messages."

"How are you?" I asked. "I called last night, but Helga said you had a headache."

"I still have it. They last a couple of days. I feel wretched. But I want you to know I'm taking your advice. I'm flying to Frankfurt just as soon as I can get ready."

"You are?" I was surprised by how relieved I felt.

"Yes. Gordon called me this morning and told me everything you said. I'm appalled. Utterly. Peter involved with something like that. I'm so grateful to you, Mr. Bix. You've done me a tremendous service. You went far beyond what any other investigator would have done, I'm sure, and Gordon was right—you're the best. When I think what I might have been exposed to! Please send me your bill immediately;

I'd like to pay it before I leave. I'm a terrible judge of people, aren't I? Anyway, you've saved me. I'm reporting the loss to my insurance company. Goodbye, Mr. Bix, and thank you again. Thank you, thank you, thank you." Anita Danton hung up.

Frank seated himself beside my desk. "All right, now, what's this other thing you've got for me?"

"Breakfast," I said, smiling. "How do you like your eggs?"

9

Zabin and Zabin was a specialty shop. Divorces only.

As such, it employed six lawyers instead of a hundred and sixty and occupied half of one floor of a building instead of, say, floors twenty-five through thirty with the corridors color coded to keep clients from getting lost. Yet the Zabin brothers had managed to spend three quarters of a million dollars, Jerry had once confided to a mutual client of ours, on furniture and fixtures.

The receptionist in the waiting room was seated at a slab of glass that was mounted on a marble pedestal, and to announce me she used a French telephone that looked as if at some point it might have belonged to General de Gaulle.

"Mr. Jerrold Zabin is in conference room B," she said then. "That's the second door on your left."

I struggled along a short hall that had carpeting so thick you had to be careful not to turn your ankle and entered the conference room. I'd come early so that I could have a few minutes with the lawyer before Mantino arrived, but Mantino had come even earlier. He and Zabin were sitting at right angles to each other on two of the four chairs that were grouped around a lacquered coffee table. Behind the grouping was a Chinese screen with panels that depicted, appropriately enough, men at war.

Zabin rose. So did Mantino. Zabin smiled. Mantino didn't; he looked like someone who was about to have a tooth pulled.

I chose the chair that faced Mantino's and had the same reaction I'd had at our first meeting: surprise that there was nothing thuggish about him. Fine-boned, pale, and blue-eyed, with thin lips and a narrow chin, he fitted my notion of preppy—and was every bit as attractive as the man in the photographs I had on my lap. If I hadn't known that this offspring of Bear Mantino's was a successful electronics dealer, I would have guessed that he was a scientist in one of the slick new fields—genetic engineering, maybe, or advanced optics. Never in a million years would I have guessed that he was the son of a man who'd got started by breaking legs and slashing noses and who'd risen to a level at which he could order assassinations. I had to remind myself that I didn't really know what was going on behind the facade; that Allen Mantino might take after his father more than I thought.

"I've just been telling Allen that you've managed to get some incriminating evidence," Zabin said, to start things off.

"That's true," I said.

Mantino's expression didn't change. It remained alert, closed.

"With these pictures," I said, "it should be clear sailing."

"The sailing is never entirely clear," Zabin put in. After all, he was planning to charge plenty for his services.

"Naturally," I said to him, and turned back to Mantino. "But in the light of these"—I tapped the envelope—"your wife won't be able to claim she's only a poor, innocent housewife and mother."

"That's what we were hoping for," Zabin said.

I looked Mantino in the eye. "Before I show them to you, though, let's go back to the talk we had a couple of weeks ago, when you told me you didn't want anything really bad to happen to your wife. A divorce settlement is one thing, you said, but—"

"I know what I said," Mantino interrupted.

"If your father should somehow get hold of these pictures—"

"He won't."

"Or if you should tell him about them—"

"Leave my father to me, Mr. Bix. I know how to handle him."

"Do you?"

Mantino didn't answer.

I glanced over his shoulder at the Chinese screen. Warlords, I thought. Early Oriental Bear Mantinos. "I don't want to feel I've contributed to an assault," I said, "or to something even worse."

The man across the table gripped the arms of his chair. " 'It takes two to make a divorce,' my father keeps telling me. And my mother agrees with him. They think I'm as much to blame as Babette is. And God knows, maybe they're right. Anyway, I'm going to let them go on thinking that. But it'll be a lot better for them, for me, for everyone, if I get custody of my son. So let's see the evidence."

I handed the envelope to Zabin. He opened it and took out the pictures. I hadn't arranged them in any particular order. The one on top showed the cellist leaning against the refrigerator, with Babette Mantino kneeling in front of him.

As Zabin studied the photograph, his eyes widened, his lips parted, his face turned slightly pink. After a while, he put it on the bottom of the pile and studied the next. His face turned even pinker.

"Jesus!" he exclaimed.

Mantino reached for the pictures, but Zabin held on to them, so Mantino got up and went around to where he could see them over the lawyer's shoulders.

After one look he turned pale. But he didn't go back to his chair. He stood there, hands clenched, jaw muscles pulsing, as Zabin went through the first dozen photographs slowly, one at a time. Finally Zabin abandoned the task. He put the photographs on the table, took a deep breath, and turned to me.

"Remarkable," he said hoarsely. "How did you get them?" Instead of answering, I inclined my head toward Mantino, who had sat down again and, white as a sheet, was going through the pictures on his own. His jaw muscles were pulsing more rapidly, his nostrils had dilated, and I was afraid he was going to break down.

He didn't, though. Doggedly he studied each photograph for some moments before placing it at the bottom of the stack and going on to the next.

"That's enough, Allen," Zabin said presently, but Mantino ignored him.

"I'll give you the man's name and address, the time and date the pictures were taken," I said to Zabin, "and any other information you want."

The lawyer nodded.

Mantino finished with the pictures and put them on the table. He opened his mouth to speak, but closed it again.

"It's everything we need," Zabin assured him. "You'll have your son. As for the settlement . . ."

"Thank you," Mantino said to me. He looked like hell.

"My job," I murmured.

He extended his hand across the table. I took it. It was very cold.

"Thank you," he said again. "If there's ever anything I can do for you . . ."

I said, "Things will work out for you. You'll see." It was the best I could do.

Five minutes later, having supplied Zabin with the pertinent facts about the photographs, I was in an elevator, riding down to the ground floor.

There was a bar off the lobby. I went in and ordered a Scotch.

*　　　*　　　*

It was a quarter past three when I left the bar and began the fifteen-minute walk across the Loop to my own office. By then I was no longer having there-must-be-a-better-way-to-earn-a-living thoughts, but I was still out of sorts.

The wind whipping along Chicago's Madison Street on its way from Saskatchewan to New York was sharp and cold. It caused my thoughts to take a different turn. For the first time in more than two years, I realized, I didn't have a single case to work on. Usually I was juggling two or three simultaneously, but now the slate was blank. Maybe I should take a vacation. Florida. Barbados. Hawaii. With luck, I might run into another CIA agent who had a useful gadget to sell.

Cheered by visions of palm trees, snorkeling gear, and bright sails in the sunset, I hurried on, arrived at my office in an up frame of mind, and got to work on the ledgers, which I'd been neglecting. My recent expenditures had been low, I noted, and my income high. Furthermore, there would be money coming in from Anita Danton and Allen Mantino. I could afford to go anywhere—and to take a friend with me. Laura McKay, for instance.

Elated by the prospect, I called her.

"I've got a great idea," I said. "How about if I come over and tell you about it?"

"Does your idea concern me, I hope?"

"It does."

"Then by all means come. I'll fix us some hors d'oeuvres."

"I'll be there in twenty minutes. You'll love my idea."

And love it she did. The only trouble was, she couldn't get away just then. She had an installation next week; an entire accounting firm was moving to new quarters, and the move was in her hands. Then the following week a construction crew was going to tear down the wall between Gladys and Lawrence Kelly's living room and den, and she had to be there to supervise. How about the week between Christmas and New Year's, though?

That was more than a month away, I pointed out. By then I might be up to my neck in clients' problems. There was no telling when I'd hit another period like this; we didn't have recess often at my school.

Laura sighed. "Clients," she said sadly.

I sighed, too. I was disappointed.

"But it was a lovely idea, duck darling. Would you mind giving me a bit more Dubonnet?"

I poured the wine for her and refilled my own glass. I was still on Scotch.

Laura eyed me over the rim of her glass. "What I don't understand is how you solved Anita's problem so soon." She paused. "It is solved, isn't it?"

"In a way," I said. "Peter Ives disappeared, and she wanted me to find him, but now she's changed her mind."

"And the last thing in the world you want is to tell me the details, right?"

"Right."

"Very well, I shall ask you no further questions." She continued to eye me. "You're not eating."

Laura was a better designer than cook. The hors d'oeuvres she'd brought out consisted of slices of apple and cheese held together with toothpicks. To be polite, I took one.

"Anyway," I said, "how about tonight? Been to Mon Goût?" Mon Goût was the new restaurant everyone said was so good. "If I can get us a reservation . . ."

But Laura couldn't have dinner with me, either. Not that night. She was invited to the Conovers'—their son and daughter-in-law were in town from New Orleans, and they were having some friends over. "In fact," she added, "I have to start dressing soon. It's almost six, and I'm supposed to be there at seven."

"If that's a hint," I said. I got no further, because the telephone rang.

Laura excused herself and went into her office. I finished my drink, decided to have another quick one, and, after pouring it, turned on the television set.

A network anchorman was assembling the pages of his script. "And that's our news for tonight," he said.

Drink in hand, I watched a string of commercials. They urged me to buy cat food, rustproof my car, and take a gentle laxative. Then the local news came on.

The top local story was the one that had been the morning's newspaper headline: the mayor denied that there had been fraud in the awarding of contracts. The video showed him walking along a corridor in City Hall, accompanied by reporters who were thrusting microphones at him. The charges were ridiculous, he was saying; drummed up by a desperate opposition, in order to discredit his administration.

The anchorman reappeared on the screen. "Chicago's Gold Coast was the scene of a grim gangland-style slaying," he said. "Early this afternoon the body of Chicago actor Peter Ives was discovered in the garage of the house belonging to prominent socialite Anita Danton. Randy Wolford was there."

The anchorman vanished. An alley appeared. In the center of the screen a body covered with a gray rubber sheet was being carried through the wide doorway of a garage on a stretcher. At the left, a red and white ambulance was parked, its rear doors open to receive the stretcher. A small cluster of bystanders looked on silently from the right.

A reporter, hatless and wearing a raincoat, stood beside the garage, reading from notes fastened to a clipboard. He said:

"Shortly after two o'clock this afternoon, the body of Chicago model and television actor Peter Ives was found sprawled across the front seat of his car, which was parked in this garage, located behind the luxurious town house owned by Anita Danton, widow of the late Howard Danton and one of Chicago's best-known social leaders.

"Ives had been shot twice in the back of the head. It is believed that the shooting occurred sometime last weekend, although police are withholding comment on the exact time until the medical examiner has delivered his findings."

The stretcher was lifted into the ambulance, and the doors were closed.

"Ives, a frequent companion of Mrs. Danton's, had parked his car in the garage on Saturday night, she said. Declining to be interviewed further, Mrs. Danton has withdrawn into the house and is now unavailable to reporters. This is Randy Wolford, outside the Danton residence on Chicago's Near North Side."

There was a quick cut from the alley to the television studio and the anchorman, who said, "We'll keep you informed as the story develops. And now, turning to the weather . . ."

I sat there, staring at the screen, unaware that Laura had come into the room.

"Did that man just mention Anita Danton?" she asked.

I glanced over my shoulder. Laura too was staring at the screen.

"They've found Peter Ives," I said. "He's dead. He was dead before I even took the case."

10

Television crews had set up camp on the sidewalk and the patch of grass in front of the Danton house. Reporters and cameramen were standing about, waiting for something to happen. A few people with nothing else to do were keeping them company.

Someone had knocked over the little tin sign that said the property was protected by the Tremaine Security Service. It was on its side, bent out of shape.

Two reporters converged on me as I turned to go up the steps. One of them was Randy Wolford. I was surprised he was still there; generally television reporters don't hang around long—they're dispatched by radio or telephone from one assignment to another, like the people who work for messenger services.

Wolford said, "Your name is . . . ?"

"Guess," I replied.

Flanked by the two reporters, I went up the steps.

"You a friend of the family's?" the other newsman wanted to know. I'd seen him on the tube but couldn't remember his name.

I didn't answer.

The newsmen stayed with me even after I rang the doorbell. My attempt to remain anonymous failed when Helga opened the door and, seeing me, cried, "Ach, Mr. Bix, Mr. Bix!"

She took my arm and more or less pulled me into the house. She looked awful. The braided halo of hair had slipped to one side, and her expression was that of someone who'd just witnessed a plane crash.

I shoved the door closed with my foot.

"Ach, Mr. Bix," Helga said, holding on to my arm. "I haf done it. Is my fault."

"Take it easy," I said. "What did you do?"

"I haf found him. Is my fault police come."

A man appeared at the top of the stairs. "Who is it?" he called.

"Calvin Bix," I replied.

He loped down the steps two at a time and came across the foyer. "Gordon Lockhart," he said. "Glad to meet you. Thank you for coming."

We shook hands. There was nothing standoffish about him now. At moments like this, apparently, detectives were O.K.

I nodded. "My answering service said 'emergency.' And I'd seen on television what happened."

He pointed to the front door. "We're under siege. And poor Anita—she's a wreck, as you can imagine. Let go of the man's arm, Helga. Nobody blames you."

As Helga released my right arm, Lockhart took my left. He said, "Come upstairs, where we can talk," and escorted me to the library.

The room seemed quite familiar. I took off my coat and threw it across a chair back.

"The police only left a few minutes ago," Lockhart said. "They were here for hours. At first they wouldn't even let me see Anita. I had to threaten."

"Where is she?" I asked.

"In her bedroom. Ellen's with her. Ellen's her daughter. I called and said I thought she should be here. Sit down."

I sat, and he pulled up a chair for himself. He was in his

fifties, I judged, but his were the athletic kind of fifties. He was tall, lean, gray-eyed and gray-haired, and somehow he reminded me of a fox—not because I thought he was tricky but because foxes handle obstacles well.

"Let me brief you," he said, leaning forward. "The police aren't actually accusing Anita of anything, but they obviously have suspicions about her. You see, they found the necklace and earrings in Ives's pocket, and she's admitted they're hers. They seem to think that she caught him walking out with them and shot him. I managed to cast some doubt by telling them what you said about someone trying to kill him last week, and about the subpoena, but still it looks bad."

"Where, exactly, did the shooting take place?" I asked.

"In the garage. As he was getting into his car. Two shots from behind. There's blood on the floor."

"Any fingerprints?"

"I don't know. Ives had left his car in the garage. He always parked there—you know how hard it is to find space on the street in this neighborhood, and Anita doesn't use the garage herself. The entrance is through the alley, and she's afraid of the alley. As she should be."

"Where does she park her own car?"

"In one of the buildings on Lake Shore Drive. Mine's there too at the moment."

I nodded. My car was also in one of those buildings; I hadn't even bothered to look for a parking spot on the street. "Helga told me she's the one who discovered the body," I said.

"She is," Lockhart confirmed. "Because of the way the dogs were acting. They didn't want to go into the backyard, and when she forced them, they simply sat by the kitchen door and whined."

He went on to explain the layout. I was generally familiar with the neighborhood, but I listened carefully anyway, because each piece of property was slightly different. The Danton house had a small backyard, he said, behind which there was a coach house with space for two cars on the ground floor and living quarters for a chauffeur above. Cars entered the garage from the alley that ran the length of the block, and there was a small door on the yard side for passengers. An outside stairway led from the yard to the chauffeur's apartment.

Most of the coach houses on the block had been converted into rental apartments, he added, but the Dantons had left theirs alone. It was rarely used. Ives had been the only one who parked in it regularly.

"I'd like to take a look," I said.

The two of us went downstairs. Helga and Sonia were at the kitchen table, conversing morosely. I noticed three bowls on the floor and asked where the dogs were. She'd put them in the basement, Helga said. She sounded as if she blamed them for all the trouble.

With Lockhart at my heels, I went out the back door and into the yard. The yard was poorly lit by two small bulbs, one above the kitchen door and the other on the coach house. The area was some fifty feet square and was no landscaper's dream. A frail tree clung to life in the middle, and shrubs lined the eight-foot-high brick walls that ran from the main house to the alley and along the alley to where the coach house stood. There was a gate to the alley in the wall near the coach house.

The small door Lockhart had spoken of was at one side of the coach house. It provided access from the yard to the garage. A wooden staircase near it led to the unoccupied chauffeur's quarters. A red, white, and black sign, posted on the door by the police department, warned against entering.

The gate to the alley was locked, I found. I guessed that it was locked most of the time, but decided that this hardly mattered, for while the yard looked safe, it really wasn't. Anyone who could scale an eight-foot wall could get into it, and its seclusion made it a good hiding place.

"Do you know whether the electronic system that monitors the house also monitors the garage?" I asked Lockhart.

He shook his head. "I have no idea."

It probably didn't, I thought. No point in monitoring an outbuilding that was seldom used.

But when we got back to the kitchen, I asked Helga anyway.

"No," she said. "Alarm is joost for house." Whereupon she reverted to what had evidently become her favorite topic— how the strange behavior of the dogs had finally prompted her to investigate the yard and coach house.

"Did Mr. Ives have a key to the garage?" I asked, as soon as I could get a word in.

"Mrs. Danton gif him one," Sonia said unhappily.

Helga sighed in agreement.

Lockhart and I returned to the library.

I said, "Anyone could have climbed that wall, hidden under the stairs to the chauffeur's quarters, and when Ives went to get his car . . ." I made a gun of my thumb and forefinger and pulled the trigger.

"You're convinced he was killed on Sunday?" Lockhart asked.

"Aren't you?" I replied.

"You'd think that after a while the odor . . ."

"The dogs noticed it, all right. Dogs' sense of smell is keener than people's. You've got to keep in mind that the temperature's been well below freezing all week, and the garage probably isn't kept heated. That would slow decomposition. And don't forget that the garage is a separate building and has no windows."

"I'm not used to thinking about things like that," Lockhart admitted. "Criminal law isn't my field."

"Do you know what Mrs. Danton told the police about the jewelry?" I asked. "Did she say she's known since Monday it was missing?"

"I wasn't in the room at that point," Lockhart said. "I assume she told the truth." He paused. "Have you any idea who the killer is?"

"There's a couple of possibilities," I said. "One is Mrs. Danton."

Lockhart looked at me as if I were the Loch Ness monster. "You can't be serious!"

I shrugged. "We only have her word that she didn't find out until Monday that the jewelry was gone. Suppose she saw Ives take it."

"That's preposterous. You know it is."

"The other possibility is, whoever tried to kill him on Thursday and failed tried again on Sunday and succeeded."

"Now you're making sense. I haven't yet told you about the Sharpe case."

"No," I said, "you haven't."

He'd found it harder than expected, Lockhart said, to get information about the upcoming trial. His New York source was "immensely capable," but the government was being tighter than usual about this particular case. There had been few leaks. It was known, however, that the U.S. Attorney's office for the Southern District of New York was under pressure from Washington to get a conviction and was leaving "no stone unturned."

"Apparently they really want to nail this Sharpe," he went on. "Partly because they hope to make an example of him, and partly because they believe he's a big cog in the wheel. They believe he's tied in with the Cyrano Trust."

"The what?"

"The Cyrano Trust. I was hoping you'd heard of it. I myself haven't. Until today, that is."

I shook my head.

"All I was told is it's a trust based in Luxembourg, managed primarily from Switzerland, but with branches everywhere, that has tremendous—and I mean *tremendous*—holdings all over the world: Europe, Asia, America ... Real estate, businesses, stocks, bonds—no one knows how much or what, because different parcels are under the umbrella of different trust entities, with the Cyrano Trust as a sort of master umbrella over them all."

"Sounds, in a way, like one of the mutual fund outfits I have money in," I observed.

Lockhart nodded. "You've hit the nail on the head, Bix. That's exactly what it is: an offshore mutual fund with worldwide holdings and shareholders on all continents—a fund that doesn't disclose its shareholders' names to their governments or report what it pays them. It's undoubtedly, among other things, a haven for drug money and money of all sorts that can't be declared."

"In other words, a superlaundry."

"Precisely."

"And Sharpe has been siphoning money into it?"

"Billions, apparently."

"What line of work does he claim to be in?" I asked. "What does he call himself?"

"A money manager," Lockhart replied.

I smiled. "Can't argue with that, I guess."

"Also a broker. He has a seat on the Big Board, I was told."

"Were you able to find out why Ives was subpoenaed?"

"That was the most difficult part," Lockhart said with a frown. "Apparently they wanted him to identify Sharpe. From a videotape, as I understand it. And to explain his relationship with the man."

"Which was?"

"I'm not certain. Evidently he'd met him and had run one or more errands for him."

I thought about Ives's apartment, his friends, his past. It was hard for me to imagine how a minor actor and hotel employee, newly arrived in New York from Arizona, and a wealthy stockbroker with a seat on the New York Stock Exchange and two middle names had met. They were an unlikely combination. Yet Peter Ives and Anita Danton had been an unlikely combination too.

"The identification was probably incidental," I said. "They wouldn't need Ives to tell them who Sharpe was. They already know. The errand or errands—that's something else again."

"I'm inclined to agree," said Lockhart.

We sat there, the lawyer and I, a couple of gloomy meditators.

"You don't really think Anita did it?" he asked presently.

"It doesn't matter what I think," I said. "What matters is what the police think. And the police like to go with the simplest explanation."

The gloom deepened. It lasted until Ellen Danton came into the room.

"Uncle Gordon!" she exclaimed. "I didn't know whether you were still here or not. The sleeping pills finally worked, but not until I gave her a second one." She noticed me and said, "Oh."

Lockhart introduced us. I was Calvin Bix, he said, a detective her mother had hired to get her jewels back.

Ellen looked me over. "You didn't, though. Obviously."

The "Uncle Gordon" surprised me. I hadn't realized until then how close Lockhart was to the Danton family. "No," I said. "She didn't hire me until two days after Peter Ives was killed."

"Oh." Ellen seated herself on an ottoman and wrapped her arms around her legs. "If only Mother had listened to me! I tried to tell her. She wouldn't listen."

Pretty girl, I thought, and decided that she must take after her father, because, with her long, straight brown hair and almond-shaped eyes, she certainly didn't resemble her mother.

"Now, now," Lockhart said soothingly.

"Well, she wouldn't," Ellen insisted. "You know she wouldn't." She turned to me. "Mother and I had some terrible rows about Peter. That's why I moved out."

"Mr. Bix isn't interested in that," Lockhart cautioned.

I didn't tell them that Mr. Bix already knew.

"Well, anyway," Ellen said, and subsided.

Lockhart glanced at his watch. "Almost time for the ten o'clock news," he said. "Can all of us bear to watch? I think we should."

Without waiting for answers, he turned on a television set that stood against the wall. We saw the last frames of what must have been a crime show. A car hurtled off a mountain road, turned a double somersault, hit the bottom of the gulch, and burst into flames. The bad guys had got what they deserved, I guessed.

The credits began to roll. Presently an anchorwoman appeared on the screen and said, "Coming up in a moment: a brutal murder on Chicago's Gold Coast. Stay tuned."

A carpet cleaner announced special November savings. A shopping mall declared itself to be *the* place to go for all your holiday needs. A beaming husband proudly showed his wife how clean he'd got the dishes.

The anchorwoman returned and got down to business. "Topping tonight's news," she said, "is the story of an actor who was found shot to death this afternoon in the garage of one of Chicago's most prominent socialites."

"Oh, God!" Ellen cried, and hurried from the room.

The story continued with an on-the-spot minicam report narrated not by Randy Wolford but by the other reporter who had accompanied me up the front steps. His name was Dean Hickok. He gave more or less the same facts Wolford had given earlier, but he made them sound worse by placing more emphasis on the necklace and earrings. Listening to him, you would have thought they were worth millions. He also said that while the murder weapon hadn't been found, a police spokesperson had said that it might be nearby. The way he said it suggested that it might still be in the Danton house.

Finally, toward the end he said, "Noted Chicago detective Calvin Bix has been called in by members of the Danton family. Bix arrived at the palatial town house this evening but refused to speak to the press. Presumably he will conduct his own independent investigation of the murder."

"Don't look at me," I said to Lockhart. "I didn't talk to him. He followed me to the front door, heard Helga mention my name, and jumped to conclusions."

The story ended. Lockhart turned off the set.
"The wrong conclusions," I added. "He doesn't know I'm not on the case."
"But you are," Lockhart said. "You have to be."

11

It took me longer than usual to fall asleep. I kept wondering whether I'd done the right thing in letting Lockhart talk me into going back to work for Anita Danton.

"I can't help her," I'd argued. "Everyone knows now that she had a young boyfriend who walked off with a necklace and earrings of hers and got shot on the way out."

"You *can* help her, Cal," Lockhart had replied. "She needs you more now, even, than she did before."

Somehow we'd reached the Cal-and-Gordon stage. Lockhart still reminded me of a fox, but I liked the way he was going to bat for his client; he obviously gave his all to those who employed him. And I admired the quiet reasonableness with which he applied pressure. He was a good arm-twister.

"You know more about Ives than the police do," he went on. "You uncovered the fact that he'd been subpoenaed to give a deposition in a money laundering-case. And from what I've sensed so far, the police aren't anxious to pursue that line of inquiry, perhaps because they're local and it's not. You said as much yourself."

I continued to resist. "Mrs. Danton's reputation is ruined. I can't change that, Gordon."

"No, but you can establish that she's a victim, just as he was."

"The innocent friend of a man who just happened to get blown away in her garage?"

"Precisely. What she needs is for the whole truth to come out."

"The whole truth isn't going to make her look any less like a fool."

"There's a principle at stake, Cal. A good woman is being victimized because of her attachment to an undesirable young man she just couldn't help liking. I don't—and I don't imagine you do, either—want her to have to live the rest of her life with people whispering that even though she was never charged with the crime, she shot Peter Ives. And that's what will happen if the person who actually did kill him isn't identified." Lockhart paused. "The retainer will be a hundred thousand dollars."

I thought it over and accepted. Partly because of the money, and partly because I had a hunch that I myself might be in danger.

The banner headline in the morning paper was SOCIALITE LINKED TO SLAYING. There was a large picture of Anita Danton on page one. Evidently she'd been surprised when the flashbulb went off; she looked panicky and old.

The article was headed "Actor's Body Found in Gold Coast Garage" and, the subhead, in a different typeface, said *"Costly Jewels in Victim's Pocket."*

I read the article carefully. Its tone was like that of the telecast. Rich widow. Young companion. Expensive necklace and earrings. Draw your own conclusion. But somehow the conclusion you drew was that the rich widow had had a hand in her young companion's murder.

Yet there was one piece of information in the newspaper story that hadn't been mentioned on television. A next-door neighbor of Mrs. Danton's, a Mrs. Virginia Hepworth, had seen a stranger lurking about the Danton house on Saturday. When questioned, she'd told the police about him, but the police weren't commenting on this aspect of the case. Putting the newspaper aside, I reached for the telephone. Television had had an effect, all right. My answering service reported eleven messages. Most of them were from people I hadn't seen in a long time who wanted me to know they'd heard Dean Hickok mention my name.

Even my son had called. This was a rare event. Usually when I wanted to talk to him I had to do the dialing.

His was the first call I returned. He'd already left for school, though. His mother relayed his message. It too was Hickok-inspired. Now that I'd been referred to on television, his civics class would be interested in me. Would I be willing to give the class a forty-five-minute talk on crime detection? He was sure his teacher would approve. Also he'd decided what he wanted for Christmas: a computer.

I fielded both requests, not brilliantly, with an "I'll see."

My ex-wife then asked me how I was.

"Fine," I said. "And you?"

"Fine," she said.

There didn't seem to be anything to talk about after that. Laura too had called. I dialed her number next.

"Duck darling!" she exclaimed almost breathlessly. "Someone said you were on the news! But how's Anita? Is there anything I can do? Oops, there goes my other phone. Well, the answering service will get it. What did you say?"

I hadn't said anything yet, but I proceeded to do so. "I haven't seen Anita," I said, "but according to her lawyer and her daughter, she's completely wiped out. The only good thing to come from it all is that her daughter's back with her, at least for the time being."

"Wonderful. And surely you're not going away now on that vacation you were talking about."

"Doesn't look that way."

"I'm glad. I was afraid . . ." Laura didn't say what she was afraid of, but I guessed that it had to do with my abandoning her friend Anita. "Damn, there goes my other phone again.

Keep in touch, duck dearest." And with that, she hung up.

Frank's name wasn't on my list of message-leavers, but he was the next one I wanted to talk with, and I called him. He hadn't seen the news on television the night before, he said; he and his wife had been baby-sitting for Maureen, the pregnant daughter he was worried about; she and her husband had gone to a farewell banquet for her husband's boss, who was, thank God, finally retiring.

Frank did know about the Ives murder, though—he'd read the morning newspaper. When I asked him if he would lend a hand with the investigation, he said, "Sure, but isn't a case like this kind of out of your line?"

"Kind of," I admitted.

He put two and two together. "This have anything to do with that other case you were working on? The one where you said you were running into a bunch of stage-struck people?"

"This *is* the other case I was working on."

"Well, I was thinking about it afterwards, Cal. Stage-struck people, actors, types like that—what I think is, they're like everybody else except in one way: they're more into playing roles. Like us when we go undercover."

Something registered, but I wasn't sure what it was. "Anyway," I said, "here's what I'd like you to do." I gave him instructions, and we arranged to touch base with each other later in the day.

After the conversation ended, I continued to sit there, frowning, trying to pinpoint what it was that had registered.

Eventually it came to me. Frank's words had triggered a memory of the feeling I'd had when looking at the photographs of Ives that Anita had shown me. The feeling that Peter Ives was more than one person, that he changed his identities with his clothes.

My thoughts then went off in a different direction. I began to fool around with an idea that had to do with television. Presently I picked up the telephone again and placed a call to Dean Hickok. He wasn't in the office, I was told by a bored-sounding man. I pictured the man slouched in a swivel chair, with one leg slung over the chair arm, his eyes half closed.

"This is Calvin Bix," I said. "I'm a private investigator. Mr. Hickok wanted to ask me some questions last night about the Ives murder. I wonder if he'd like an interview now."

The boredom vanished. Alertness replaced it. "Could be," the man said, and I pictured him swinging his leg off the chair arm. "Where can he get back to you?"

I gave my number and hung up. Then I detached myself temporarily from my answering service.

Five minutes later my telephone rang.

"This is Dean Hickok," the caller said. "I understand you're willing to give an interview."

"Yes."

"Exclusive?"

"I can't promise."

Hickok hesitated, then said, "O.K.," and we made the necessary arrangements.

Pleased, I went on to try the other stations. I was successful with all of them. In less than fifteen minutes, I'd set up a press conference. It had been far easier than I'd imagined.

As soon as the first mobile unit arrived, a crowd began to collect. By the time all the TV crews had their equipment set up on the sidewalk, the crowd was considerable, and curious apartment dwellers were leaning out of their windows.

I stood in front of the building in which Ives had lived. With the collar of my raincoat turned up and my hands in the pockets, I hoped that I looked like Humphrey Bogart being grim.

Dean Hickok started things off. He introduced himself, then he introduced me. I was, he said, the celebrated private detective Calvin Bix, who had been hired by socialite Anita

Danton, in whose house the body of actor Peter Ives was found shot to death.

I squelched an urge to remind him that the body had been found in the garage, not the house. And to add that I really hadn't been celebrated until the night before, when he'd mentioned me in his telecast.

He threw the first question. "Have you turned up any new evidence, Mr. Bix?"

"Yes," I said, keeping the grim expression going. "The shooting that resulted in Peter Ives's death wasn't the first attempt on his life. Someone tried to kill him here, where he lived, a week ago last night."

Dean Hickok sounded very surprised as he said, "How did you find this out?"

"By questioning his friends and neighbors," I replied. "Peter Ives was anything but a loner. In fact, one of his closest friends, a woman he knew in Arizona before coming to Chicago, has an apartment right across the hall from his in this building. She and other friends of his told me what happened. I can't mention their names, because I don't want to endanger them." I shoved my hands deeper into the pockets of the raincoat and added, darkly, "You never know."

Hickok tilted the microphone toward himself. "Can you tell us more about this previous attempt on Ives's life?" He tilted the microphone back toward me.

I said, "Ives was walking into the parking lot behind this building when suddenly a young man jumped out from between two cars and began firing an automatic handgun at him. Fortunately, the young man was blinded by the headlights of a tow truck that just at that moment turned into the area." I paused. "The police know of the incident. They were called to the scene."

Hickok again drew the microphone toward himself. "As you know, some valuable jewelry belonging to Mrs. Danton was found in the victim's pocket. What's the connection between that and the murder?"

"There is none," I replied when the head of the microphone was again leaning my way. "I suspect that Mrs. Danton gave Ives the jewelry as they were leaving a party last Saturday night. She was afraid of muggers. Ives put the jewelry in his pocket, and both of them forgot it was there."

One of the other reporters piped up. "Are you saying the motive for the killing was something *other* than the jewelry?"

"Right."

"Can you be more specific?"

"I'd rather not. I'm looking into a number of possible motives. I don't want to comment on them yet, but I will say that Ives had important connections in New York and in other cities."

All of the reporters began talking at once. They wanted to know about the important connections. I gave short answers to their questions and added nothing to what I'd already said. Finally, looking squarely at Hickok, I declared flatly, "That's all I can tell you at this point. There are angles to this case I'm just not ready to talk about."

The reporters hung around for another few minutes, but they'd got their story and seemed satisfied. Presently I turned and walked toward the building, not sure whether I was on camera or not, but hoping that I looked competent and knowledgeable even from the back. Letting myself into the building's inner lobby with the key Dennis had given me, I waited until the reporters and cameramen had driven away and the crowd had dispersed. Then I got into my car and headed for the Danton house.

Ellen opened the front door. She appeared to be worn out and discouraged.

"Mother's a total wreck," she said, shaking her head sadly. "She really shouldn't have visitors."

"I only need a minute of her time," I said.

I followed her up to the third floor and waited outside Anita Danton's bedroom until Ellen said it was all right for me to go in.

Anita was pale and gaunt. She seemed to have lost ten pounds since I'd last seen her. Propped against the pillows in a half-sitting position, she gazed at me as if she wasn't entirely sure who I was.

"How are you, Mrs. Danton?" I asked.

She made a vague, careless gesture with one hand.

"Pull yourself together," I said. "The end of the world isn't here yet. I've got a question for you."

She nodded.

"When the police interrogated you yesterday, what did you tell them about the necklace and earrings? Did you say Ives had stolen them? Did you tell them about hiding them in your shoe?"

She made another vague, careless gesture.

"Concentrate!"

"Mr. Bix!" Ellen protested.

"It's for her own good," I said. "I'm on her side."

Anita Danton blinked, turned her head toward me, and said in a faint voice, "I don't know."

"Try to remember," I said. "It's important."

"I said, 'I don't know.' I was so confused. I couldn't explain things."

"You *didn't* tell them about the shoe?"

"It was all so awful. Poor Peter."

"Continue to tell them you don't know," I said. "I've given an interview to some television reporters and I claimed you gave Peter the jewelry as you were leaving the party because you were afraid of being mugged. Can you remember that?"

"I'll keep reminding her," Ellen promised.

"Please do," I said, and taking her arm, I guided her from the room.

"Who's she being?" I asked. "Meryl Streep?"

"She really is upset," Ellen assured me. "But she does dramatize. Always has. It's her way of getting through difficult periods."

"Peter wasn't worth it, though, was he?" I said as we started down the stairs to the second floor.

Ellen shook her head emphatically. "No, he wasn't."

"You probably know things about him that your mother doesn't," I suggested. "Those are the things I'd like to hear about."

Ellen paused before descending to the next step. "You mean it?"

I nodded.

"All right," she said. "Let's go into the library. I'd love to tell you what I found out about Peter. Just love to."

12

On the whole, I believed, Ellen was a nice young woman. A little too sure of herself, perhaps, a little spoiled, but basically well-meaning.

So her vindictiveness toward Peter Ives surprised me. She'd evidently resented him intensely, and she wasn't about to stop resenting him merely because he was dead. He'd been a scumbag, she insisted; he'd intended to take her mother for millions.

I kept my mouth shut about her hiring a private investigator to look into Ives's past, but she brought the matter up herself. She wanted me to know that she wasn't just, as she put it, being snotty; she had *facts*.

The investigator's name was Kevin Cameron. I'd heard of him, but we'd never met. Like me, he was an independent operator. Our paths had almost crossed once in the office of Clark Andrews—Andrews had fired Cameron twenty minutes before I arrived to be hired—but that was as close as I'd ever come to him.

Listening to Ellen, I was reminded of the Andrews case. Two brothers, Johannes and Clark Andrews, had been spying on and suing each other for years over a family trust fund. Each claimed that the other was incapable of managing it. They went through private investigators the way hypochondriacs go through doctors. Cameron was one of the discards, and I was another. I'd antagonized Clark Andrews right off the bat by telling him that I wouldn't give him a hundred percent of my time. Too bad, he'd said; he would have to get someone else.

Cameron, I gathered, had been more flexible. He'd given a hundred percent of his time and had tried to dig up as much dirt as possible about the hated brother. The trouble was, he hadn't dug up enough.

And it was the same with Peter Ives. Cameron must have sensed that Ellen wasn't the average client. She wasn't looking for evidence that would stand up in court; she simply wanted to see all the warts. Which Cameron had set out to find.

But he hadn't found any really big ones. What difference did it make, I wondered, that at the age of ten Ives had been arrested for stealing a bicycle? Or that he'd been in six foster homes and run away from four of them, or that his mother had had a steady stream of boyfriends flowing through the apartment? What difference did it make, even, that as a teenager Ives had tried to earn a few bucks as a male hustler? The guy had come through rotten times and survived—that was the important thing. Not only had he survived, but he'd acquired enough polish to mingle with the likes of Anita Danton.

Even the one major felony he'd committed—the theft of some jewelry from someone named Harper or Harkinson; Ellen wasn't sure of the name—didn't seem so awful, as she described it. And it couldn't have been such a big theft, because the police hadn't followed through; Ives had skipped town, and that was that.

The only useful information I picked up from Ellen was the fact that Peter's last name wasn't Ives but Aves. He'd changed it.

"Ah-ves," she said, repeating it and accenting the first syllable. "The Spanish word for 'birds.' His father, for whatever it's worth, is part Mexican. For a while he was a nothing sort of movie actor—Ramon Aves. Nobody's ever heard of him."

Latin blood, I thought. That would account for the feeling I'd had when Anita Danton had shown me the photographs of Ives—the feeling that the toreador outfit was more right for him than any of the others. And I was almost positive I'd seen "Aves" in the address book; I simply hadn't made the connection.

"Peter's changing his name like that," Ellen said, "shows what a scumbag he was. He was afraid to use his real name."

"Lots of actors change their names," I pointed out.

Her chin shot forward. "His father didn't."

"Where's his father now?" I asked.

"He owns this gas station in Tucson, Mr. Cameron said. I don't know what it's called, but it's on one of the main streets. He lived with his father when he first got to Tucson—his father and stepmother. His father's been remarried for years. Peter has two half-brothers." Ellen paused and went back to her favorite theme. "How Mother ever could have seen anything in a scumbag like that . . ." She shook her head.

I looked at her. She was on the ottoman where she'd been sitting the night before. Her arms were clasped around her knees now, as they'd been then. Her expression was sad.

Father dead at an early age, I thought. Brother dead a few years later. Mother and daughter alone, grieving, in a big, lonely house. And then betrayal by the mother.

I could understand. I could sympathize. Ellen had reason to be sad.

But at the same time I couldn't forget what Laura had said: that Ives had been genuinely fond of Anita Danton. It couldn't have been easy for him in that house, frowned on by the servants, hated by the daughter. I began to sympathize with him too.

"He would have taken Mother for everything she had!" Ellen erupted.

"But he didn't, did he?" I reminded her. "All he got were a few dinners, a few presents. Your mother didn't exactly spend a ton of money on him."

She glowered at me. "It was leading up to that."

There was no point in arguing, I decided. Or in prolonging the conversation. Ellen had unburdened herself but had told me little I didn't already know.

"Well, anyway," I said, getting up, "I appreciate your being so frank. Every little bit helps."

She got up too, and began to look ashamed. "I hope I wasn't too snotty about Peter," she said.

I smiled. "You were honest. There's nothing wrong with honesty."

She went downstairs with me. We shook hands at the door.

"I'm sure you're doing everything you can," were her parting words.

"Everything," I said, and turned up the collar of my coat. It was getting colder.

Frank reported by telephone at a quarter to four. I was at home, watching the end of a soap opera. It was almost time for the late afternoon newscasts to begin. I hadn't seen a soap opera in years and was fascinated. All those beautiful people bravely blinking back tears, plotting revenge, giving in to lust. Reminded me of my clients.

"Had a hard time catching up with the guy who was driving the tow truck," Frank said. "It cost me fifty bucks to the dispatcher. Hope you don't mind."

"It's O.K.," I said.

Frank became policeman-like. I could picture him with the telephone in one hand, his notebook in the other. "The incident occurred, to the best of his recollection, between seven-twenty-five and seven-forty. He'd just turned the corner from the parking area at the side of the building to the parking area in back. Suddenly the suspect stepped from between two cars, pointed an automatic handgun at the truck, and fired several shots. One shot penetrated the right headlight, another the windshield, and a third—"

"Skip that part," I interrupted. "What did the kid look like?"

"He's not so sure it was a kid. It might have been a small adult. And Mrs. Danton's next-door neighbor, the Hepworth woman, says it definitely was an adult. Description as follows: height between five foot, five foot three; weight between a hundred ten and a hundred twenty; small frame, skinny legs, blond hair, big head in relation to the body size. Black pants, according to the tow truck driver, black leather jacket with lots of metal on it. Same jacket the Hepworth woman described, but she thinks blue jeans. Also she noticed the shoes. White, with stripes, like jogging shoes, heavy-looking."

"So they agree, the two of them."

"A few differences, but basically yes. I trust the Hepworth woman's memory more; she saw the guy in broad daylight and for longer, and she wasn't all shook up like the driver— nobody had been firing a gun in her direction. She says the man is close to thirty."

"If you could get any of your buddies on the force to run it through the computer—"

"There's not enough to feed *into* the computer, Cal. No fingerprints, no name, hardly anything. The computer needs more to go on."

I nodded to myself. Frank was right.

"There's something Mrs. Hepworth told me that wasn't in the newspaper," he continued. "Might matter, might not. Has to do with a garbage can in the alley."

"A garbage can?"

"Police are asking questions about it," Frank said. "Seems someone moved a garbage can from one side of the alley to the other. The owner of the property across the alley from the Danton house noticed this last Monday morning. It was her garbage can, she says, and it wasn't where it belonged— it was across the alley, next to the back wall of the Danton yard, near the Danton coach house. This woman—Mrs. Hepworth doesn't know her name—didn't think anything of it at the time; she just shoved the can back to her side of the alley. But when the police canvassed the neighborhood, looking for people who might have seen something, she remembered. And they've been following up the lead. What I think is, a short guy might have needed a little help getting over the wall."

"Sure," I said.

"Anything else I can do?" Frank asked, after a moment.

"Not unless you can think of a way to get a name to go with the description."

"That's a tough one, Cal. We don't have enough specifics."

I smiled at the "we." "I've got to go now," I said. "I'm waiting to see if I'm on TV this afternoon."

"TV?" Frank said wonderingly. "You?"

"Turn on your set," I said. "I don't know which channel. I'm liable to be on at least one of them, though."

"Goddamn," said Frank. He hung up.

I went back to the soap opera. I could no longer keep my mind on it, though. I was seeing a different scene—a dark alley, a small man standing on a garbage can, boosting himself onto a wall, dropping from the wall into the Danton backyard. I saw him look around for a hiding place, find one under the stairway that led to the unoccupied chauffeur's quarters. Saw him waiting there patiently, as he'd waited in the parking lot on Thursday night, until Ives appeared, and then silently following Ives into the garage. . . .

The scene I was visualizing was interrupted by a message. The message was delivered by an irritated-looking woman whose skirt was stuck to her legs. It had to do with static cling.

The next commercial was for one of the soaps that made the soap opera possible. But then a talking head appeared. The head belonged to a pretty young lady who was wearing a dress with a big yellow bow at the neck and was sitting at a long table.

"The City Council turns thumbs down on plans for a new community center," she said, "and the mystery deepens in the Gold Coast murder of Peter Ives. Stay tuned for the news. Coming up in just a moment."

After two more commercials, the anchorwoman reappeared. She and her partner, a man who knew how to keep his eyes serious while his lips were smiling, took turns with the stories. He led off with the City Council story, which, because a couple of council members got into a shouting match, was the most dramatic one of the day. The murder story had less action; it merely showed "celebrated private investigator Calvin Bix" standing on the sidewalk in front of the building in which the murder victim had "resided," describing a previous attempt on the victim's life.

I didn't look as much like Humphrey Bogart as I'd hoped, but I came across all right. With my hands in the pockets of my raincoat and my words about Ives's important connections in New York and other places, I managed to suggest that the murder had been motivated by something big and sinister.

Without waiting for Dean Hickok's closing remarks, I flipped to another channel. And then to a third.

I'd made all three networks.

I turned off the set and waited.

The telephone rang.

"Why'd you do such a dumb thing?" Frank demanded. "Now for the rest of your life everybody's going to know what you look like. You've blown our whole future."

"A week from today nobody'll remember," I replied. "And it was the only way. I have to shake something loose."

"But you've made it dangerous for yourself, Cal."

"It was dangerous for me before, Frank. The best defense is offense—ever hear that one?"

"In football maybe, but not in life. Jesus, Cal, I thought you had more sense!"

"Don't worry," I said. "I know what I'm doing." But inside I wasn't so sure.

Frank hung up, and I did some more waiting.

The wait was a long one. My telephone didn't ring again until ten minutes past six.

"Oh, Mr. Bix," Jill Cranmer said, sounding as if she was having a hard time catching her breath. "I was so afraid you wouldn't be there. Can you come over? I've got to talk to you. I lied to you before. Now I'm worried."

13

The Ganges Palace smelled of strange spices. Curry powder was the main one. There was a multicolored glass peacock in the foyer. The entrance to the dining room was draped with a satiny material that had a 1930s look. The general effect was more art deco than Ganges.

Panjit Gupta was overjoyed to see me. "You came!" he cried, beaming.

When I told him I wasn't planning to stay for dinner, his face fell. But when I said I needed his help in my investigation, he was happy again.

"I'm all participation," he said.

He insisted on consulting Mr. Judal, however. Mr. Judal, he explained in case I didn't remember, was his employer and a very severe man. "I can't risk him," he added.

Judal either approved or didn't give a damn, because Gupta was back in no time flat. "I'm able to assist," he informed me with a big smile. "What do you wish me to do?"

"I'd like to use your apartment for a little while."

His smile faded. Participation had its limits.

"I'm not a citizen of these United States," he said gravely. "If I commit an illegality, I will be deported. Banished from this wonderful land."

I had nothing illegal in mind, I assured him. I merely needed a place to conduct a secret interview. I was as interested in upholding the law as he was.

He was skeptical, a harder sell than I'd expected. But I kept talking and in the end was able to persuade him to give me his keys. I promised to bring them back before he went off duty.

Inside Gupta's apartment, I set up the recorder on the table beside the lounge chair. Then I let myself out and, with the smallest of my transmitters and a strip of two-way tape in my pants pocket, went down to the vestibule and rang the bell marked "Cranmer."

Jill had rearranged her hair. She'd added a fall and worked it into a bun at the nape of her neck. With no makeup on her face and Andy in her arms, she reminded me of a madonna, which, I guessed, was what she'd intended to do. And the pale-blue robelike dress added to the overall image. This evening she was purity, motherhood, sweetness.

"I thought you'd never get here," she said.

"Sorry," I apologized. "I got hung up."

She led me to the sofa and, seating herself, began to sway gently from side to side, rocking Andy. I dropped my coat across the sofa's arm and sat down next to her. The telephone, I noted, was where I remembered its being—on the end table. The nearest picture, a framed print of a ballerina on a stool with her legs extended, was above it and to the left. I estimated the distance between picture and telephone at four feet.

No problem, I thought.

"I don't know how to begin," Jill said with lowered eyes. "You'll hate me. I didn't tell the truth."

"Before you begin at all," I said, "how about a cup of coffee? I haven't had time for dinner. I need something to tide me over."

"Oh, gosh! Sure. It didn't occur to me. Here, hold Andy."

She handed the baby to me and hurried into the kitchen. I put him down and in less than thirty seconds attached the transmitter to the back of the picture. Then, picking him up again, I said in a very low voice, "Don't tell."

He kicked me in the chest.

Presently a teakettle hissed, screeched, and went silent. Then Jill came in with a mug of steaming coffee.

"Cream? Sugar?" she said.

I shook my head and suggested we put Andy to bed.

Her response was, "I'll hold him." Evidently she considered him an important prop.

I gave him to her and took a sip of coffee. She began to rock him some more.

"The first time you were here," she said, not looking at me, "and then the day before yesterday, when I found you in Peter's apartment . . ." She sighed heavily. "Poor Peter!" Her eyes got misty. "I said I hadn't seen him since Thursday. That was true. He was here Thursday afternoon. He came over here a lot; I liked to have him; it gets lonesome sometimes. He was sitting where you are and was in a good mood. He'd had an audition that morning. Nothing big—a radio commercial—but he was feeling up; he thought he was going to get the job. He was here for like half an hour, then he went back to his own apartment and I never saw him again." She heaved another heavy sigh. "But I wasn't telling the truth when I said I didn't know about the shooting that night. I heard the shots. I didn't know what they were, but then in a little while I heard sirens and there was all this fuss outside, and after a while two policemen came to the door, asking if I'd seen anything. There'd been a shooting, they said, but no one had been hurt. I didn't know it had anything to do with Peter, though. I didn't know that until tonight, when I saw you on TV. Now you've got me in trouble, because when you said what you did about Peter's friend from across the hall, people are going to think I know more than I do."

She looked innocent, troubled, appealing.

"You're still not telling the truth," I said. "You did know the shooting had to do with Peter."

She clutched her baby more tightly. "I swear!"

"You were used to hearing Peter come and go, used to having him knock on your door, and suddenly it was quiet. That's one way you knew. Another is, Dennis Close told you."

"Honestly, Cal!"

"Dennis told you what Peter had told him when Peter got to his apartment—that someone had tried to kill him. Not the driver of a tow truck, but *him*. The only way he could have been sure of that is if he recognized the guy who fired the shots. Not only recognized him but knew his motive." I drank some more coffee. "Now let's go back to square one and begin again."

She stopped rocking. Andy had fallen asleep.

"I don't know where square one is," she said, after a silence.

"It's in Tucson, Arizona."

There was another silence, a longer one.

"Why don't you ever believe me?" Jill asked finally.

I didn't reply.

"All right, yes, Dennis told me. Last Saturday, when he came to get Peter's car. Peter'd said someone had shot at him and he was afraid and he was going to go away for a while to where he'd be safe. But Peter hadn't said *who.*"

"Square one," I reminded her. "Tucson. Start there."

"I met Peter when he joined the Cholla Players. I was already a member—I'd joined a little while before."

"What was Peter doing then?"

"Working at a gas station. But pretty soon he quit that and got a job at a hotel."

"Which hotel?"

"I don't remember the name."

"The Mountain Mirage?"

"That's it." Jill was obviously startled.

"Did you work there too?"

115

"No. I was a secretary."

"Who did you work for?"

"I'm not going to tell you. You'll go around asking about me."

"All right, you were a secretary. Continue."

Jill told a tale of plays and performances, parties and good times. The Cholla Players, according to her, wasn't your average amateur theatrical group. It had a good local reputation and some well-heeled local sponsors. The sponsors took care of its annual deficit.

The number of the people who were part of the company varied. It grew in the winter and shrank in the summer, but averaged around twenty. There was a lot of sociability among the members. They went out together and spent time at one another's houses.

"We were like a club, some of us," Jill said wistfully.

"You miss it?"

She nodded.

"So why are you in Chicago? Because of Andy's father?"

"Andy doesn't have a father."

"Oh? The first immaculate conception in two thousand years."

"That's not funny, Cal. Not funny at all. Andy's father split before Andy was born. He's never even seen him."

"That doesn't explain why you're in Chicago."

"Things just happen."

"Did you come here because of Peter?"

"In a way, yes, but not exactly."

I frowned.

"I needed a place to go. I had to get away. Don't ask me to explain; I had my reasons. Anyway, I was pregnant and I needed a place to go, and Peter was living here in this building and he heard there was going to be a vacant apartment on his floor and he told me about it, and I said to myself, 'All right, you have to go somewhere, why not there?' And I came."

"Told you about it how? On the telephone?"

"Yes."

"You'd kept in touch with him?"

"Some of us did."

Jill looked away. She'd been telling the truth, I felt, but now she was starting to lie.

"How did *he* get here?" I asked.

She turned to face me again. Peter had left Tucson a year ago, she said. He'd moved to New York, but after six months he'd decided to give up on New York and try somewhere else. She didn't know why; all he'd ever answered when she'd asked him was that New York was too tough a town for him. Knowing that Dennis was in Chicago, and having heard that Chicago was a good town for actors, he'd driven there and found that he liked the city. Then he'd met Mrs. Danton, and, well, Jill said, I knew the rest.

"But he drove me to the hospital when Andy was born," she added as an afterthought. "Stayed there all night, too."

She gazed at her son. "Maybe I *should* put him to bed."

I nodded.

She got up and took Andy into the bedroom. I hurried into the kitchen and had a quick look around. I saw a saucepan of water on the stove, with no heat under it. Open boxes of Wheaties and Grape-Nuts stood on the countertop. An assortment of unwashed dishes half filled the sink. A printed list of foods and the number of calories they contained was stuck to the door of the refrigerator, with "chocolate chip cookies (two)" circled. A plastic shopping bag leaned against the wall—it was being used as a wastebasket. Riffling through the shopping bag, I found an empty milk carton, two eggshells, the wrapper of a package of frozen string beans, an advertisement for laundry bleach addressed to "Occupant," an old television guide, and a business-sized envelope that had been torn open.

I picked up the envelope, noted the logo for the Mountain Mirage in the upper-left-hand corner, and put the envelope in my pocket.

Moments after I got back to the sofa, Jill returned from her mission.

"He hasn't been crying as much the past couple of days," she said. "I wonder if the wine had anything to do with it."

I shrugged and said, "Don't overdo the wine bit."

Jill sat down beside me again.

"I've got to be going soon," I said, "but before I do, I'd like to know why, exactly, you wanted me to come over tonight."

She tucked her legs under her. "I told you, Cal. I lied about what happened and I want you to know the truth. In case it matters."

"That's nice of you," I said. "I appreciate it. There are a couple of other points that maybe you can help me with too. One is, did Peter ever mention a man named Sharpe?"

"Sharpe?" Jill's face was blank.

"Sharpe with an *e*. Frederick W. Cahill Sharpe. Lives in New York."

She shook her head. "I'm pretty sure he didn't. Is it important?"

"Could be," I said. I believed she was telling the truth. "The other point is, is there a man in the Cholla Players who's particularly short?"

Jill frowned but said nothing.

"Not much more than five feet tall," I went on. "Big head, skinny body. Blond hair. Ring any bells?"

The frown disappeared. "No. Sounds funny-looking, though. Why do you ask?"

"Just wondered." I got up and took my coat from the arm of the sofa.

"Must you go?" Jill asked. "Seems like you just got here."

She walked me to the door and, when we got there, squeezed my hand as a parting gesture.

"I'm sorry I was so awful the day before yesterday," she said. "Most of the time I'm not like that."

I smiled and said, "Goodbye, Jill," and walked into the corridor. She closed the door behind me.

*   *   *

In Gupta's apartment, I sat down in the lounge chair, put on the headset, made sure that the recording tape was pushed into the slot as far as it would go, and settled back to wait.

I heard sounds almost immediately. The musical notes made by the telephone as Jill punched the buttons on the dial.

Presently she spoke. "Juanita?" she said. "Is Chili there? This is Jill."

There was a silence. I wished I'd been able to tap the telephone line, so that I could hear both sides of the conversation, but I'd known I wouldn't have enough time to do that.

"Tell him to call me as soon as he can," Jill said. "Tell him it's important."

A clatter indicated that Jill was putting the telephone back on its stand.

I glanced at my watch. The hands showed nine-thirty.

Taking the envelope from my pocket, I studied it. The logo in the upper-left-hand corner declared that the Mountain Mirage offered "Luxury Under the Sun." Jill's name and address were typewritten. The postmark was so blurred that I couldn't read the date.

After a while I put the envelope back in my pocket, closed my eyes, and tried to imagine what luxury under the sun included.

At eight minutes past ten, Jill's telephone rang. She answered quickly.

"Darling," she said, "he came. . . . Yes, just as you said. Everything. . . . Yes, I think he did. At least he seemed to. . . . About half an hour ago. . . . There's something else, though, dearest. . . . I know. I'm sorry. I can't seem to help it. Anyway, Mr. Bix mentioned the Mountain Mirage. I don't know how he got the name, but he mentioned it. And he asked me who I worked for in Tucson. I told him it was none of his business. I didn't want to get Mr. Chadler involved. Did I do right? . . . He also asked me about a man I never heard of, named Sharpe. Said he lived in New York. Does 'Sharpe' mean anything to you? . . . O.K., I won't. But, Chili, he described someone like Sparrow. . . . Yes, he did. I swear. Could Sparrow have done it, dar—Chili? . . . I *know* it's wrong to ask, I *know* I'm better off not knowing, but it's been on my mind so much. . . . Well, all right, I will. . . . Of *course* I won't call unless it's import— Chili? Darling? Are you there?"

Again there was a clatter as Jill put down the telephone. And then there was sobbing.

Jill sobbed brokenheartedly for a long while. Finally I stopped listening. Detaching the headset, I put on my coat, picked up the recorder, and left the building.

The Ganges Palace still had customers when I went in to return Gupta's keys.

14

The fields were brown. The Mississippi River was a snaky silver thread. There was a bridge five miles down and to the north of us, and a smudge that the pilot said was Cape Girardeau, Missouri. It was not a breathtaking view, any of it.

I sipped my Bloody Mary and waited for lunch. Our flying time to Tucson would be two hours and fifty-eight minutes, the pilot had announced after takeoff. There would be a bit of turbulence over Illinois, but the rest of the flight would be smooth. We should sit back and leave the driving to him.

We'd passed through the turbulence, and now the smoothness was upon us. The plane was uncrowded. Despite the fact that Thanksgiving was only a few days off, not many people were flying from Chicago to Tucson that Saturday morning. I gazed down at the great midwestern tundra and wondered why I had such a strong feeling that Peter Ives was sitting beside me.

I knew he wasn't. Yet as the plane sped southwestward at five hundred and fifty miles an hour, I had a real sense of his presence. It was like traveling with a ghost. A friendly one, who approved of what I was doing.

Strange, I thought. At first Peter Ives had been nothing

more to me than a name and some photographs. Then, in his apartment, browsing among his possessions, I'd begun to be aware of him as a person who actually existed. With the news of his murder, the awareness vanished, but now it was back.

Mentally, I had a sort of conversation with him. I said I was trying to find out who'd killed him, and asked whether he had any advice or suggestions. His answer was that I was on the right track and should keep going.

I realized it was my own unconscious I was talking to, but that didn't stop me.

"Chicken or lasagna?" a cabin attendant inquired.

"Lasagna," I said. I'd had too many bad experiences with airline chicken.

She put the tray on my tray table, and I unwrapped the utensils.

I fooled around with the meal, but my thoughts weren't on it. They were on my invisible companion.

I was experienced in most kinds of investigative work, I told him, with divorce being my specialty, but I'd never handled a murder case. I was simply relying on my belief that there are two kinds of murder—random and specific. The terrorist who plants a bomb in a department store commits random murder—he doesn't care whom he kills. The other kind of murderer intends to kill a particular person and does so.

Your case, I went on, is an example of the latter. Someone set out to kill you, decided on a method, and put his plan into action. In fact, he put it into action twice, because the first attempt failed. Which means that getting you out of the way was a high-priority matter.

Off to the left, the pilot announced, we could see Tulsa.

I was sitting on the right, but I didn't want to see Tulsa anyway.

The victim in a murder like yours, I told Ives, contributes to his own death. He's been singled out because of something he did. He might have done it a long time ago, and unknowingly, but he had done it and it was going to get him wiped out. In other words, Pete, I believe that the cause of your death lies in your life, and that if I can find the cause I can find the killer.

I felt positive vibes coming from the vacant seat next to mine. And denied that I was generating them myself.

I've known a lot of people like you, I continued. The world is full of them. As kids, in order to survive, they had to lie and cheat and steal and say that black was white and blue was red. They learned to live by their wits. They didn't go out of their way to bend rules or break laws, but if they felt the bending and breaking was necessary they did it. And after a while they quit thinking about right and wrong; all they thought about was what was convenient.

The positive vibes stopped.

In California and Chicago you were willing to steal your friends' jewelry, I said to Ives. What were you willing to do in Arizona?

Ives didn't answer, and my sense of his nearness vanished.

The ground changed color. It went from shades of brown to shades of gray and pink and purple. It began to look less flat too. Faintly, in the distance, I saw snow-covered mountains.

I felt good. I like going to new places, and to me Tucson was new. I'd been to Phoenix once. I'd caught up with a very rich orphan there. She'd given her guardian the slip, climbed behind the wheel of his Rolls-Royce, and headed west, not realizing how conspicuous a Rolls is on a desert highway. But that had been my only trip to Arizona.

Frank Norris had spent a couple of vacations in Tucson, though—his wife's sister had lived there for a while. Nice town, he'd told me, but too much crime for its size.

"Worse than Chicago?" I'd said, not believing.

"As bad," he'd replied. "Drugs. You can drive from Nogales and the Mexican border to Tucson in a little over an hour, and some folks do, regularly, with a million or so in coke stashed in the trunk of their cars, or a few bales of

123

grass in their vans. The murder rate is about as high there as here, and there's so much open space that the police have to patrol by helicopter."

"They do?" That was hard for me to imagine. A helicopter isn't much good in a Chicago alley.

"This loud noise woke me up one night," Frank said. "Sounded like someone was running a power mower under the bedroom window, but when I looked out the window I couldn't see anything. Next day I told my sister-in-law about it. It was just the police patrolling, up the wash, she said."

"The wash?"

"A dry creekbed, like. Tucson's not built up, the way Chicago is. There's patches of desert between neighborhoods. My sister-in-law's house backed up to one of these washes. Saw a coyote trotting along it one afternoon. And jackrabbits—you'd have thought that wash was their singles bar. Yet we were only half a mile from a Sears."

A cabin attendant picked up my lunch tray. I tilted my head back and closed my eyes. My thoughts returned to Peter Ives. Not one of the people I'd talked to about him had mentioned drugs. Not even Ellen Danton, who had hired an investigator to dig up all the bad in his past. Even though he'd lived for several years in a city that was a major stop on the drug caravan route, and was, when it came to legal and illegal, flexible.

In his apartment I'd found no sign of drugs. Nor had I noticed any in Jill's. And Dennis Close, weird as he was, hadn't struck me as being either a user or a pusher.

Why, then, did the idea of drugs keep buzzing in my brain? Simply because of what I'd heard about Tucson? Because Ives had known a money launderer? Or was I being influenced by other cases I'd had?

So much of my work these days was bringing me into contact with people who got their kicks from little white crystals. Clients whose problems didn't seem at first to be drug-related turned out to be addicts. As did the friends and relatives they wanted me to investigate. I was beginning to

124

think that everyone I rubbed shoulders with had something to do with narcotics. Even my son, who was not quite fifteen, spoke knowledgeably about crack.

Still, I reminded myself, most of the world was clean. It was wrong to believe that every crime was linked to drugs. Not only wrong but misleading.

Erase the blackboard, Bix. Clear your head. Don't get off the plane thinking you've got it all figured out.

The air pressure in the cabin changed as the plane started its descent. I opened my eyes and sat up. The pilot announced that we were crossing the Continental Divide. He estimated that we would arrive in Tucson in approximately twenty minutes. The temperature there was seventy-eight degrees.

The ground grew nearer, its features more distinct. This was the West, all right; we were coming down into an enormous sun-baked plain surrounded by treeless mountains. Hot-looking, vast, barren—it was the sort of landscape I knew mainly from the westerns I'd seen on television as a kid.

Television. Actors. Peter Ives.

We landed. I collected my gear from the overhead bin and entered the jetway.

For the first two hours I just drove. I'd bought a street map of the city at the airport newsstand, and I kept it spread out on the seat beside me, but I didn't refer to it much; I wasn't trying to find any particular street; I was merely familiarizing myself with the rental car and the area. Getting the feel.

It was more or less as Frank had described. A patchy sort of place that had grown away from its original downtown and was crawling up the lower slopes of the mountains that formed the north rim of the valley. Few tall buildings. Only one limited-access expressway, which didn't cross the city but skirted its western edge and went on to Phoenix. Low population density; no thirty-, forty-, or fifty-story apartment houses, as in Chicago; instead, the same number of units in low-rise complexes that covered acres. Hardly any in-town parks, but quite a bit of vacant land, uncultivated and deserty, in unexpected places.

Not many sidewalks. If you were tailing someone, he would be in a car and so would you. Also, you had to know where streets began and ended; except for main thoroughfares, most streets didn't go very far. And on main thoroughfares the traffic regulations were confusing. Center lanes were used by cars going in one direction during the morning rush hour and the other direction during the afternoon rush hour, and during the rest of the day as left-turn lanes by cars going in either direction. A high-speed chase could easily result in a head-on collision.

By late afternoon I decided I'd seen enough. I checked into a motel called the Livermore. There was nothing special about it, but its location was central and its Vacancy sign caught my eye. It was one of the few motels I'd passed that didn't have "palm" or "oasis" or something Spanish in its name.

I hung up my extra suit and took the recording gear from my carry-on case, along with the tape of Jill and Chili. I also loaded the Leica. Then, sitting on the bed with my feet up and my tie off, I direct-dialed my answering service.

Chloe answered.

"How come you're working on Saturday?" I asked.

"Patrick has a game today," she replied. "I said I'd fill in."

Patrick was the service's only male employee. He was studying to be a data processor and was defensive tackle on a non-pro football team called the Jaguars.

"Any messages?"

"Two. Your son called at ten-twenty-three, and at one-oh-five you had a call from a Jill Cranmer."

"Thanks, Chloe." I hung up.

My son still wanted to know about the talk at his school. His civics teacher wasn't exactly enthusiastic, but he thought he could persuade her. And he'd checked into computers, in case I was interested. There were two models he liked, and neither was *that* expensive. Should he tell me the prices?

"O.K.," I said. "I'm sitting down."

He told me. The prices weren't unreasonable.

"We'll see," I said. "And about the talk—I think your teacher is right."

"What about next weekend?" he suggested. "I'm not doing anything then."

Our weekends together were usually at his request. He didn't like it when I did the requesting.

"I'll try to clear the deck," I said. "At the moment I'm out of town."

"Oh? Where?"

"Out west."

He accepted that. He knew better than to try to pin me down.

"I'll call you," I promised, "and let you know for sure."

"O.K.," he said, and the conversation ended on a hopeful note.

But my conversation with Jill didn't.

She was slow to answer the telephone. When I mentioned this, she said that she was giving Andy a bath and he was slippery—she was afraid of dropping him.

"Can't do that," I agreed.

"I wanted to ask you something," she went on after a moment's hesitation. "This morning I was going out with Andy—we were going to the grocery store—and in the lobby I met one of my neighbors. He was talking to our maintenance man, and I heard him say your name, so I stopped." Jill hesitated again. "He was helping you discover who shot Peter, he said. Helping you with something very secret."

I said nothing.

"Is it true?" Jill sounded uneasy.

"Who are we talking about?" I asked, although I damn well knew.

"His name is Gupta," Jill said. "He's an Indian from India and he works in a restaurant. I hardly know him. But when

I heard him telling Art Lindquist about helping you, I stood there and listened. He said you used his apartment last night for a very secret meeting with somebody that even the police don't know about. Is that true, Cal? I mean, I know you were at my place last night and you were late and, well, you didn't say anything to me about it. I don't understand."

"You're not supposed to understand," I said. "It's nothing that concerns you. Anyhow, nothing happened. The guy didn't show. But if you want advice, stay away from Gupta. He's strange. Is that all you wanted to tell me?"

"No, there's something else. I have a feeling you're in danger. I mean, I can't help thinking that maybe whoever killed Peter might not like all the questions you've been going around asking."

"Is that a warning?"

"No. Just a hunch. Intuition, like."

"Thanks," I said. "I'll keep your hunch in mind."

15

The lawn, like others I'd seen while driving around, consisted of gravel. The gravel was painted green and, in the last light of day, could almost be mistaken for grass. A flagstone walk led from the driveway to the house, which was dun-colored and resembled all the other houses on the street; they were obviously the work of a developer who believed with all his heart in mass production. A Ford pickup truck was parked in the carport, and a Honda Civic stood in the driveway. Near the pickup truck, a bicycle leaned against the wall of the house.

I parked in back of the Honda and crossed the flagstones to the front door. The door had a plastic replica of an Aztec god on it and was flanked by plants that reminded me of big, angry porcupines. Before ringing the bell I took a deep breath—I wasn't expecting the interview to be easy.

The man who opened the door was tall and lean and had a deep tan. The resemblance between him and the photographs I'd seen of his son was uncanny.

"Mr. Aves?" I said. "I'm Calvin Bix."

He nodded unsmilingly and said, "Come in."

I'd called from the motel. He wasn't home then, his wife had told me, but he would be in a few minutes.

I went inside. A waist-high divider separated the entrance area from the living room. The ledge of the divider had an empty vase on it, and a statue of a cowboy on a bucking horse. Ramon Aves escorted me around the divider to a couch. The living room was small but well-kept. An oil painting of a cowboy hung on the wall above the couch. This cowboy was also on a horse, but the horse wasn't bucking and the rider was swinging a lasso.

"You told my wife it's about my son Peter," Aves said, motioning for me to sit down.

"Yes," I said.

Before I could explain, however, a woman joined us. She was tall too, and very attractive, with black hair that was just beginning to turn gray. Her expression was grave.

"My wife," said Aves. "Norma, this is Mr. Bix."

She sat down next to her husband.

He made it easier for me by asking, "Is it good news or bad?"

I said, "Bad, I'm afraid. Unless you already know?"

"Know what?"

I took another deep breath. "I hate to have to break this to you, Mr. Aves, but Peter was shot last Sunday."

Mrs. Aves gave a little cry. Her husband's shoulders sagged.

"Is he hurt bad?" he asked unsteadily.

"He's dead."

Mrs. Aves seized her husband's arm.

"Dead?" Suddenly he looked much older.

"Yes, sir."

For several moments they just sat there, the two of them, side by side under the painting of the cowboy, the wife holding her husband's arm, the husband motionless and staring at the blank screen of a television set across the room.

"Dead," he said again.

"He died instantly," I said, almost sure that I was right. "He didn't suffer."

"No one told me," he said, after an interval.

"It happened in Chicago," I explained. "I guess the police there didn't know about you." Most likely this was true. Ellen could have spoken up, and so could Jill, but evidently neither of them had done so.

"Does his mother know?" Mrs. Aves asked.

"I doubt it," I said.

She nodded.

"Dead," Aves said for the third time.

I looked at him. Then I looked away. He was still staring at the television set, his face as bleak as frost. "I'm a private investigator," I said. "From Chicago. The reason I'm here is, I'm investigating your son's death. It's one of those cases where the killer got away and no one knows who it is. I'm looking for leads and I'm hoping you can help me."

A teenager who also resembled Peter Ives barged into the room. "I'm on my way to—" he began. But one glance at the three of us was enough to silence him. He beat a hasty retreat.

"It was all in the script," Aves said, after a while. "From the very beginning. All in the goddamn script."

His wife gripped his arm even more tightly. "It's not your fault, Ray. Don't blame yourself."

"Poor Pete," he said. "What a script." He turned to me. "How can I help?"

He wasn't a man who was good at describing his life. He didn't seem to understand how one thing leads to another. To him, things "just sort of happened." "The script" was his way of accounting for turning points. His way of letting himself off the hook.

One of five sons of an American mother and a half-Mexican father, he'd grown up on a ranch in west Texas. He couldn't remember a time when he wasn't able to ride a horse. At seventeen he'd "hit the road," drifting north to Wyoming. There he'd worked at first one thing and then another until he landed a job he liked—riding in a rodeo.

He stayed with the rodeo until a woman came along who

was assistant to a Hollywood agent. She persuaded him that there might be a career for him in the movies. He went with her to Los Angeles and she proved that, sure enough, there was a career for him in the movies. He was twenty years old when he got his first part.

"I was never in anything that didn't have horses," he told me, "and I never did anything real big. I wasn't just an extra, though. I was usually the deputy or one of the bank robbers or a captain of the *Federales*—know what I mean? I got credits, and it was more money than I'd been making in the rodeo, and I was having a good time."

A couple of cracked vertebrae interrupted his career temporarily and kept him out of the army permanently, but eventually he managed to go back to work again, this time in the television series *The Navajo Trail,* which ran for three years and was shot on location near Tucson.

"The cracked vertebrae," I said. "You got thrown by a horse?"

"No," he replied. "Hit a telephone pole, doing sixty. In those days, I lived kind of free. I was feisty."

It was after *The Navajo Trail* got canceled that he met Dorothy, Peter's mother. She was a waitress in a restaurant where he sometimes ate. He couldn't say what it was about her that appealed to him. All he could say was, "It sure must have been something."

The marriage was a terrible mistake, he admitted. He found that out right away. Dorothy was even feistier than he was. She didn't give a damn about *anything*.

Peter was born in the first year of the marriage. Recalling this event, Aves got misty-eyed. "He was a cute kid," he said. "Real cute. I liked him." After that he cleared his throat, but was unable to speak for several moments.

Regaining his self-control, he said his luck changed just about then. The public was getting tired of westerns, for one thing. For another, more westerns were being made in Spain. The little American guy who wasn't a star, which was how Aves described himself, had a tough time finding work.

After his stint on *The Navajo Trail,* he never was able to get a continuing part in a series, and the competition was keen for a part of any kind. He auditioned for straight roles, but wasn't good at them. On a horse he was O.K., it seemed, but on his feet he wasn't—he didn't know why.

"At the end I hit a dry spell that lasted eight months," he said. "I was divorced by then, I was broke, they were threatening to throw me in the clink for being behind in my child support. I finally got a job in a car wash—that's how bad it was. Then one morning I looked in the mirror, I saw I was thirty-seven and beginning to look beat-up, and I was going nowhere. I decided maybe it was time to quit trying, time to move on. So that's what I did. That same day. Instead of going to the car wash, I packed up and came here to Tucson. Best thing I ever did."

"Why Tucson?" I asked.

"Because it was someplace I knew," he said with a shrug. "Because I'd had some good times here. Why does anyone do anything? It was just part of the script, I suppose."

At first his luck wasn't any better in Arizona than it had been in California. But then he met Norma, and her father owned a gas station. He went to work for her father, married Norma, and after a while her father died. Now he and Norma had been married for eighteen years. Their sons were seventeen and fourteen. The family had lived in its present house for six years.

Aves no longer rode horses, he said. Didn't have the desire. He'd taken up bowling, though, and liked it. Norma liked it too. And the church had bingo on Wednesday nights. Both of them got a kick out of bingo.

He was no longer feisty, it appeared. He'd been tamed.

"Now when Peter turned up," I said, "you had no idea he was coming?"

Aves shook his head. "It was completely sudden. I just answered the doorbell one day and there he was. I didn't even know who he was at first."

"We were glad to see him, of course," his wife put in quickly.

I didn't comment. There were a lot of questions I hadn't asked, though; a lot of gaps in the story. What about the back child support? Had Aves ever returned to Los Angeles on a visit? Did he know what had become of his firstborn? Had he ever tried to help him?

At some point he must have done something for the boy, I thought. According to Ellen's investigator, Peter and his father had been in touch. And Peter had known where to come when he needed a refuge. But the onetime cowboy actor hadn't exactly been a model parent. Not even a model divorced parent.

"He slept here in the living room," his wife added. "We put up a folding cot."

"And you all got along all right?" I asked.

"Yes," said Norma Aves.

"No," said her husband.

She released his arm and gave him a look.

"Well, at first we did," he conceded. "I mean, I hadn't seen him in so long, and he was grown up now, and he was good company—he was easy to like, you know. It was like a big party. The boys took to him, and pretty soon he began helping me at the station, and then, I suppose, I got ahead of myself. I shouldn't blame Pete; it wasn't his fault. I just got ahead of myself."

"In what way?" I said.

"I started seeing what wasn't there. For the future, I mean. It's hard to explain. Suddenly I have these three sons, and the younger two have already told me they don't want to work in a gas station ever, no way, but Pete . . . I started looking ahead and seeing him as a partner, with us maybe owning two stations instead of one. But that wasn't what Pete had in mind at all. And I should have thought of that. He was, when you come right down to it, a stranger. I hadn't seen him since he was little. How was I to know what he had in mind for himself?"

"I tried," Norma Aves said. "We all tried."

Her husband's eyes misted up again, but he pulled himself together and asked me, "Am I helping you? Is this what you want?"

"Yes," I said. "Go on."

"Well, the first thing that happens is, he goes out and gets a job on his own. At a hotel. The Mountain Mirage, if you know where that is. The job ain't so aye-aye-aye—night manager—and it don't pay more than I was paying him, but it's more what he has in mind, so he goes ahead and takes it without even telling me."

"It's not your fault," his wife said.

"Not his, either," said Aves. "But anyway."

"How'd he happen to get the job?" I asked.

"Fellow who used to come into my station. One of my regulars. They took to each other. The fellow worked there. He talked him into it."

"You know the fellow's name?"

"Solana. He don't come in anymore, I'm glad to say. Can't stand him personally. Big sunglasses, big hat, lots of after-shave . . . you know what I mean."

"So Pete took the job," I said. "Then what?"

"Then he moves out of the house. That's not so bad, actually—we didn't have room for him on a steady basis; he's living in the middle of the living room, like Norma said. He rents this apartment at the Oasis Plaza, a place that was new then, up in the foothills. He joins an acting company, too. I'm kind of happy about that, in a way; it's what I used to do. But what happens after that is, he buys a new car. A Trans Am." He drifted off into his private thoughts.

"Did he have a car when he got here?" I asked, to bring him back. "Did he have any money?"

It took a while. Finally Aves said, "He had a car, a little Chevy. And he must have had some money; he never asked me for any. He furnished up that apartment of his, besides. But the Trans Am—well, it made for trouble between me and my other two boys." He paused. "They liked Pete, and he liked them and he took them around, here and there, and all of a sudden I wasn't good enough for them."

"You're not being fair," his wife said.

"The hell I'm not!" he shot back.

She turned to me. "What Ray is trying to say is, Terry— he's our older—Terry wasn't quite fourteen at the time, and you know how boys are at that age; they want everything under the sun from the latest hi-fi equipment to motorbikes. And Seth, our younger—he's just an echo of Terry; whatever Terry says Seth says five minutes later. Anyway, Ray wasn't about to buy the boys most of the things they wanted, and it seemed to them that their half-brother, who was only— what?—twenty-five, was already living better than their father. It made for some hard feelings."

Aves sighed heavily. "I didn't handle it as well as I could've. Terry and Seth—I busted their butts a couple of times. And Pete—I told him I didn't exactly appreciate him showing off around here with his car and all. Well, one word led to another. Both of us said things we shouldn't have. Now I'm sorry. But you can't undo, or at least we couldn't." He heaved another sigh. "That was the last I saw of Pete. Saw him going into a movie house one time, but that's as close as we came. I didn't even know if he was still in town or not. . . . Chicago, you say?" His voice failed him.

"Maybe I ought to get us all a drink," Norma Aves said. "Rye all right with you, Mr. Bix? We don't drink much, but when we do it's rye."

"Anything," I said.

She left the room. Aves remained on the couch, shoulders drooping, staring at his knees. Neither of us spoke.

Sounds came from the kitchen, and in a little while Norma Aves returned with a tray on which there was a bottle of rye, three glasses, and a mixing bowl with ice cubes in it.

"I thought we had some ginger ale left," she said as she put the tray on a table, "but we don't. The boys must have drunk it."

She poured three small drinks, squinting as she measured with her eyes, and handed the glasses around.

"This'll make you feel better," she said to her husband.

He drank the rye in one gulp and went back to staring at his knees.

"This hotel," I said, "the Mountain Mirage—what kind of place is it?"

Norma Aves said, "We haven't been there in years. But I remember when I was a girl it was the best place in town. Swimming pool, tennis courts . . . People came there from all over the country. I don't suppose it's so popular now; we have all these beautiful new hotels—places like no one ever would have imagined back then. The Mountain Mirage must have slipped, wouldn't you say so, Ray?"

Aves came out of his funk. "It's still all right, but not what it used to be, is what I hear."

I took a sip of rye. The taste startled me. I put the glass down. "I'm going to run a few names past you," I said. "Tell me if anything registers. Jill Cranmer."

Aves and his wife regarded me with no change of expression.

"Young woman," I explained, "middle to late twenties, pretty." I told them Jill's coloring and approximate measurements.

Still no reaction.

"O.K.," I said. "Dennis Close. He's a painter. Spends his winters in this part of the country. Specializes in pictures of desert plants." I described Dennis.

No reaction there, either.

"Chadler," I said. "I don't know his first name."

Norma Aves perked up "*William* Chadler?"

"Might be," I said.

"He's a very fine man. Does lots of things for the city. I read about him just the other day. What was it, Ray? I showed you the article."

"Something about a building he's buying," Aves said. "He's head of a company called Chadler Management," he added, to me. "It owns a couple of shopping malls, other things. He supports this and that. Did he have anything to do with Pete?" He sounded impressed.

"Possibly," I said. "I just don't know. I believe he knows Jill Cranmer and Solana."

"The Solana I was telling you about?"

"Most likely."

"Hard to imagine," Aves said. "That guy was mostly flash, in my opinion. Chadler I don't think is."

"Sparrow," I said.

"Sparrow?"

"That's all I know. Sparrow. A man."

He shook his head.

"What a funny name," his wife said.

"It might be a nickname," I suggested.

She finished her rye and said, "He must be awfully small."

"Any other names?" Aves asked.

"No," I replied, "that's all. And now I guess I'll be going. I appreciate your help. I'm sorry I had to be the one . . ."

Both of them walked me to the door.

"Just one thing," Aves said as I reached for the knob. "If there's a funeral . . . I mean, the body. Is there anyone who's in charge?"

"At the moment, the police," I said.

"Well, if it's all the same to them, I'd like to handle the burying, Mr. Bix. It's the least I can do."

"I'll put in a word," I promised. I was glad that someone cared.

16

The gateposts were low. Each had a little sign in black wrought-iron letters that said MOUNTAIN MIRAGE, but the T had come loose from the left gatepost and was hanging upside down by a single bolt.

Even with the map, it had taken me a while to find the place. It was closer to downtown than I'd thought, in what must have once been a nice residential neighborhood. The neighborhood had changed, though. Across the street from the entrance was an animal hospital, and next to that was a discount carpet outlet.

The driveway was well tended and was bordered by orange trees that had lots of oranges on them. Beyond the orange trees were some tall coconut palms with spotlights pointing up at the fronds and giving them a romantic, moon-over-Miami look. I followed the driveway to the parking lot, which was located beyond the main building, an adobe structure with a tiled roof and hacienda features—arches, iron grilles over the windows, and a veranda with big pots of flowers on its floor. The parking lot had spaces for maybe fifty cars, but less than half of the spaces were occupied. One of the cars was a Mercedes, and another was a Porsche, but the rest were ordinary middle-America vehicles. Most of the license plates I checked were from Arizona and California, but there was one from Ohio and another from Indiana.

In a far corner of the parking lot I saw a motorcycle and went over to inspect it. It was a Japanese import with California plates and had the high handlebars that I associate with bikes that are used for cross-country touring.

I walked along a dimly lit cement path that skirted the main building. It took me past a row of adobe bungalows, two beds of petunias, and some croquet wickets to a nice little swimming pool from which, in the cold evening air, steam was rising. Beyond the swimming pool was a tall chain-link fence that I guessed enclosed tennis courts. There were some blooming shrubs along the fence, and I smelled what I thought was honeysuckle. A stiff breeze was blowing, and clouds were scudding swiftly across the starry sky, but no moon was visible, and the only sound I could hear was the rustling of palm fronds.

The windows of most of the bungalows were dark, but from two or three a pale glow indicated television viewing in progress. Approaching one such window, I observed a pair of eighty-year-old swingers sitting in front of their television set with their shoes off, drinking wine and watching a show that had been filmed on a ship. They were typical of the clientele, I imagined. Even in its best days the Mountain Mirage had probably not catered to the young and restless.

I moved away from the window just in time. Seconds later a very deep voice startled the hell out of me with a "Nice evening, sir."

I swung around. The speaker was a two-hundred-pound, bald-headed character who was wearing a black suit, white shirt, bolo necktie, and gun belt with a gun in it. "Very," I said.

We eyed each other briefly and unsmilingly. Then I walked on. Most resort hotels had security guards, I knew, but generally the guards weren't good for much besides escorting drunks to their rooms. This one was an exception; he had real stealth.

The guard, the elderly couple watching television, the two motorcycles with California plates—I put the combination together, took it apart, put it together again. And was still playing with it when I walked into the main building.

The lobby was small, with stucco walls, a beamed ceiling, and a fireplace, in which a log fire was crackling. The furniture, what there was of it, was old and slightly shabby. A jigsaw puzzle covered most of one of the tables. No one was working on the puzzle, though; the room was deserted.

Across the entrance hall from the lobby was a counter that served as a reception desk. The corner of a switchboard was visible at the far end of it. A dark-complected young woman was leaning on the counter, reading a magazine. I wondered whether she was the Juanita to whom Jill had spoken on the telephone.

Hearing my footsteps, she glanced up, saw me, and came to attention with an alert smile. She said nothing, however, and neither did I. I felt her eyes on me as I continued down the hall toward an archway. Soft music was drifting into the hall from that direction.

Beyond the archway was the bar. It too was a small room with stucco walls and a fireplace. The fire in this fireplace was almost out, though. All that remained were some glowing embers.

I didn't know the title of the song that was coming from the speaker mounted high on one wall, but I recognized it as one of the golden oldies I so often heard on late-night radio in my car.

The bartender was a nice-looking young fellow with big biceps and lots of blow-dried blond hair. He was talking with his one barstool customer, who was also one of the golden oldies—a faded little lady who couldn't have weighed more than a hundred pounds or been a day younger than seventy-five. Perched on the high stool, she seemed very fragile, but I guessed she wasn't—she had a martini in front of her and was knitting and talking with great energy. Her knitting bag was on the floor. A single strand of yellow yarn linked knitting bag with lap.

Only two of the room's tables were occupied—one by a middle-aged couple that appeared to be painfully bored, and the other by a young man in a black leather jacket and a gold-colored shirt that even from a distance said pure silk. One glance at him and I immediately thought of the motorcycle. He was drinking a beer and tapping his finger on the table in time with the music.

I seated myself two stools down from the knitter. The bartender approached me.

"Yes?" he said. There was distrust in his eyes.

"Scotch and water," I said.

He fixed the drink and brought it to me. "Charge it to your room?" he asked, still distrustful.

I shook my head and put a twenty-dollar bill on the bar.

He left the money there and went back to the old lady. They didn't resume their conversation, however, and both of them kept glancing my way.

"Chilly night," I said.

Neither of them responded, and I was afraid that neither of them intended to. But after some moments the old lady spoke up.

"You're new here," she declared.

"Just got in today," I said.

"Well, it's always chilly at night. Always." She'd stopped knitting, but now she started again.

"And hot during the day," I said.

"Not always hot during the day," she contradicted, and put her knitting down long enough to take a sip of her martini. "Remember last January, Robert?" she said to the bartender. "Remember how cold it was then?"

"Sure do," he said. "Real cold that was. Below freezing."

"Below freezing," she agreed, and lapsed into silence. But her silence didn't last long. Looking at me, she stated in the take-it-or-leave-it tone that seemed to be characteristic of her, "I'm Susan Germond. Been coming here thirty-two years. Wouldn't go anywhere else. Come the first of November, leave the first of April."

"Gosh," I said.

"Started coming because of my knees," she went on. "Arthritis. In my case it set in early. Eight years ago I had replacements, but I still come. Wouldn't go anywhere else. I'm from Seattle. You?"

"Kansas City," I said.

She nodded approvingly. Kansas City was acceptable, apparently.

"And you always stay at the Mountain Mirage?" I asked.

"Always. Wouldn't stay anywhere else. Thirty-two years. Come the first of November, leave the first of April." She put down her knitting, took another sip of her martini, and told the bartender in no uncertain terms, "You weren't even born thirty-two years ago."

"Sure wasn't," he acknowledged cheerfully. He seemed to be getting over his distrust of me. Susan Germond's approval made me O.K.

The man in the leather jacket and silk shirt came up to the bar.

"Another Carta Blanca, Roberto," he said. But he didn't have a Spanish accent or look like a Latin. He was as blond as the bartender and reminded me of California surfers I'd seen on television. Courier, I thought.

Robert gave him the bottle of beer, and he went back to his table.

"Thirty-two years is a long time," I said to Susan Germond. "You must have seen quite a few changes in this place."

"Yes," she said. "In some ways it's slipped, especially since Mr. Chadler bought it. But some of us still come. Wouldn't go anywhere else."

"Mr. Chadler?" I said.

"The owner. Local man. Only met him once. He doesn't take a personal interest the way Freddie Parson did. But the food is good, especially the fish. It's flown in daily."

"That so?"

"Daily."

"How long ago did the hotel change hands?" I asked.

"Six years. Or is it seven? Do you know, Robert?"

Robert shook his head. "Before my time."

"Freddie Parson, the old owner, died," Susan Germond told me. "That's when Mr. Chadler bought the place. It was different under Freddie. We were all one big family. The same people year after year. That's changed now. Some of my best friends have left. A few of us still come, though." She finished her martini and pushed the glass toward Robert. "One more and that's all. I'm going to bed early."

He made the drink. She sampled it.

"A friend of my nephew's used to work here," I said to her. "Name of Peter Ives. Maybe you remember him."

She frowned. "What'd he do?"

"I don't know," I said.

She repeated the name a couple of times, then said, "Afraid I can't recall. How about you, Robert?"

The bartender thought for a moment. "Doesn't ring any bells with me."

"The help comes and goes," said Susan Germond. "Guests too, these days. There are a lot more transients than there used to be. People no sooner check in than they check out. Makes it hard to get acquainted."

"How long have you worked here?" I asked Robert.

"Two years," he said.

"And you don't remember Peter Ives?"

"Nope."

I said nothing. He looked as if he was telling the truth. Figure that one out, I thought. Everyone else says yes, but these two say no.

"He might have been part of the pool," Susan Germond suggested. "For some reason, the pool people don't mix much with the rest of the help. They keep to themselves. Like specialists."

Robert disagreed. "I know the pool people. Larry's a friend

of my roommate's. And I know Phil from when we both were going to Community College."

"Well, anyway," said Susan Germond.

The couple that had appeared so bored stood up. The female half strolled toward the archway. The male half came up to the bar.

"Charge it," he said to Robert. "Room thirty-eight."

"Yes, Mr. Olmstead," Robert said, and promptly made a note on a bar check.

Mr. Olmstead caught up with the woman, and the two of them left the room.

"New people," Susan Germond muttered to me. "First year." She took a swallow of her martini. Her face brightened. "Before dinner I saw Sparrow," she said to Robert. "It's such a pleasure to have him back."

I kept calm. "Sparrow?"

"One of our security men," Susan Germond explained. "You probably don't know him."

"Is Sparrow his first name or his last?"

"Neither. It's just what people call him. Started when he was in grade school, he told me, because he was so small. His real name, unfortunately, is Simon Smith."

"Unfortunately?"

"Yes. He can't pronounce it right. He lisps."

I finished my Scotch and water.

Robert noticed. "Another?"

"Please," I said.

He gave me the drink.

"Sparrow," I prompted.

Susan Germond smiled. "He's so dear. I always feel much happier when he's around. And last week he was off for a few days. Virus, he says."

"Is he from the old days?"

"Heavens, no. He's from Mr. Chadler's time. Mr. Chadler added more security when he took over. Good thing, in my opinion. Things aren't as safe as they used to be. Anywhere."

"How many security people are there?" I asked.

"Six," said Susan Germond authoritatively. "Two, days; three, nights; and one for filling in. I'm friends with all of them." She lowered her eyes flirtatiously, like an old-fashioned belle. "A woman alone, you know."

"Come on, now," Robert said, grinning. "You know they're madly in love with you. Every one of them."

The old woman blushed with pleasure. "Robert!"

Robert winked at me. I winked back.

Susan Germond finished her martini and ate the olive. "Time to go beddy-bye," she said, and struggled to get off the barstool.

I helped her. She gathered up her knitting bag and said to me, "Nice meeting you, Mr.—you didn't tell me your name."

"Baxter," I said. "Cliff Baxter. A pleasure, Ms. Germond."

"Indeed," she said, "but don't call me Ms. I'm not liberated. I'm prewar." She drew herself up and, without explaining which war she was pre, made a dignified exit.

"You get many like that?" I asked Robert.

"A few," he said. "Goes with the territory."

I drank the rest of my Scotch and water at a moderate pace. The man in the leather jacket came to the bar for another beer, and he and Robert got into a conversation. They were standing some distance away from me and speaking in low voices, so I couldn't hear what they were saying.

"I'd like to settle up," I said, loudly enough to interrupt the conversation.

Robert came over and gave me change. I left a dollar tip.

The woman at the desk looked at me as I passed, but neither of us said a word.

Strolling along the path to the parking lot, I thought over what I'd seen and heard. A theory began to take shape.

There were no additional cars in the parking lot. I didn't check any more license plates. I merely walked quietly toward my car and toward the little man who was studying it.

But as quiet as I was, he nevertheless heard me. He turned

around quickly. I was maybe fifteen feet away by then. He stayed near the car. I continued walking toward him. There was no doubt in my mind who he was.

No more than five feet tall, with a large head and hair that even in the poorly lit parking lot appeared to be blond, Simon Smith, also known as Sparrow, was exactly as he'd been described.

Like the other security guard, he was wearing a bolo necktie and a gun belt. When I came up to him I stopped. Despite an awful tightness in my chest, I managed to smile. I was positive that I was looking at a killer. One whose natural habitat was parking areas.

"Cold out," I said.

"Yeth," he replied.

I opened the door of the car and got in.

Sparrow moved away.

I backed the car out of the parking space and stopped. The Leica was in my pocket, and Sparrow was within range, but the film was wrong—it wasn't the supersensitive kind that produced clear pictures at night.

No point in trying, I decided. And with that, I turned the car, shifted into Drive, and headed out to the street, certain that I'd just come face to face with danger.

17

I woke early and couldn't fall asleep again. The things Susan Germond had said kept running through my mind. A change in the hotel's ownership. Beefed-up security. A few old-time guests, but mostly new ones who didn't stay long. No recollection of Peter Ives.

I thought about a little boy named Simon Smith, who couldn't pronounce his name properly because he lisped. Who was given a nickname that he also couldn't pronounce and that suggested something small. I imagined him being laughed at because of his size and speech problem and growing up to be a hater.

For a while I studied Ives's address book. Nothing I'd seen in Tucson provided a clue to the list on the back pages. And there was no entry in the book for the Oasis Plaza or for anyone named Chadler. But the Oasis Plaza was listed in the telephone directory, and so was Chadler Management. I decided to visit both places.

The Oasis Plaza was within shouting distance of a shopping mall. It was located at the base of one of the cactus-dotted mountains at the northern edge of the city, and was one of many apartment complexes on that particular road.

The road had a lot of traffic on it and was the main drag of a neighborhood that was growing fast. NOW RENTING and VISIT MODELS signs were everywhere.

Driving along the Oasis Plaza's central street, I passed a couple of dozen identical square white two-story buildings that looked like big sugar cubes with windows. At the street's midpoint was a quart-size swimming pool surrounded by a spiked fence, and not far from that was a small building with a sign above the door that said: LAUNDRY. TENANTS ONLY. I parked the car and walked around. Not much was going on. A man was playing catch with a little girl in front of one of the buildings. They were using a beach ball, and the little girl was having trouble holding on to it. An elderly man and woman were unloading the trunk of a car. Evidently they'd been to a grocery store and laid in a large supply of food; there were four shopping bags in the trunk. These people and the few others I saw appeared to be neither rich nor poor. They were your average office manager, data processor, or retired school principal. Peter Ives hadn't leaped from his father's house into the lap of luxury. He'd merely taken quarters of his own in a place where it was easy to go unnoticed. The same sort of anonymous setting he'd chosen for himself in Chicago.

As I left the housing development, I remembered that Ramon Aves had said something about William Chadler owning shopping malls. Did Chadler, I wondered, own the one down the road from the Oasis Plaza? And did he own the Oasis Plaza too? How much of this booming part of the city belonged to the man who had bought the Mountain Mirage?

The building in which Chadler Management was headquartered was several miles away, downtown. On my swing around the city the day before, I'd driven past the downtown area but hadn't paid much attention to it. Now I noticed that it contained interesting contrasts. Old office buildings with turn-of-the-century facades, narrow streets, Southern Pacific railroad viaducts, aging shops that had no doubt been built in the days when cowboys-and-Indians was played for real. And next to these relics of the Old West were a Las Vegas-y community center with vast halls for conventions and cultural events, and glitzy new high-rises.

Chadler Management was in one of the glitzy high-rises. I was relieved to find that the building was open on Sunday. Crossing the marble-walled lobby, I consulted the directory of tenants. Chadler Management was on the seventh floor. So was Cholla Players.

Looking at the two names, I thought: Coincidence?

I shook my head.

Cholla Players occupied a small space between a law firm and something called Media Specifics. It appeared to be about the same size as my own office—just right for a one-man operation run by someone who didn't spend much time at a desk.

The Chadler spread was directly across the corridor. William Chadler's name appeared below the company name. It wasn't as large a setup as I'd expected; I estimated its corridor length at maybe seventy-five feet. Evidently Chadler didn't have a big staff; he held his hand close to his vest.

The door was locked, but I could hear noises coming from inside. The noises sounded like those made by a computer. I eavesdropped for several minutes. There were no voices, no footsteps; only the uneven rhythm of a machine. I finally came to the conclusion that the computer was conducting business on its own, communicating with another computer that was located somewhere else.

Yep, I thought, close to the vest. Computers don't gossip.

Gordon Lockhart had called, Veronica said. So had Laura McKay.

"How come you're working on Sunday?" I asked Veronica.

"I need the money," she replied.

I returned Laura's call first.

"Duck darling!" she cried. "Where on earth have you

been? I've been waiting for hours to hear from you." She sounded very up.

"I'm working," I explained. "Out of town."

"Oh? And is one permitted to ask where?"

"One is better off not knowing."

"Very well, but you sound paranoid, duck darling, you really do. Anyway, what I wanted to ask you is: What are you doing for Thanksgiving? I thought maybe a quiet little dinner somewhere, just the two of us. Will you be home by Thursday?"

Since my divorce, Thanksgiving hadn't been a big event in my life, and the prospect of a quiet holiday dinner with Laura was appealing. "I'll be home, I think. It depends on how things break. I won't know till the last minute."

"Honestly!" Exasperation crept into Laura's voice. "Well, you warned me. Let's hope I'm not like all those other women, who you said got tired of it." She hung up before I could think of a reply.

Lockhart wanted a progress report. The police had interviewed Anita Danton again, he said—they just wouldn't leave her alone. She looked god-awful, and he was afraid she was on the verge of a serious illness.

"I was hoping you'd have some good news," he said pointedly.

"Well, I do," I said. "Last night I met the man who shot Ives."

Lockhart's voice cracked like a teenager's. "You *did?*"

"Yes. I'm in Tucson. That's where he lives. His name is Simon Smith. He's a security guard at a hotel named the Mountain Mirage, which is where Ives worked before going to New York. Smith exactly fits the description of the man who was hanging around the Danton house the day before the murder and who shot at Ives as he was going to his car a few days before."

"Well *done,* Cal."

"So far it's only guesswork on my part, but I believe the

Mountain Mirage is a stop on the route from the cocaine producers in South America to distributors in the U.S. Tucson is one of those cities like Miami and San Diego; tons of drugs get handled here. The Mountain Mirage changed hands some years ago, and various things I've seen and heard lead me to think that under the new ownership it's a terminal for mules."

"Mules?"

"People who carry illegal goods. Couriers. The Mountain Mirage is a secluded place with individual bungalows that you can get to directly from the parking lot without going through any of the public rooms. It has good cover too; for years it was a refuge for very respectable people. A courier could go into one of the bungalows, drop off the merchandise, get paid, and leave. A distributor could pick it up the same way. The two of them wouldn't even have to meet; the whole exchange could be handled by a middleman who works for the hotel."

"And you're saying that Ives . . . ?"

"I don't know where Ives fitted in. All I'm saying is that Smith is a security guard at the hotel. And that's another thing that makes me suspicious—the hotel's got more guards than it needs. And they're not the kind that most hotels have, the kind who are there mainly for show."

"Smith would have to be extradited to Illinois," Lockhart pointed out.

"I know," I said, "and for that we need evidence, which is what I haven't yet come up with. No prosecuting attorney could build a case around what we have so far—the word of the truckdriver and of Mrs. Danton's neighbor. Assuming the two of them could be made to testify. Assuming they'd be convincing. And assuming a smart defense lawyer wouldn't make fools of them."

"True. So what's the answer?"

"I don't know, but I need something from you, Gordon: an introduction to Tucson's best divorce lawyer."

"Divorce lawyer?"

"Yes."

"I'll have to find out who that is. Where can I reach you?"

"My answering service. It's best that way."

Lockhart promised to go right to work on the matter.

The T was still hanging upside down on the gatepost. I wondered whether its being upside down was a signal of some sort. I didn't suppose it was, but it could be.

The approach to the hotel wasn't as pretty during the day as at night. There were puddles of rotting oranges under the orange trees, and some of the fruit had rolled onto the driveway and been squashed. The palms, without floodlighting, looked dusty and disheveled.

There were fewer cars in the parking lot than before. The Porsche was still there, but was in a different spot. The motorcycle was gone, as, I suspected, was the fellow with the leather jacket I'd seen in the bar the night before. And I didn't see Sparrow.

I parked facing the tall hedge that separated the parking lot from the hotel's side lawn, made sure that the car doors were locked, and strolled onto the hotel grounds. Before I'd gone thirty yards, I got a shock. Coming toward me was the man whose photograph I'd seen in Jill Cranmer's apartment.

There was no mistaking him. He wasn't grinning now, but he was squinting into the sun as he'd been doing when the photograph was taken. He smiled as we got close.

"Hi, Chili," I said.

He nodded pleasantly.

I got a powerful whiff of aftershave lotion.

We continued in opposite directions, but after counting to thirty I turned and followed him as far as the parking lot. He climbed into the Porsche and drove away without a backward look.

I recalled Jill's sobs. Her "Chili? Darling? Are you there?"

Yes, he's there, I thought. All there.

And some of the other words she'd said to him came back to me, as well: "Could Sparrow have done it?"

It's on tape, I thought with satisfaction. In my motel room.

I retraced my steps across the hotel grounds.

Chili. Darling. Mastermind?

No, probably not. Merely the mastermind's right-hand man. But ruthless. With all the sexual magnetism that so often goes with ruthlessness.

I had no particular plan. All I wanted were some pictures of Sparrow. Pictures that could be used to help the police in an investigation. I might have to wait a long while or even come back later. Meanwhile, though, it wouldn't hurt to poke about some more.

Almost immediately I saw things I hadn't noticed before. The Mountain Mirage was larger than I'd thought. Behind the bungalows that faced the flower beds and croquet lawn was a second row of bungalows. I detoured to get closer to them. They were separated from the others by a putting green, but were of the same whitewashed adobe and had the same kind of patios. And behind them were still more buildings. These too I checked. They were larger than the rest of the bungalows, of brick rather than adobe, and not as well landscaped.

Skirting the putting green, I continued in the direction of the swimming pool. On the patio in front of one of the bungalows I saw the bored-looking couple I'd seen in the bar the night before. He was stretched out on one lounge chair, dozing; she was on the other, half covered by various sections of the Sunday newspaper. She glanced up and fluttered the fingers of one hand at me as I went by. I was surprised. I hadn't thought she'd paid any attention.

There were only two people at the pool. One was a well-built, bronzed young man in very brief swimming trunks who was skimming dead insects from the surface of the water with a net on a long pole. The other was Susan Germond. She was seated on a wrought-iron chair and was wearing a green eyeshade. Her knitting bag was at her feet. She was watching the young man as he guided the net across the water with graceful, rhythmic strokes. However, she saw me enter the pool area and waved.

I joined her. "Nice afternoon."

"Lovely," she agreed.

Pulling up another chair, I sat down beside her and said, "I just saw Chili Solana."

She went back to watching the pool attendant.

"Does Mr. Solana usually work on Sunday?" I asked.

"I don't interest myself in when Mr. Solana works," Susan Germond said stiffly.

"Oh?"

"He isn't in the least accommodating, and ever since the wasp I merely tolerate him, because he is the manager."

"Wasp?"

Susan Germond looked at me. Her eyes flashed with remembered anger. "There was a wasp in my room!"

"No!" I exclaimed. "When?"

"Last year. The day after Christmas. In the middle of the afternoon. A wasp! And I'm afraid of wasps."

"As you should be."

"I insisted on being moved immediately to a different room, but Mr. Solana wouldn't move me. He was quite unpleasant about it. We had words. I threatened to leave the hotel. In Freddie Parson's day that never would have happened. I was most upset."

"Understandably. What was the outcome?"

"After an unconscionable delay, during which I sat on the patio with my jewel case and my fur jacket, Mr. Solana finally sent one of the security men. He killed the wasp with some sort of spray. Then he sprayed the entire room for me, including the bathroom, in case there were any more wasps. But I still don't think Mr. Solana behaved properly to an old guest like me."

"Of course," I said. "Which security man? Sparrow?"

"However did you guess, Mr.—ah—?"

"Baxter. You mentioned Sparrow last night."

"Did I? You have an excellent memory. Yes, it was Sparrow. That's when I really got to know him, poor dear. It must be awful to lisp."

"It must. Would you know whether he's here today?"

"He's here all the time. All the security men are. They have their own cottages on the grounds. That's one of the fringe benefits Mr. Chadler provides for them. Freddie Parson wasn't very modern when it comes to fringe benefits, I'm afraid."

"Where are the cottages?"

"Over there." Susan Germond gestured airily toward the area beyond the putting green.

"Those little brick buildings?" I said.

She nodded.

The pool attendant finished skimming the far side of the pool and came around to the side where Susan Germond and I were. Inclining my head in his direction, I said, "Does he have a cottage here too?"

"Oh, no," Susan Germond replied. "Only the security men actually live at the hotel. Everyone else commutes."

The pool attendant leaned forward to sweep in a leaf. The old lady eyed the taut muscles of his thighs and buttocks with an admiring smile.

"Don't you just love Arizona?" she said to me.

"Sure do," I said, getting up. "Great scenery."

I left her to her pleasures and returned to the cottages. Cautiously approaching the nearest of them, I edged around a cluster of mean-looking prickly pears and squinted into one of the windows.

It was a bedroom. A man was sitting on one of the twin beds in his underpants. He was wearing a headset and absentmindedly massaging his right knee. A second man, in a jumpsuit of camouflage material and pointed-toe cowboy

156

boots, was sprawled on the floor, toying with a deck of cards. Somehow the two of them made me think of a couple of mercenary soldiers relaxing in their tent between battles.

I moved on to the other cottages and peered through windows, but didn't see anyone else. One cottage, though, had recently had someone in it—the television set was on, and there was a steaming cup of coffee on a table.

I thought: Where are you, Sparrow? There's a wasp in my room.

He'd been on duty Saturday night, I reminded myself. It might be too soon for him to be on duty again. But I decided to check the parking lot once more, in case. The parking lot seemed to be his special responsibility.

At the spot where I'd passed Solana, I left the cement path and crossed the grass to the hedge that separated lawn from parking area. The hedge was at least twelve feet high and quite thick. Something about it appealed to birds, though. Clusters of them were perched somewhere within it, chattering loudly. I walked along the hedge until I came to the spot opposite where I thought my car was parked. Quietly parting the branches, I surveyed the paved area on the other side. And suddenly my adrenal glands began secreting like crazy.

Sparrow was standing behind the trunk of my car, writing something in a notebook. The car's license number, I guessed.

I had an unobstructed view of him. Holding the branches apart with one hand, I took the Leica from my pocket, focused, and snapped two pictures in rapid succession. Then Sparrow obliged me by putting pencil and notebook into a pocket and turning sideways. I snapped two more pictures.

He moved away from my car, toward the far side of the lot. I released the branches.

A voice behind me said, softly, "I'll take that."

I whirled around.

The fat, bald-headed guard I'd met the night before was pointing a gun at me and holding out his free hand.

I closed my fist around the camera.

He took a step forward and pressed the gun against my breastbone, hard. "Now."

I remembered police academy. And gave him the camera. I wondered how long he'd been tracking me and whether the headset I'd seen on the man in the cottage had to do with the security system.

He dropped the camera into his pocket.

I said, "Put the gun away."

He wasn't about to do that, however. He merely stepped backward, widening the distance between us. "Get out," he said in that same quiet voice. "Don't come back. This is private property."

I glanced toward the path, inhaled sharply, and called, "Hey, Chili! I'm over here!"

For an instant the guard's gaze left me. That was long enough. I seized his gun hand and pushed it away from me, half twisting as I did so, and chopping down in a cleaverlike motion with the edge of my other hand. The blow caught him just above the wrist of his gun hand.

"Ai," he said, his eyes widening. The gun dropped to the grass.

He aimed a kick at my knee, but his foot merely grazed my calf. I jabbed my knee into his stomach, and as his head came forward I chopped at his throat. He uttered a funny-sounding "Uff," and his knees started to buckle. I chopped at his collarbone.

He landed on his knees, but remembered the gun and reached for it. I thrust it away with the side of my foot. Then I brought my foot up and connected with his chin. The pupils of his eyes rolled upward, and he toppled onto his side.

I removed the Leica from his pocket and picked up his gun. He remained motionless. I headed for the parking lot.

Sparrow and I almost collided as I came around the hedge.

Pointing, I said breathlessly, "A man's hurt back there. He's lying on the grass."

Sparrow hesitated, as if not sure whether to believe me or not. Then he went off to investigate.

I made a dash for my car, got it started, and left.

18

The adrenaline didn't stop flowing right away. I kept glancing at the rearview mirror to see whether I was being followed, even after I was sure I wasn't.

Sparrow had made a note of the car's license number. That was bad. I'd had to show my driver's license when I'd leased the car. Through the rental contract he could eventually learn my name and address. There was no way I could prevent that, but I could, by renting a different car, make it harder for him to pick up my trail in Tucson. So I drove to the airport, turned in one car, and rented another. A small gain was better than no gain at all.

After completing the transaction, I bought myself a drink at the cocktail lounge in the airport. Sitting beside a window, watching private planes come and go, I thought about how easy it would be to move drugs from the Mountain Mirage to virtually any part of the United States. I had to make a conscious effort not to play policeman. You're not Drug Enforcement, I told myself. You're not Customs, FBI, or even local cop on the beat. You're a private investigator working for a Chicago widow whose boyfriend was shot to death in her garage. Your job is different.

Still, I was going to have to deal with Chili Solana, and the best way to do that, it seemed to me, was to come at him sideways.

Use divorce tactics, said the little voice that gives me advice. But first make sure he's married.

I finished my drink and went to a telephone. The flow of adrenaline had slowed. I was calm now. Making use of Ives's address book, I dialed Solana's number.

A woman answered.

"Is Mistah Solana they-ah?" I asked in a southern accent.

"No, he isn't," the woman replied.

"Is this his wife?"

"Yes, it is."

"Will Mr. Solana be home soon?"

"No, I don't think so."

I tried to sell her a subscription to a magazine called *Sports Month*. She said she didn't think her husband would be interested and hung up.

Eagle Drive, the address book said. I got into my newly rented Ford, checked my map of Tucson, and took off.

The map called it the Rillito River and showed it in blue, so I supposed that at certain times of the year it had water in it. But right now it was totally dry, a wide, stony trench with a bridge across it. Sprouting from its banks were clumps of mesquite, tumbleweed, and various other growths that I knew from John Wayne movies.

I crossed the bridge and kept going. Soon I was in an area where the houses sat on lots that covered at least an acre. The land was hilly, forbidding, and strewn with boulders. The only green was the green of plants that were all thorns and barbs. But the view of the mountains was unobstructed, and the houses were classy-looking.

Eagle Drive was marked by two gateposts as well as a street sign. The gateposts were status symbols—there was no gate or fence—and flanked a narrow asphalt road that wound among the rock-strewn hills. The Solana house was a quarter of a mile in from the gateposts, near the top of one of the hills. It had a two-car garage, a glassed-in loggia, and a front yard that, except for a couple of baby date palms, was as barren as the moon. Eight or nine rooms, I guessed, with maybe a swimming pool in back.

As precautions, I turned the car around so that it was facing the direction I'd come from, parked it some distance beyond the house, and walked back. The garage door was open. There was only one car in the garage, and it wasn't a Porsche. In addition to the car, there was a small fleet of children's vehicles—two tricycles, a wagon, a junior-size bicycle, and a stroller.

A cocker spaniel came charging around the side of the house, barking furiously, but when he was within a few feet of me he stopped, as if not sure what his next move should be. I told him to go chase a bird, but he didn't. I pushed the doorbell. Chimes played the first two bars of "Joy to the World." Moments later the door opened. The opener was a pretty, blond woman. She had a baby in the crook of one arm.

"Is Mr. Solana in?" I asked.

"No," she said. "He had to go back to his office."

A boy of about three came running to the woman, in tears. "Janie bwoke my twuck," he sobbed.

The woman sighed. "Play with something else," she suggested.

"She *bwoke* it."

The woman led him away from the door, knelt, still holding the baby, and had a conference with the three-year-old. He stopped crying and went back to wherever he'd come from. She returned to me.

"My name is Hopkins," I said. "I hope you don't mind my barging in like this, unannounced, but I'm with the Glengate Community Theater in Chicago, and a friend of mine, when I said I was coming to Tucson, told me to be sure and look up Chili Solana. He's with the Cholla Players, I understand."

162

The woman's expression became less guarded. "Do come in."

I walked into the house. She led the way to the loggia, a nice, sunny space with an entire wall of glass. Children's debris was generously distributed on chairs, tables, and floor—a half-eaten cookie, a coloring book and some crayons, a single small sneaker.

"I'm Frances Solana," the woman said, and after she put the baby down on a shag rug we shook hands.

Then, as the baby kicked and waved its arms, Frances Solana and I got acquainted. Watching the child, I kept thinking of Jill and Andrew. Andrew and this child had been born at about the same time. I wondered how Chili Solana had felt, knowing that two women were about to have babies by him only weeks apart.

Frances seemed nice enough, and I found myself liking her. We spent a few minutes talking about our families. I said I had three children, because three sounded better than one. She had five, she said. The oldest was eight. A woman came in to help with the housework Mondays through Fridays, but even so she had her hands full.

"It's a three-ring circus all the time," she added. "The washing machine just goes and goes. I live in constant fear that it'll break down."

Gradually I edged the conversation around to the subject of theaters and her husband's interest in the Cholla Players. He wasn't an actor, she said; he was the company's business manager. She herself wasn't involved—she had her hands full at home—but she kept up with what the group was doing. Most of the members were friends of hers. And she went to all the plays.

Does she know? I asked myself. Does she even suspect? "Chicago's a great city for community theaters," I said, "but we do have our problems. That's why Jill suggested I talk to your husband. Jill Cranmer, that is."

Did a shadow cross Frances's face? I wasn't sure.

"One of the problems we have at the moment," I went on,

"is whether to produce the work of an unknown local playwright. Whether to risk it. The play is called *Double Delivery*. It's a comedy about a man who gets two women pregnant at more or less the same time. One is his wife and the other is his boss's secretary."

"Good heavens," Frances exclaimed, "what a situation!"

"Yes," I said, "but will the play pull an audience? I don't want the theater to lose money. We can't afford it."

"How does the play end?"

"It's kind of complicated. The easy ending would be for the boss's secretary to get an abortion or offer the baby for adoption, but she isn't willing to do that—she insists on having it and keeping it. She thinks it will give her a hold over the baby's father, which in a way it does. I mean, he has to support the child; he'll be in all kinds of trouble if he doesn't. On the other hand, the woman loves him. Secretly she's hoping that someday he'll leave his wife."

Frances eyed me thoughtfully. "It doesn't sound much like a comedy to me."

"Maybe that's the problem," I said. "It's not such a funny predicament." She doesn't know, I decided. "Anyway, what I wanted to talk to your husband about is financing. Glengate isn't subsidized, the way the Cholla Players are. I was wondering if there's any chance I could interest Mr. Chadler in our group."

"I doubt it." She sounded positive.

"Oh? You know Mr. Chadler well?"

"Heavens, yes," said Frances Solana. "He's my father."

I sat behind the wheel of the Ford, arms folded across my chest, feet apart, watching. This was the part about being a private investigator I'd found hardest to get used to, but now I was good at it. I could keep a house, doorway or window under surveillance for hours without becoming impatient. The secret lay in remaining alert while letting your thoughts wander.

I'd moved the car closer to the Solana property, so as to

get a better view of it. For a long time nothing happened. The only member of the household I could see was the cocker spaniel. But then a boy of about eight emerged from the garage on a bicycle that he'd evidently just learned to ride, and rode shakily down the driveway to the street. After pausing to check the traffic, he pedaled over to the driveway of a house a hundred yards down the hill, where I guessed he had a friend. The cocker spaniel followed him part of the way, but presently returned to the Solanas' front yard.

The boy looked like his mother, I thought.

It was very quiet on Eagle Drive. The quiet reminded me of the last time I'd done what I was doing now. That street, the street on which Babette Mantino lived, had been quiet too.

Less than six days ago, I thought. Seems longer.

Was the Mantino boy already living with his father? He was about the same age as the boy who had pedaled down the hill.

A fat little bird with a long tail strutted across the street. A quail?

Yes, by gosh, a quail.

The cocker spaniel noticed the bird and went into action. The bird took off.

A big rabbit with very long ears bounded across the Solana property in great, athletic leaps. A jackrabbit?

Yes, by gosh, a jackrabbit.

I wasn't sure why I was waiting. I was mildly curious as to how long Chili Solana would be gone. Also, I had nothing else to do. But I was sitting there mainly because I remembered times in the past when aimless surveillance had paid off. So I stayed, relaxed but attentive, as the afternoon shadows lengthened and the air turned cooler. I began to plan what I was going to say to Solana when I finally took him on. Gradually the scene took shape in my mind. . . .

The divorce lawyer would have a nice office. Nice offices were part of the divorce *gestalt;* they made it easier to get nice settlements.

The divorce lawyer would be respectful toward me. Suspicious, perhaps, but respectful. After all, I'd been vouched for by a senior partner of Lockhart, Fratern, Ney and Wright. I too would be respectful. Toward the lawyer, toward Solana, even toward my bodyguards if I decided I needed bodyguards. I still wasn't sure about the bodyguard bit, but I thought it might be a sensible precaution. Also it would impress Solana. I could easily enough find a couple of men in that line of work; Tucson undoubtedly had its share of frightened businessmen and nervous hostesses.

I heard myself saying to Solana in the lawyer's office: "This tape is of a telephone conversation that took place last Friday night between you and a Miss Jill Cranmer. It was made without her knowledge, and the making of it was illegal, so no court would permit it to be used as evidence. But then, I don't intend to use it in court."

I tried to picture the expression on Solana's face, but couldn't.

"Before playing it, though," I went on, in my head, "let me explain why I'm here. As I said on the phone, I'm a private investigator and I'm working for a Chicago woman named Anita Danton. She's in the news back home because a former friend and co-worker of yours—Peter Ives—was found murdered in her garage. The police have been questioning her, and the press has been making a big deal out of her connection with Ives, and the whole thing is causing her a great deal of embarrassment. She hired me to establish that she had nothing to do with the murder, which of course she didn't. Are you with me so far, Chili? You don't mind my calling you Chili, do you? If you do, please don't hesitate to say so."

"Keep going," I heard Solana say.

I saw myself nodding. "O.K., that's the background. Now to get down to the nitty-gritty. What I want from you is a statement about a man named Simon Smith, nicknamed Sparrow, who works for you as a security guard at the Mountain Mirage. I've already sent photographs and a description of him to the Chicago police department and the National Crime Information Center, in Washington, to find out whether or not he has a criminal record. My guess is that he does. But that's more or less beside the point, because there are witnesses in Chicago who can identify him from my photographs. They can link him to the scene of the Ives murder and to a previous attempt on Ives's life, which failed. Do you know about the previous attempt? Well, it doesn't really matter except as something that would come up at his trial, most likely. Are you still with me?"

No response from Solana. Just silence.

"As for the statement," I continued, "it should say that during the time of the two shootings—the one that didn't get the job done and the one that did—Sparrow was absent from work, that he'd said he was going to Chicago and he intended to settle a score with Ives. I'd like the whole thing to be specific enough to get the police onto the right track. As for the exact motive, you can mention the subpoena that Ives got to testify against Fred Sharpe or not—it's up to you. As for your mentioning how the Mountain Mirage is being used by drug dealers—that's up to you, too, but I'd just as soon you didn't. I mean, Mrs. Danton doesn't need to be linked to anything extra.

"In other words, Chili, I want a statement from you that will help get a murderer caught. What's your reaction?"

I anticipated various reactions and tried to counter them one at a time. The important thing was to convince Solana that I would play the tape to his wife and father-in-law and tell them how I'd found a Mountain Mirage envelope in Jill's trash bag. It was the envelope, I would explain, that had led me to believe that he'd put her on the hotel's payroll to keep his wife from finding out about the support payments.

The reaction I couldn't figure how to handle was indifference. Suppose Solana told me I could play the tape to anyone I pleased—that it didn't matter to him. Suppose he denied flat out that the child was his.

I still had some thinking to do, I realized. I didn't have it all worked out.

Questions and answers came and went as I sat in the car. So did desert creatures. Another jackrabbit. A roadrunner with her brood of youngsters. The birds looked surprisingly like the roadrunners in the cartoon and reminded me I was on unfamiliar turf.

The Solana boy came home from his friend's, walking his bicycle up the hill.

And eventually the Porsche swept up the hill too. It turned into the driveway and came to a stop in the garage; the object of my surveillance got out. He disappeared into the house.

Soon, I guessed, his wife would be telling him about the man from the Glengate Community Theater. Would he connect that man with the one who had decked one of his security guards?

There was no reason for me to linger in the neighborhood. Yet I did linger, my thoughts on what might be taking place inside the house.

Finally, though, I decided it was time to leave. The air had got cold. I was hungry. Perhaps Lockhart had left a message with my answering service.

I turned the key in the ignition and started to pull away from the curb. But at that moment I heard a noisy engine and saw an odd-looking van coming up the hill. The van was painted the color of an eggplant.

Something clicked in my memory. I uttered a silent whistle.

The van turned into the Solanas' driveway and stopped. Dennis Close stepped onto the pavement.

19

I switched off the engine and prepared to wait as long as necessary.

The sun set the sky on fire, then dropped behind the mountains, putting the fire out. Stars appeared. Houses, brightly lit and at different heights on the hills, looked like stars too.

After a while I got out of the car, relieved myself, turned up the collar of my jacket, and paced back and forth to stretch my legs. My stomach began to growl. I had a perverse urge to ring the Solanas' doorbell and ask what the hell was going on.

It didn't surprise me that Dennis was there. What surprised me was that he'd come so soon. It was only four days since I'd seen him in Chicago.

Think, Bix. Think about Dennis Close. Willowy, raven-haired, kinky painter of thorny plants. Frail, flighty, frightened friend of actors and crooks. Here. Now. Why?

Consider the sequence of events. You interviewed him on Wednesday afternoon. The next day Ives's body was discovered and the story appeared on television. You were mentioned in connection with it. And seventy-two hours later, Dennis is in Tucson, having driven eighteen hundred miles in an old van. At what point did he decide to clear out of Chicago? How long has he been here?

The only person who can answer those questions is Dennis himself. So be patient. Don't think about food. Forget how cold you are. Just wait.

The wait was a long one. But finally, at twenty minutes past seven by my watch, the front door opened and, silhouetted by the glow from the loggia, Dennis crossed the yard to the driveway. Moments later, the van backed onto Eagle Drive.

I followed in the Ford, headlights off. After passing between the gateposts, the van turned left into a stream of traffic. I flicked the headlights on and continued to follow. A mile north of Eagle Drive, at a busy intersection, Dennis made a left turn and I almost lost him, but I soon managed to catch up. The street began to seem familiar. Presently I realized that this was the street on which the Oasis Plaza was located.

The van entered the apartment complex. I switched off the Ford's headlights and trailed at a distance. When the van pulled into one of the parking areas, I stopped the car and prepared to follow on foot.

Dennis went into one of the two-story buildings. I got there just in time to see him disappear around a corner at the top of the stairs. Taking the steps two at a time, I reached the second floor an instant before the door to one of the apartments closed. I noted the apartment number, just in case. Then I returned to the car and drove off to a drugstore to buy a roll of adhesive tape. Near the drugstore was a gas station. I stopped there and bought an air pressure gauge for tires.

My mental alarm clock woke me at five-thirty. Within minutes I was in the car, my recorder in the trunk and a microphone taped to my right side, under my shirt. In the pocket of my jacket, along with Ives's address book, were the tire gauge and the roll of adhesive tape. The gun I'd taken from the security guard at the Mountain Mirage was in the waistband of my slacks. I'd had to do some arguing with myself about the gun; I hadn't brought my permit with me, and in general I'm against carrying firearms. In this case, though, I'd decided that a gun was safer than a rock. Less jagged.

By the time I reached the Oasis Plaza, there was a narrow band of gray in the sky to the east, but a few stars were still out and the air was very cold.

The van was where I'd last seen it. With the air pressure gauge, I let the air out of all four tires. Then I got back into the car and drove off to reconnoiter.

There were, I found, plenty of isolated spots nearby. Streets that looked as if they would cross other streets didn't; they merely curved in and out among scattered housing and continued on over humpy, undeveloped land, ending abruptly a long way from where anyone lived.

The spot I finally chose was almost a mile beyond any reminder of human life on that particular road. A sign said: NO DUMPING. The ground was hard-packed and rutted, and a half circle of big century plants created a secluded cove.

After familiarizing myself with the route, I drove back to the Oasis Plaza. It was twenty minutes past seven when I got there. The van with its four flat tires was exactly as I'd left it. I parked nearby and waited in the car. There wasn't much action. People emerged from the various apartment buildings one at a time and drove away. One or two paused to look at the van, but nobody went to find the owner. And nobody paid any attention to me.

At eight-thirty, the parking space to the left of the van became vacant. I moved the Ford into it and continued to wait. But finally, around nine o'clock, I made a sortie to Dennis's apartment. Listening outside the door, I heard the sounds of water running and of rock music played low. Reassured, I returned to the car and renewed my vigil.

Nothing happened until almost ten o'clock. Then things happened fast.

Wearing jeans and a denim jacket, Dennis came out of the building, a camera case slung over one shoulder. He paused to study the sky and seemed pleased. Nice day for taking pictures.

I slid out of the Ford and positioned myself at the rear of the van. The muzzle of the gun was in my hand; the safety catch was on. Peering around the corner, I watched Dennis approach. He didn't notice the flat tires until he was right beside the van. His eyes widened. He ran his right hand through his hair. Not believing what he saw, he knelt for a closer look. And that was when I made my move.

He heard my footsteps on the cement and turned his head. His eyes got even wider, and he tried to straighten up, but it was too late. In one short, sharp stroke I brought the butt of the gun down across the back of his head hard enough to stun him. As he sagged, I stepped behind him. Supporting his body with my legs, I shoved the gun back into the waistband of my slacks. Then I whipped out the tape, tore off a piece, and slapped it across his mouth. He began to recover and to struggle, but was so disoriented that I had no trouble pinning his arms behind him and wrapping some tape around his wrists. He writhed and tried to shout, but the shouts didn't get past his lips. I managed to pull him to his feet, drag him around the rear of the van, and shove him headfirst onto the floor between the Ford's front and back seats. The whole scuffle took less than a minute.

Without looking around to see whether there had been any witnesses, I jumped into the car, started the engine, and headed for the street.

In what seemed like no time at all, I was at the spot beyond the NO DUMPING sign where the century plants were. Parking the Ford on the hard gray earth beside them, I got out, opened the trunk, and turned on the recorder. Then I pulled my passenger out of the car and walked him to our conference site. He didn't want to go, but a couple of yanks on his ear persuaded him. He was already beginning to lose his bounce. His skin had developed a pallor, a lump was forming on the back of his head, and the camera case was no longer slung across his chest at a jaunty angle—the strap was caught under his armpit and the case kept hitting his elbow.

I pointed to the ground. "Sit down."

He tried, but with his arms taped behind his back he couldn't do it. I had to help him.

"I'm going to take the tape off," I said, "but it won't do any good to yell. There's no one around to hear."

I pulled the tape from his lips. He winced and looked very frightened.

"We can do this easy or hard," I said. "Understand?"

"Please don't crucify me," he said in the same faint voice.

He'd used the word "crucify" in Chicago, I recalled. I wondered what he meant by it.

"First question," I said. "When did you get to Tucson?"

He hesitated, then answered. "Yesterday."

"You left Chicago when?"

"Thursday."

"Louder," I said. I was afraid that the recorder might not be picking it all up.

"Thursday," Dennis said in a stronger voice.

"That's better. Why did you leave?"

"I was afraid."

"Of what?"

"Of you."

"You'd heard my name on television, after Peter's body was found?"

He looked around wildly and began to struggle, twisting the upper part of his body.

I watched him for a little while. Then I said, "Don't tire yourself. I'd been to see you, you'd told me about Peter, and after they found the body it hit you that I'd eventually figure out you were the one who set him up."

He gave a few more convulsive twists, straining to free his wrists. The camera case flapped, sweat appeared on his forehead. But soon he gave up. "Please," he said. "I didn't set him up. Let me go."

"You told Sparrow where he was going to be on Saturday night. Where to find him. You're an accessory, Dennis. You helped Sparrow commit a murder."

"I didn't. I swear I didn't. I told Jill, when I went there to get his things, that Peter was at my house. Jill must have told Sparrow. Sparrow must have waited for him outside my house and followed him. I'm not an accessory. I swear to God!"

"So it *was* Sparrow." I felt a surge of relief. Dennis's words supported Jill's. This was what I'd been hoping for. "Simon Smith," I added for the benefit of the recording, "nicknamed Sparrow. A security guard at the Mountain Mirage Hotel. That's who we're talking about. Right?"

Dennis nodded.

"Say it."

"Sparrow. Security guard. I swear to God, I didn't tell him anything!"

This was the truth, I guessed. "Sparrow works for Chili Solana. Doesn't he?"

Dennis nodded again.

"Say it."

"He does. He works at the Mountain Mirage."

"Which Chili Solana manages for William Chadler. Right?"

"Yes."

"Now why, Dennis, would Sparrow want to kill Peter? We both know Sparrow's the one who did it. Peter recognized him when he shot at him the first time, behind the building where he lived. Right?"

"Yes. Please, Mr. Bix, I didn't have anything to do with it. Don't crucify me. Let me go home."

"Answer my question. Why would Sparrow want to kill Peter?"

"I don't know. I swear I don't."

"Would it have anything to do with the subpoena Peter

174

was served with? The subpoena to give a deposition about a man in New York who's about to go on trial, Frederick W. Cahill Sharpe?"

Shock appeared on Dennis's face. He was putting two and two together, as I'd done.

"Peter told you about the subpoena, didn't he?"

No answer.

"I've got all the time in the world, Dennis. If you'd like, I can drive off and leave you here to think things over. I can come back tomorrow and we can talk about it then. If in the meanwhile a rattlesnake should come out from behind those rocks over there, or a scorpion, or a tarantula, or if you should get very cold during the night—"

"He told Jill. Jill told me."

"So you knew about the subpoena. And you knew he'd called Chili to ask what to do about it."

No answer. Just more of that shocked expression. What hadn't made sense to him before was beginning to make sense to him now.

"Do you need time to think about it?" I asked.

"He did call Chili. But I—"

"—had nothing to do with it. That's not the question. The question is why Sparrow turned up in Chicago not long after that telephone call and killed Peter. Peter is served with a subpoena, he calls Chili, and pretty soon a goon who works for Chili comes to Chicago and shoots him. How do you explain that, Dennis? What, in your opinion, led to what?"

"I don't know. I swear I don't."

"But you're beginning to figure it out, though. Same as me."

"I don't know. I swear."

"Let's look at it another way, then. Let's ask why Chili is the one Peter called, in the first place, why he needed Chili's advice instead of, say, a lawyer's. Think about that, Dennis. Why *would* he?"

"You're asking me things I don't *know*. I've *told* you what I know. Let me go home. Please."

"Then let me tell you what I think, Dennis. I think Peter called Chili Solana because Chili is the one who *introduced* him to the man in New York. Peter wasn't killed because of anything he knew about Sharpe; he was killed because he could link Sharpe with Chili, Chadler, and the Mountain Mirage. Chili—and more important, even, Chadler— couldn't let that happen. So Sparrow was sent to Chicago."

"Maybe. I don't know. Honest to God."

I didn't push it. I just sat there, watching him watch me. I could feel the tension building in him.

Finally I took Ives's address book from my pocket and said, "I'm going to show you something, Dennis, and I'm going to ask you what it means." I held the book in front of him. "I found this in Peter's apartment. It's his address book. Your name is in it. So is Chili's. So are a lot of other names that a U.S. Attorney might be interested in." I opened the book to the list at the back. "See these numbers, these letters. What I want to know is, what do they mean?"

Dennis stared. First at the page I was showing him, then at me. And began to sweat heavily.

"What do those letters mean?" I turned the pages. *"T, P, F . . . VOS, FO, CC . . .* What's the significance, Dennis? Explain it to me."

"I don't know," he said in a parched kind of voice.

"You *do* know."

"I don't. I don't, I don't, I don't. Please."

I said nothing and let the silence work on him. I dropped the address book into my pocket. "Want to see it again?" I asked after a while.

He didn't answer.

The sun was almost directly above us now, and the air was hot.

"O.K.," I said, getting up. "I'll give you time to think it over." I walked over to the car, turned off the recorder, and drove away.

*   *   *

It was almost two o'clock when I returned. The time in between had been hard to get through. I'd driven around the area, afraid to get too far but not wanting to arouse suspicion in the neighborhood by going down the same streets too often, worried that Dennis might somehow have managed to make enough noise to attract a rescuer, but also worried about his safety.

I stuck it out, though. For three hours. Then I went back.

He hadn't been rescued. He was exactly where I'd left him. But he wasn't in great shape. The nice black hair was wet and limp, the face was wet with tears and sweat and red from the sun, and there was a dark stain in the crotch of his jeans.

"Changed your mind?" I asked.

"Please," he said in a hoarse whisper.

I showed him the address book. "Want to explain it to me?"

He said nothing.

"O.K.," I said. "I'll be back tomorrow." I started to walk away. I got almost to the car.

He uttered a cry. It sounded like "Don't!"

I turned on the recorder, went back, and sat down beside him. "Ready?"

He nodded. "It's bank accounts," he said. And went on to answer all my questions.

By two-thirty we were finished. I untaped his wrists, drove him to the nearest thoroughfare, told him how to get back to the Oasis Plaza, and let him out of the car.

The last I saw of him, he was walking toward the housing complex, shoulders sagging, camera case swinging, a very tired young man. And at last I could let myself feel sorry for him. The poor guy had had a terrible day.

On the way back to the motel I thought about what he'd told me. The whole thing was extremely simple, yet I never would have been able to figure it out for myself.

Ives had devised the abbreviations on his own. His job was to deposit money into and withdraw it from thirty different bank accounts. The main headings—*T, P,* and *F*—stood for the three areas he covered: Tucson, Phoenix, and Flagstaff. The subheads were the initials of banks. *VOS* was Valley of the Sun National Bank, FO was First Orvetta Trust Company, RSL was Ranchers Savings and Loan, and so on. Some banks had branches in more than one city, others didn't; all in all, there were nine banks. The other entries represented names and account numbers.

Dennis didn't know the meaning of all the symbols, because he wasn't a regular member of the team. But on a couple of occasions he'd been present when Ives had made deposits. Based on what Dennis had told me, I would, if I ever had to, be able to explain to whoever was interested that "Rose 219865" meant an account, thus numbered, in the name of Rose.

Dummy accounts. Dozens of them. Each transaction under ten thousand dollars.

A lot of things were now clear to me. The importance of the Cholla Players. The reason Susan Germond didn't remember Ives. My initial reaction to the photographs of him. And above all, the reason for his murder.

A current of excitement crackled through me. It started as a series of little ripples, which got stronger as I neared the motel. I began to refine the scenario of my interview with Chili. And to wonder if there was some way to protect Jill and Dennis.

I wondered which lawyer Lockhart had decided on. What had he told him about me? How soon could I get an appointment?

I swung the Ford into the motel's parking area, jumped out, and removed the recorder from the trunk. Then, going into my room, I placed the recorder on the bed and went to the telephone.

Veronica answered.

"Veronica," I said, "this is Calvin Bix. Is there a message

for me from Gordon Lockhart?"

"Mr. Bix," Veronica said with obvious relief. "Yes, there is. People have been calling you all day. There's, let me see, five messages from a Miss Laura McKay. She's very anxious to get in touch with you. And a Mrs. Thomas called. And a Mrs. Gilbert. Also—"

"Forget about the others," I said. "Tell me about Mr. Lockhart's?"

"He called at nine-twenty-five this morning. Wanted you to get touch with him immediately."

"Thanks," I said, and hung up, wondering what Laura was so excited about.

I immediately dialed Lockhart's number.

"Lockhart, Fratern, Ney and Wright," said the woman who answered. "May I help you?"

"Gordon Lockhart," I said.

There was a slight click as the call was transferred.

"Gordon Lockhart's office," said another woman, whose voice I recognized. She was the one I'd spoken to the first time I'd called.

"This is Calvin Bix," I told her. "I understand Mr. Lockhart wants to talk to me."

"Oh, yes," she said. "He isn't in the office now, but he left a message for you. It's a very sad one, I'm afraid. Mr. Lockhart wants you to know, Mr. Bix, that your client, Mrs. Danton, suffered a heart attack last night. She passed away at seven-thirty this morning. Mr. Lockhart wants you to discontinue the investigation and return to Chicago at once."

20

The funeral took place at eleven o'clock on Wednesday morning. I didn't go. I saw a clip of it, though, on the five o'clock news. It had been a media event. Not as big a one as a Super Bowl, but bigger than, say, a visit to Chicago by the Vice-President of the United States, which in some ways it resembled. A convoy of police cars with flashing lights and a procession of black limousines.

The reporter who did the voice-over summed things up pretty well, I thought. "And so," she said as the video showed the coffin being carried down the steps from the gothic doorway to the hearse, "one of Chicago's most prominent social leaders begins her final journey, with questions still unanswered about her role in the fatal shooting of Chicago actor Peter Ives. Anita Danton, dead of a massive coronary at fifty-one, is borne from Saint Edward's Cathedral through a throng of family, friends, and the merely curious. This is Gloria Tremaine, Channel Four News, Chicago."

Prominent? I thought. Well, now she is, after getting tangled up with a good-looking young operator from California who had too much jungle in him. But before, Anita Danton had merely been one of the lonely rich widows who populate some of the most expensive houses and apartments on Chicago's Gold Coast and meet one another for lunch three times a week.

Laura, of course, did attend the funeral. She was sincerely saddened by the loss of her friend. The many messages she'd left with my answering service on Monday had been prompted partly by a wish to tell me about the death and partly by a need to be comforted. I did the comforting on Tuesday night. At that time she urged me to go with her to the funeral, but I said no, funerals aren't my thing. Besides, I thought it best to keep a low profile.

So I spent Wednesday morning and afternoon at home, nursing a growing resentment over the runaround I was getting from Gordon Lockhart. He hadn't returned any of my calls, and his secretary said she hadn't the slightest idea when he would be available—"Mr. Lockhart has a very busy schedule."

Finally, on Wednesday evening, I decided to confront him, and on the chance that he would be there, I went to the Danton house to offer my condolences to the bereaved daughter.

My hunch was on the mark. Lockhart was there, along with at least a hundred other people. I buttonholed him in the living room and said, "Gordon, we have to talk."

He gave me the sort of look that turns water to ice and said, "This isn't the time or place."

Taking a firm grip on his elbow, I said, "It's as good a time and place as any," and steered him toward the door.

We had our conference upstairs, in the hall outside Anita Danton's bedroom. It was obvious that Lockhart, feeling he no longer needed me, had again become anti-investigator. In his eyes he was estates, trusts, and taxes, and estates, trusts, and taxes are part of a different galaxy from private detectives. A superior galaxy.

"I know what's on your mind," he began, before I could say anything. "You're worried about your fee. Well, I haven't had a chance to discuss it with Ellen. As you can see, she's upset, and there are more crucial items than your fee on our agenda. I'll recommend that she honor my verbal agreement with you, but I can't guarantee that she'll take my advice. She may want to arrive at some sort of settlement with you. You didn't complete the investigation, and whatever you did accomplish—ouch, you're hurting me."

I'd taken his elbow again, and this time I was digging my fingertips into the pressure points. "I didn't come here to discuss my fee," I said, "but since you bring it up, I'll tell you there's going to be no 'settlement.' Ellen or your firm is going to pay the whole hundred thousand, plus expenses. If not, the two of you are going to have trouble in the reputation department. That's a promise. But what I want to talk to you about now is the investigation itself. I've stirred up a hornet's nest out there in Tucson."

"Let go of my arm, damn it."

I let go of his arm. "Ives was part of a money-laundering operation, Gordon. Originally marijuana and cocaine, but now mainly cocaine and crack. I think there's a connection between that operation and the Cyrano Trust you told me about. Ives himself, as near as I can estimate, helped launder as much as a quarter of a million dollars a week. And he was just one of a number of people in the network."

Lockhart gave me another chilling glance. "I fail to see what any of this has to do with Ellen. Or, for that matter, with her poor mother."

"And you don't care that—"

"I care about Ellen Danton. Just as I cared about Anita. Very much. Period. Whatever kind of nest you stirred up in Tucson has nothing to do with Ellen, and Anita's past being helped or hurt. You're right about your fee, I suppose. Even though our agreement was only verbal and you didn't finish the investigation, you should be paid and you will be. But that ends our association in this case, Bix—yours, mine, and the Danton estate's."

He walked away.

I didn't try to stop him. Because in some respects he was right.

But I did put the matter to Ellen. I found her in the dining room, instructing Helga to bring out more sandwiches. She was, as Lockhart had said, upset. Her eyes were red-rimmed and she appeared to be very tired, but she was holding up as well as could be expected.

She recognized me and gave me a quick little nod. "Mr. Bix," she said. "So nice of you to come."

"My deepest sympathy," I said. "I know how you must feel."

I hadn't intended any irony, but she misunderstood. "Mother and I didn't always see eye to eye," she said, "but I did love her."

"I'm sure," I said. "And I was trying to help her cause. I was out in Tucson—"

"Yes, Uncle Gordon told me. What you were doing was probably in Mother's best interest, but now that she's gone there's no point in your continuing. I mean, what good would it do?"

"Peter Ives—"

"Don't mention that name to me! I never want to hear it again!"

"You aren't interested in solving his murder?"

"None whatsoever. I blame him for Mother's death. As far as I'm concerned, he got what he deserved."

"But for your own peace of mind—"

"For my own peace of mind I intend to leave Chicago, Mr. Bix, just as soon as I possibly can. And I may never come back."

"Oh?"

"I'm going to Japan. I'm interested in Japanese ceramics."

There wasn't much I could say to that. "Well, then," I said, "good luck." I left the dining room and started down the stairs to get my coat.

"Wait for me!" Laura cried.

I turned around. She was behind me. I'd kept an eye out

for her while I was searching for Lockhart but hadn't seen her. "I looked for you," I said.

"And I you." She came down to the step I was on and took my arm. "Let's go to my place. I've had enough humanity for one evening."

"I'm human," I said.

She smiled. "So you are."

We spent that night together. The next day too. It was the best Thanksgiving I'd had in years, even though—and partly because—the quiet little Thanksgiving dinner we'd talked about on the telephone didn't turn out as planned. Five of the seven restaurants at which I tried to make reservations were closed for the holiday, and the other two were booked solid. So we ate caviar and scrambled eggs and smoked salmon, and drank wine, and watched the Christmas Parade on television, and enjoyed each other's company, and neither of us got dressed until Friday morning.

Except for a brief period on Thursday afternoon, we didn't discuss the death of Anita Danton or anything connected with it. But when the subject did come up, we just missed getting into an argument. Laura saw Anita Danton's life in one way, I in another. To Laura, she was a star-crossed woman who'd had a miserable childhood, a disastrous marriage, and suffered the tragic loss of a child. It was no wonder, Laura said, that the poor thing had developed a heart condition. Laura, it turned out, was one of the few people who knew about the heart condition; Anita hadn't confided in many.

"She was gallant," was the way Laura summed her up.

"She was a damn fool," I said.

Laura flared up. "Now wait just a minute!"

"No," I said, shaking my head, "I won't wait just a minute. She was her own hard luck. All that being crazy about movies, all those movie magazines you said she collected—she was always playing a part, Laura. The real Anita Danton was buried so deep under all the Elizabeth Taylors and

Sophia Lorens and Meryl Streeps and the parts *they* played that you couldn't find her if you tried. People like her don't live in the real world. That's why they're always making wrong decisions.

"But that wasn't her worst quality," I went on. "Her worst quality was wanting to have her cake and eat it too. She wanted her fling with a guy twenty years younger than herself, but at the same time she wanted to be a pillar of Society—capital *S*. She wasn't worried that he'd stolen her necklace and earrings; she was worried that people would find out. That's why she hired me. And in the end that's what did her in. The world—her world—had found out her boyfriend was a thief, and, even worse, she was suspected of having had something to do with his murder."

"You're unfeeling, Cal."

"I'm an expert on people like Anita Danton, Laura. Two thirds of the clients I've had have been like her—wanting to have their cake and eat it too. That's what got them in trouble."

"Anita was in love with Peter, don't you understand? And I honestly believe he was in love with her."

"So you said before. And yes, I do understand. I don't agree, that's all. I don't know what kept them together, but it wasn't love. Most likely it was the combination of his looks and her money."

"Why are you such a cynic? Because you used to be a policeman?"

"Beats me," I said. I didn't think I was especially cynical, but I didn't want to argue anymore.

Laura calmed down. She changed the subject. "What were you doing out there in Arizona? Is it all right for you to tell me now?"

"It's a long story," I said, "I was trying to find something in Ives's past that would explain his murder and get your friend Anita out from under the cloud."

"Did you find it?"

"Yes."

185

"May I know what it is?"

"He'd been mixed up with some very bad people, Laura. And he'd become a threat to them."

"What are you going to do now?"

"I haven't decided. Anita's daughter doesn't want me to follow through, and the Danton lawyer doesn't either."

"So you're going to let sleeping dogs lie?"

I shrugged.

"Well, if you want my advice, duck darling, you will let sleeping dogs lie. Erase the blackboard. Go on to other things."

"Because of Ellen?"

"Because of you."

On Friday morning Laura packed a couple of dozen fabric swatches and an order book into a tote bag and took off by taxi to meet a client at the Merchandise Mart. I went back to my apartment and treated myself to a shave with a razor that was designed for men, and then placed a call to Patrick Mooney. Pat had gone through police academy with me. Now he was a lieutenant of detectives. We'd kept in touch.

"Bix?" he said. "What's this I hear about you being on television? You bucking to become famous or something?"

"Right. I'm going for the gold, Pat. How're things with you?"

"Not bad, but I haven't been on TV lately like you. You want to buy me a drink? That why you're calling?"

"Drink? Sure, but not now. I need a favor. I want to get together with whoever's doing the legwork on the Ives murder. Can you fix it up for me?"

"Shouldn't be hard, Cal. Let me put you on hold."

I was on hold for almost ten minutes.

"Harder than I thought," Pat said at the end of that time. "Detectives Rolfe and Acer are the guys. I don't know them personally. Anyway, the best I could do was get Acer to agree to talk to you on the phone; Rolfe was out of the office. Here's the number."

I wrote it down, thanked Pat, and we talked about getting together soon.

Acer had a chip-on-the-shoulder voice. I began to understand what Anita Danton had gone through. But he was interested when I said I had photographs of the man who had killed Peter Ives.

"I'd like to turn them over to you, Detective," I added in my most respectful tone. "At your convenience."

His convenience was noon. In his office. I promised to be there.

My next call was to my son and was disappointing. He couldn't spend the weekend with me after all. Jimmy Herder's dad had got tickets for the hockey game and Jimmy had invited Eddie to go along as his guest.

"Would next weekend be all right instead?" Eddie wanted to know.

"What can I say?" I replied. I wondered whether things would ever change.

"Thanks," said a relieved Eddie.

I drove downtown, took the film that was in the Leica to a one-hour processing center, and had it developed. The results were neither good nor bad. Sparrow was recognizable, but there was a fuzziness to his features. However, when I recalled how I'd had to focus through the hedge, I figured I'd been luckier than I might have been.

It was ten minutes to twelve when I arrived at the police station. Lieutenant Acer was busy, I was told; he would be with me shortly.

Shortly turned out to be twelve-thirty. Rolfe was there too.

Neither of the detectives offered to shake hands. Acer merely pointed to a chair and said, like someone who had no time to waste, "Sit down. Now what's your story?"

"I have photographs of the man who killed Peter Ives."

Both men eyed me narrowly.

I handed Acer the pictures. He frowned over them for a

few moments and passed them to Rolfe, who frowned over them too.

"His name is Simon Smith," I said. "His nickname is Sparrow. He's about five feet, weighs, I'd say, a hundred fifteen, twenty pounds, and, as you can see, is blond and blue-eyed. He works as a security guard at a resort hotel in Tucson, Arizona. I believe that Mrs. Danton's neighbor will recognize him from those. And he may be in the computer at the National Crime Information Center."

Rolfe looked at the photographs again. Then he put them on the desk and asked, irritably, "What makes you so sure he's the perpetrator?"

I had a feeling that I wasn't among friends. It was understandable, I supposed. These men were probably two of the department's best investigators; otherwise they wouldn't have been assigned to the case. As such, they didn't welcome a kibitzer. In addition, they might have a thing about private detectives as alternatives to public ones.

Still, I was annoyed. "Are you sure you want to hear?" I said.

"By all means," Acer replied, gazing not at me but at the ceiling.

"Then let me give you some background on Ives." In as few words as possible, I outlined the trouble Ives had had with the law in California, his flight to Arizona, his association with the Mountain Mirage and the Cholla Players.

Acer continued to gaze at the ceiling. Rolfe began to clean his fingernails with a straightened paper clip.

I told them about Sparrow's first attempt to kill Ives and about the subpoena. I suggested that they check with the U.S. Attorney's office.

"O.K.," said Rolfe. "What else?"

Acer looked at me. "Any real *evidence?*"

I thought about my tape of Dennis's statement. And imagined trying to explain to these men how I'd forced the statement from him. I shuddered.

"Afraid not," I said. "All the rest is up to you."

There was a long silence. I looked out the window at the police parking lot and saw a small fleet of patrol cars. Each had WE SERVE AND PROTECT painted on it. Mentally I added: SOMETIMES.

"In Tucson I interviewed Ives's father," I said. "He'd like the body released to him. You want the address?"

Rolfe nodded. I gave him the address. It was the only thing I said that he wrote down.

After another silence, Acer stood up. "Thank you," he said, and flicked a finger toward the photographs. "Nice of you to bring these over. What's your next move?"

"My next move?"

"Now that your client's dead."

"Get another client," I said.

He smiled, proving that he could. "Great line of work you're in. You can walk away from a case at any time."

"Yep," I said. "A pleasure to meet you two."

Chicago's finest, I thought sourly as I drove toward downtown. Three cheers for law and order.

But I reminded myself that there were people like Acer and Rolfe in all professions, people who felt they had the answers before they asked the questions. Some of them did quite well. An open mind wasn't always necessary for success.

Maybe the two detectives had already known some of the things I'd told them. Maybe they'd made more progress than it appeared. At any rate, I'd done my bit.

I stopped at a classy pizza place for lunch. Brass chandeliers, carpeting, and a wine list. I had a glass of the house red wine with my pizza and considered the immediate future. New clients or a dry spell? I'd already lost the two prospects who had called while I was in Tucson. Mrs. Thomas had said, when I'd got in touch with her, that she'd hired another investigator—one who returned calls more promptly. And Mrs. Gilbert had solved her problem, such as it was, on her own. She'd located her husband. It had all been a misunderstanding.

My mind began to wander. It went from subject to subject, hovering briefly over each. Why hadn't I ever taken Eddie to a hockey game? Could Japanese ceramics be the key to a new life for anyone? Where were Laura and her client having lunch?

Poor Dennis, I thought. A scared kid in search of protectors. Well, one of his protectors had arranged for the murder of another.

Too bad I hadn't applied more imagination. My first reaction to the pictures of Ives had been on target; he'd had a rare talent for appearing to be different people. I simply hadn't imagined that such a talent could be put to use by someone making banking transactions under more than one name.

Did the envelope from the Mountain Mirage that Jill Cranmer had thrown away really prove that she was on the hotel's payroll? And was that why Susan Germond didn't remember Ives? Because although he'd been on the payroll as night manager, he'd never put in much time there?

I ordered a second glass of wine and lingered. What about Drug Enforcement? I wondered. What about the FBI? Would any federal agency ever get around to investigating Chadler and his hotel? Or was it possible that an investigation of them was already, thanks to Frederick Sharpe, under way?

The wine made me mellow. I leaned back and noticed the people around me. Young executives, mostly. They appeared to be happy. Well, why not? Life wasn't so bad— when you took the time to savor it.

I paid the check, and went on to my office to itemize my expenses for Lockhart. Aside from that, I had little to do. Unless another client was sitting by her telephone, desperately anxious for me to return her call.

When I checked in with my answering service, Veronica said I sounded different somehow. So relaxed.

"An eight-inch pizza," I explained, "and two glasses of wine."

"No wonder."

"Any messages?"

"Not exactly."

"Not exactly? What's that supposed to mean?"

"Well, a man called, but he didn't leave a message. He just wanted to know if you were in." Veronica giggled. "He sounded awfully funny, though. He lisped."

21

"How can you do this to me?" Phyllis made a lament out of it.

"I'm not doing it *to* you," I said. "I'm doing it *for* you. You and Eddie. Now get moving."

"If only you'd stayed on the force!"

I bit back the reply that was on the tip of my tongue. Phyllis's explanation for everything that had gone wrong in our marriage and since our divorce was: You stopped being a policeman; you got rich.

"I'd like the two of you to be gone within an hour," I said.

"We can't. I've got to pack."

"Pack fast. Take only what you need. But go. Understand?"

"Yes. We will. But if only you'd stayed on the force!"

" 'Bye," I said. "Call when you get there. Leave word with my answering service, but don't mention where you are."

"All right. But what about you?"

"I'll be O.K. Out of reach, though."

"Cal . . ." Phyllis hesitated. "Whatever it is, be careful."

"I will." I put down the telephone.

I felt better. In a pinch, I knew, Phyllis would follow instructions. Especially these instructions. I'd told her to take

Eddie and go to Sarasota, Florida. She had friends there and liked the place.

I left my office and got my car out of the garage. Not until I was driving along Michigan Avenue did I start thinking about where to go. It didn't matter, I decided; any large hotel would do.

Since I was near the Drake, I went there, and was able to get a room. The room faced the lake. From the windows I could almost, but not quite, see the building I lived in.

Sitting on the bed, I considered my options. And chose one.

Mr. Allen Mantino was out of the office, his secretary said. He would be gone for the rest of the day.

"It's very important," I said. "If he calls in, would you ask him to get in touch with me right away?"

She said she would. I told her who and where I was. Then I settled down to wait.

For once I wasn't a good waiter. I paced, sat, paced some more, threw myself on the bed, only to get up and resume pacing. I couldn't stay put.

And all the while I was second-guessing myself.

I'd asked for trouble at the very beginning, I now realized, when I'd questioned Jill. She'd immediately alerted Solana. Dennis had probably done the same. At that point Solana might not have felt I was a threat. But after the body was discovered, when I went on television . . .

It had probably been a mistake to let Lockhart talk me into staying on the case. But Lockhart hadn't been my only reason; even then I'd had a sense that I was in danger, and I'd believed that the best way to deal with danger was to meet it head-on. The trouble was, I'd met it too head-on. Prowling about the Mountain Mirage, going to Solana's house . . .

Had Dennis been crazy enough to tell Solana about our conference among the cactus? Apparently he had.

Would it have been any different if Anita Danton hadn't died, and if I'd had my meeting with Solana? As it was, I'd become the new danger, the new Peter Ives.

The afternoon wore on. The telephone didn't ring. I continued to second-guess myself.

Had it really been necessary to send Phyllis and Eddie away? Would Sparrow have used them to get at me? Did he even know they existed?

Would Bear Mantino be willing? Would he be able? If not, then what? The U.S. Attorney's office?

I shook my head. The U.S. Attorney's office was concerned with prosecution. Any lawyer I talked with there would only send me to another agency, most likely the FBI or the Drug Enforcement Agency, where I might or might not be taken seriously. Even if I was, an investigation would require months. And the odds favored the hit man.

I'd made the right decision, it seemed to me. There were times when the back door was better than the front. This was one of them.

Finally, at five-thirty, Allen Mantino called. He was sorry to have taken so long to get back to me, he said. He'd been shopping. He needed all kinds of things, because on Saturday his son was coming to live with him. Babette had caved in on the custody issue. He sounded extremely happy.

I smiled at the telephone. "I'm glad," I said. "And along those lines, you told me that if I ever needed a favor . . ."

All I did for the next three and a half days was sit around. It was like convalescing. Except for one trip down to the hotel's arcade to buy toilet articles, haberdashery, and reading matter, I stayed in my room, which seemed to get smaller with each passing hour.

Laura, with whom I spoke twice on the telephone, said she couldn't understand why I was being so vague and mysterious. Phyllis left word with my answering service that she and Eddie had arrived at, as she put it, "the destination."

Sparrow hovered constantly on the rim of my thoughts. I knew he was out there somewhere. I began to understand what it was like to live on a fault line; you couldn't predict when the earthquake would occur, but you could be damn sure that sooner or later there would be one.

On Monday morning I called Milton, my tax man. He gave me a short discourse on the Bank Secrecy Act. It was really very simple, he said. The act required banks and financial institutions to report to the Internal Revenue Service all cash transactions in excess of ten thousand dollars. It was designed to stop money laundering and had been partly successful, although millions of dollars were still leaving the country in suitcases and aboard private planes and boats.

"What about transactions under ten thousand?" I asked.

"Exempt," Milton replied.

"So if you want to deposit a million dollars in cash—"

"You have to do it in amounts of less than ten thousand. The same with withdrawals."

"So you need a lot of accounts."

"Exactly."

"And it's being done that way?"

"Sure."

I told him what I knew about Frederick W. Cahill Sharpe.

"He's not the first to get caught," Milton said. "There've been others. What he probably did was accept large sums of cash, deposit them in his own account in small amounts, then transfer it to a branch office overseas—the Bahamas, say, or Bermuda—from where it would be forwarded to banks in Panama or Switzerland that would eventually invest it in legitimate businesses."

"Anyone ever mention the Cyrano Trust to you?" I asked.

"No," said Milton. "What is it?"

"One of the legitimate businesses," I said.

After hanging up, I thought about the relationship between Sharpe and Chadler. The money from all the little accounts in the Arizona banks had, most likely, been sent to the New York broker, who had moved it along in the manner Milton had described, until it became shares in apartment buildings, shopping malls, steel mills, oil tankers, and God knows what else, with the names of the real owners of the shares on file only in Luxembourg.

I recalled the computer I'd heard through the door of the Chadler Management office. That computer had a lot to keep track of. No wonder it had to work on Sunday.

Mantino had said he would let me know one way or the other as soon as he could, but he didn't know when that would be.

It turned out to be four o'clock Monday afternoon.

"Good news," he reported, "but I'm supposed to give you the instructions in person. May I come over?"

"And how!" I said.

The Allen Mantino who appeared in my hotel room thirty minutes later was a different man from the one I'd seen in Jerry Zabin's office. There was something shining about him now, even when he asked me questions like was the room bugged.

I assured him it wasn't.

"My father worries constantly about bugs," he explained.

"No need here," I said.

He glanced around, then nodded. "O.K. This is what he said. He's never had anything to do with the Cyrano Trust. He's heard of it, though, and friends of his have connections. As you said, the money comes from all over the world and is invested all over the world. Not all of it is dirty, either. Anyway, the trust is managed from Switzerland. The name of the top man doesn't matter as far as you're concerned—it's been arranged for you to meet with one of his chief assistants. You'll have to go to Switzerland, though. If you don't have a passport, you'll have to get one quick. They're expecting you this week."

"I have one," I said.

"Good. Then here's what you do."

The instructions were simple. I was to fly to Zurich, dial 88 98 60 between ten in the morning and noon any day during the coming week. I was to ask for a Mr. Grendle, give him my name, and do what he said. He was someone I could trust.

"What about the other thing?" I asked.

196

Mantino shook his head. "Impossible. My father isn't about to step on anyone's toes. If there's a contract on you, it's your problem." He paused. "But if there's a connection between the people in Arizona and the Cyrano Trust . . ."

"I understand," I said. "Thank you."

We talked for a few more minutes. The divorce would be granted without delay, he said. He would have sole custody of his son, but Babette would be able to take the boy out on Sundays. She'd lowered her alimony demand too.

"Thanks to you," he added.

Neither of us said anything about debts being canceled. We simply shook hands and exchanged smiles, and he left. He was anxious to get home, he said, to supervise dinner. The new cook hadn't yet proved herself.

I made a reservation to fly to Zurich the next evening. Then I gave some thought to survival. My passport, Ives's address book, and the tape of Dennis's explanation were in my apartment, and I had to have them.

Lower the risk, I decided at last. Call Frank.

"What are you carrying?" I asked, in the car.

"A thirty-eight," Frank replied. "You?"

"Nothing," I said. "My gun's in the apartment."

He relaxed his grip on the steering wheel and began a lecture. The odds were ninety-nine point nine nine nine to one that we didn't need the hardware, he said, because there wasn't any danger. "No one can manage a twenty-four-hour-a-day stakeout single-handed," he added. "It just ain't possible. A guy's got to sleep, eat, pee, do all those things—hell, you know the trouble we ourselves have when we try to do it."

I did indeed, I said. But this particular guy had managed two successful one-man stakeouts. He was good at it.

"It's been—what?—three days," Frank argued, "and you haven't shown your face. Even if he'd started out watching your building, he'd have given up by now. And shit, you don't even know if the call came from Chicago. The lady at your answering service, you said, couldn't tell whether it was local or long-distance."

I didn't disagree with anything Frank said. But although Sparrow might not have been in Chicago then, he could be now. And if Solana had said, "Get that bastard Bix," the little man with the lisp wouldn't be eager to return without my scalp.

Frank kept talking. I only half listened. I was thinking about the quickest, safest way to get in and out of the building.

"Don't pull into the garage," I said, when we approached the entrance. "Pull into the driveway that leads to the loading dock."

Frank grunted.

The building was L-shaped. The short part of the L was set back about a hundred feet from the street. That was where the loading dock was. A driveway connected the dock with the street.

Frank guided the car into the driveway, turned it around on the paved apron in front of the loading dock, and parked it near the sidewalk, facing the street. We sat there for some moments, observing. Everything appeared to be normal. The street was a thoroughfare and a bus route, but parking was allowed on both sides. Traffic was seldom more than medium heavy. At the moment there were a few cars going in each direction, and a bus was approaching from the north. Every parking space was occupied. No pedestrians were in sight.

"Let's go," Frank said presently, and started to get out of the car.

"Wait," I said. I'd noticed a camper parked just north of the driveway.

"What for?"

"Give me your gun."

Frank looked at me.

I indicated the camper. "I'm going to check it out, just in case."

He shrugged and gave me the gun. I got out of the car and started toward the camper. Then things began to happen fast.

The door on the passenger side of the camper opened. A stocky man jumped out. He was wearing a padded jacket with a hood and had something in his hand.

"Cal!" Frank shouted, and started the car.

At that moment the man raised his hand, and I saw that he had a gun. I threw myself to the pavement. He fired as I was going down. Something struck the pavement beside me, and I felt a sting on my neck.

Frank turned on the headlights, and I saw with terrible clarity who the man was. He was the fat security guard from the Mountain Mirage. I fired at him from the prone position, but missed. Squinting in the beam from the headlights, he pulled the trigger again. I heard the gun's *pfft,* but this time the bullet didn't come close.

With the car bearing down on him, he didn't have time to get off a third shot. All he could do was leap out of the way and run toward the camper. The camper lurched forward just as he reached it.

Frank jammed on the brakes. The car stopped with a screech. But the camper kept going, moving away from the curb, heading into the street, its front door open and swinging wildly.

The fat man grabbed at the passenger-side door, dropping his gun. He got hold of the outside handle, but then lost his balance.

"Sparrow!" he screamed as the camper sped down the street, dragging him along as he clung to the door handle.

I got up. Frank hurried toward me.

"You all right?" he asked breathlessly.

I put my hand to my neck and felt a wet spot. I'd been nicked by a chip of concrete. "Um," I said, and handed him his gun.

The two of us went to the curb. We got there just in time

to see the fat man lose his grip on the door handle and fall to the pavement.

The camper swerved from one side of the street to the other as the driver reached across the front seat, trying to close the flapping door. And a moment later the vehicle went out of control. It swung into the path of a truck that was going in the opposite direction.

There were loud sounds of rending metal and shattering glass. The camper ended up crosswise in the street.

Frank and I ran down the block to the crash site. By the time we got there, other cars had stopped. Traffic was beginning to back up in both directions.

The truck had staved in one side of the camper. Sparrow was slumped against the window, unconscious and bleeding. The driver of the truck was hunched over the truck's steering wheel, holding his head.

Twenty feet away, the fat man lay on the pavement. He was dead.

22

Gradually the pictures in my mind began to fade. By the time we were flying over Newfoundland, I was no longer seeing the camper with its side crushed. Or Sparrow. Or Jack Horton lying on the pavement, his neck broken, his head pulpy.

I hadn't known that the fat man's name was Jack Horton until I read it in the newspaper. The story of the crash had been short, but I guessed that whoever had written it had got the fat man's name right, because Sparrow's was. The article referred to him as Simon Smith, driver of the recreational vehicle.

Great recreation, I thought. Hunting a human being.

On the way back to my building, Frank had paused over the gun Horton had dropped.

"Should I?" he'd asked, stooping and reaching out with his hand.

"Not unless you want to spend the next six months explaining," I'd said. ·

So we'd left the gun where it was. The police who arrived didn't find it, because they didn't look. Someone else did find it, though. By morning it was gone. I checked.

The entire incident, from the time I got out of Frank's car

to the moment the truck hit the camper, had lasted less than a minute. But the images stayed with me throughout the next day as I did the few things that needed to be done before I went to the airport—things such as sounding the all-clear for Phyllis and Eddie, making duplicate tapes of my conversation with Dennis, photocopying the pages of Ives's address book, and following up, through Frank, on the state of Sparrow's health.

Ruptured spleen, Frank reported, a skull fracture that resulted in a subdural hematoma and required surgery, and assorted internal abdominal injuries the seriousness of which wasn't yet known. "I hope he has plenty of insurance," he added. "He's going to need it."

"How about the truckdriver?" I asked.

"Not as bad," Frank replied. "Broken leg, concussion, and three loose teeth."

"Eyewitnesses?"

"Four. People in other cars. Conflicting stories, but they saw the guy hanging from the door and say the truckdriver wasn't at fault. So your boy is going to have a lot of explaining to do."

"Good," I said.

After talking to Frank, I called Detective Acer. The individual I'd told him about, I said, the man who'd killed Peter Ives, was in Chicago. He'd been in an automobile accident and was in the hospital. When Acer asked me how I knew, I said I'd read it in the newspaper.

One of the duplicate tapes and one set of photocopies went into my safe-deposit box; another went to my lawyer. The originals and a tape player were part of my hand luggage.

After dinner they showed a movie on the plane, but I had my own movie to watch. Mine was based on fact. It had to do with my going to rent a camper for a surveillance but changing my mind at the last minute because campers attract attention. Also with a couple of men from Arizona who, if they'd worried at all about attracting attention, hadn't worried enough. Then the movie's locale shifted from Chicago to Switzerland, and I saw a shadowy figure with a name but no distinct face who had probably never heard of the two men from Arizona but, I hoped, had heard of me. I watched my own movie until, somewhere near Ireland, I fell asleep.

It was late morning when we landed at the Zurich airport. I decided not to call Grendle until I could tell him where I was staying. I had to make several phone calls in order to get a room at a hotel. I also had to stand in line at the money exchange, at passport control, and at the taxi rank. So it was after twelve o'clock when I finally settled down.

The hotel was located on the city's main street, Bahnhofstrasse. It was one of those places that serve tea in the lobby and have real Oriental rugs on the floor and blimp-size flower arrangements. The men I saw as I glanced about the lobby were businessman types with fur-collared overcoats and calfskin attaché cases. The women were the sort that have their own Mercedes-Benzes. And there was one fellow I couldn't help staring at—an Arab in a white robe and headcloth, with a mink coat across his shoulders and a long-haired dachshund on a leash. Both Arab and dachshund had an OPEC look.

I spent the afternoon window-shopping. The stores were decorated for Christmas, and lots of people were buying things, and a wet snow was falling. If it weren't for the fact that so many of the buildings seemed to be part of an opera set and that there were trams on the street, I would have thought I was back in Chicago.

Darkness fell early. I walked along the lake. The lights of the buildings beside the lake were reflected in the water, and when I crossed the bridge at the point where the Limmat River meets the lake, I saw other, older buildings that must have been standing there when Columbus was a kid.

Dinner was the most expensive I'd ever eaten. And, just possibly, the best. Up in my room, I watched television and tried to figure out what the people were saying. One channel was French, another German, a third Italian. I couldn't do much with any of them. Finally I gave up and went to sleep.

At ten-thirty the next morning I placed the call.

A man answered. *"Achtundachtzig achtundneunzig sechzig, guten Tag."*

I said, "Mr. Grendle, please. This is Calvin Bix."

"Bitte?" he said. "Who iss?"

"Bix," I said. "From Chicago, Illinois."

There was a pause and then a click. "Mr. Bix," another man said presently, in very good English. "Welcome. Where are you?"

I gave him the name of my hotel and the room number.

"Excellent," he said. "Are you available now?"

"Yes."

"Excellent. Please stay there. A car will come for you in half an hour. The driver will be wearing a gray uniform. He will knock on the door of your room. Describe yourself."

I told him what I looked like.

"Excellent," he said. "Please bring your passport with you." He hung up.

I put the address book and the tape in my pocket and got the tape player out of my suitcase. And for the next thirty-two minutes I waited.

Thirty-two minutes exactly. I timed it.

The driver was a short, pale man with black eyes and thin lips.

"Please come," he said, after looking me over.

I accompanied him downstairs and out of the building. A black Mercedes was parked in the turnaround. He pointed to it. I got in. Then he handed me a pair of wraparound dark glasses.

"Wear these, please."

I put the glasses on. They didn't shut out the glare; they shut out everything. It was like suddenly going blind.

We started. Because of not being able to see, I lost track of time. The drive seemed to take forever. We turned right

204

and left and went up a hill and then down and then up another, steeper hill. I had the feeling that we were traveling in a circle, that the driver was deliberately trying to confuse me, but I didn't really know.

At last the car came to a stop. "Keep the glasses on," the driver said. "I will help you walk."

He did just that, too. He even put his hand on my head as I got out of the car, so that I wouldn't bump myself.

We went up some steps. I heard a door open. We entered a warm room.

"Now you may remove the glasses," the driver said.

I found myself in the foyer of a large house. There was a broad stairway at the far end of the foyer and some expensive-looking furniture between where we were standing and the stairway.

"Come this way," the driver said, and led the way to an anteroom on our right. Then he closed the door and said, "Please take off your clothes."

I frowned.

He repeated the instructions and added, "Everything."

I sighed and began to strip. He examined the pockets of my clothes and subjected me to the sort of body search that isn't usually allowed in democratic countries.

Satisfied that I wasn't armed or wired, he said, "You may dress."

I put my clothes back on and followed him up the stairs. He carried the tape player and my topcoat. At the top of the stairs we went into a room that had paneled walls, two crystal chandeliers, half a dozen oil paintings, and some nice antique cabinets and tables. A man was standing by one of the narrow windows. He came forward, hand outstretched.

"Mr. Bix," he said. "A pleasure."

We shook hands.

The driver deposited the tape player on a table and folded my coat beside it. Then he left.

"I'm Frank Grendle," the man said. "Sorry for the security precautions. Hope you weren't embarrassed. Now there's just one more thing: May I see your passport?"

I took it out of my pocket and gave it to him. He compared me with my photograph.

"Excellent," he said, returning the passport. "Come and sit down, Mr. Bix. Coffee? Tea?"

"I wouldn't mind some coffee," I said.

He went across to a tapestry bell pull, gave it a tug, and returned. Pointing to a long couch that was upholstered in plum-colored velvet, he said, "There."

I sat down near one end, he near the other. He extended his arm across the back, as if to narrow the space between us.

"You're a detective," he said. "Am I correct?"

Before I could answer, a side door opened and a middle-aged man in a black suit, white shirt, and black necktie came in. Grendle spoke to him in German. Through the open door I could hear the faint, irregular sound of a computer in operation. It took me back to the corridor outside Chadler's office.

The man in the black suit bowed and backed out of the room, as if Grendle were a king.

"Yes," I said. "A private investigator." I tried to size him up, but it was hard. In his middle thirties, he was tall and slim, and there was something oddly preppy about him, although his clothes were boardroom and his manners Continental. The preppiness was due to his blue eyes, I decided, and to his blond crew-cut hair. "You sure speak English well," I said, fishing.

"Thank you," he said. "Harvard Business School. But tell me, how may I help you?"

I dove in. "Partly," I said, "I'm here to help *you*, Mr. Grendle. I believe the Cyrano Trust has a problem."

"Ah?"

"One of its pipelines is threatened."

He watched me with a polite expression that revealed nothing.

"I was hired," I went on, "by a client who wanted me to

206

find a man named Peter Ives, who'd disappeared. As it turned out, he'd been murdered, but my client didn't know that. Looking for leads, I interviewed a couple of Ives's friends and searched his apartment. In the apartment I found an address book. This." I handed the address book to Grendle.

He slowly leafed through the pages.

"At the back is a sort of code," I said, "although to Ives it wasn't so much a code as a way of keeping everything straight. He had a lot to remember."

Frowning, Grendle studied the back pages. If the letters and numerals meant anything to him, it didn't show on his face. "Continue," he said.

"It's those pages that translate into trouble for your trust's pipeline," I told him.

"It's not *my* trust, Mr. Bix."

"The Cyrano Trust's, then. Because what you're looking at is a list of bank accounts. And in the front are the names and addresses of the men who run that particular show and a few people who are in the cast. 'Show' and 'cast' are the right words too, because the people are members of a theater company called the Cholla Players, in Tucson, Arizona. It's subsidized by a businessman named William Chadler. He uses certain of the actors to make cash deposits and withdrawals in a string of little bank accounts. It's a way of getting around the Bank Secrecy Act, with which I guess you're familiar."

Grendle said nothing.

I gave him a rundown of Chadler's money-laundering methods, starting with the operation of the Mountain Mirage. He listened with no show of feeling, until I mentioned Sharpe, who I said was about to go on trial in New York. At that point his right eyelid twitched. The movement was barely noticeable, but I caught it and guessed that the name had registered.

The side door opened again, and the man in the black suit

brought in a silver tray with coffee things on it. He put the tray on the table and backed out.

Grendle got up to do the pouring. "Black or white?"

"Black. No sugar."

He gave me a cup of coffee and poured one for himself.

"Anyway," I said after he sat down, "Ives was one of Chadler's runners. He took orders from Chili Solana, the manager of the Mountain Mirage and Chadler's son-in-law. He was murdered because Solana had sent him, or introduced him, to Sharpe. He ran some errands for Sharpe, and someone must have given his name to the U.S. Attorney in New York, because he was subpoenaed to give a deposition for Sharpe's trial. In other words, what I'm saying is, he was murdered because he could link Sharpe with Chadler, which might lead to an investigation of Chadler. Follow me?"

"Of course. But I don't see how any of this affects my principals."

"Bear with me. I want to play a tape for you." I went over to the table, slid the tape into the player, and turned the player on. When I returned, I noticed that the address book had vanished.

The tape ran for half an hour. I watched Grendle as he listened. If they taught self-control at Harvard's business school, I thought, this guy must have got an A in the course. For all the emotion he showed, he might have been listening to a musician playing the scales. But he didn't tell me to turn the machine off.

When the tape ended, the silence was heavy.

"Whose voice was I listening to?" Grendle asked, at last.

"A friend of Ives's who hung around with the Cholla Players. His name doesn't matter. Does it?"

Grendle gave one shoulder the slightest of shrugs.

"His name is in the address book," I added. "You have the book in your pocket, I believe."

He didn't bat an eyelash. "Would you like it back?"

"Not really," I said. "I have copies. I've spread them around in safe places. Also of the tape."

"No doubt. But you still haven't explained how my principals are affected."

Principals, not bosses. European, I supposed. "A lot of people make fun of U.S. lawmen," I said. "They think the guys who work for the FBI, DEA, IRS, and all those other bureaus and agencies with the initials are a bunch of clowns who are always tripping over their own feet and screwing up. Well, a few *are* like that, but from what I've seen, most aren't. Most have been to college, and some have been to law school or business school besides, and just about all of them have plenty of street smarts and patience and whatever else it takes to catch criminals. And if there's one thing they're better at than anything else, it's in following a trail. They're slow sometimes, but they know how to fit all the little pieces together, one after another, to get a big picture."

"And so?"

"Let me finish. Of all the different kinds of trails there are, the ones they're best at following are money trails. Because with money there's usually a record somewhere. Banks' microfilms, brokers' computer disks, certificates and receipts of one sort or another—you know what I mean. Even something as simple as the notes Ives made in his address book, if they're turned over to a team of government investigators, become important, because they help with the big picture." I took a deep breath, then went on. "When it comes to money laundering, what the investigators are after is not how the money is moved—they pretty much know that—but whose money it is. They want names. And Chadler could give them names. American names, Mexican names, Colombian names, names from all over. So a lot of people the Cyrano Trust pays dividends to could end up with problems."

Grendle gave me a thin smile. "The voice of doom."

I closed my eyes and opened them and felt I was seeing the room for the first time. Chandeliers, paintings, antiques—a handsome room in a handsome house, a house not too different, actually, from Anita Danton's. For Grendle this was probably a combination residence and office. At any rate, it certainly wasn't the world headquarters of the Cyrano Trust. But then, perhaps the trust didn't have a world headquarters. Perhaps it was run from various computer-equipped houses like this one.

"No," I said. "The voice of a man who doesn't want to get killed."

"And you think you will be?"

"Unless someone does something to prevent it, yes."

"So you want magic," Grendle said with another of those thin smiles. "And you seem to think that the Cyrano Trust is an arm of the Mafia or the Syndicate or the Colombian Connection—one of those groups the American press is so fond of pointing to as the cause of America's problems. You don't seem to realize that the Cyrano Trust is an extremely respectable entity that engages in legal transactions and employs lawyers all over the globe to make sure that the transactions *are* legal."

"Yes, I do realize that, Mr. Grendle. But I believe that some of the trust's—what shall I call them? beneficiaries? investors?—are members of the groups you just mentioned. And I believe that if those investors thought that their names might be turned over to the FBI or the Drug Enforcement Agency or, in some cases, their own governments, they'd be willing to do whatever has to be done to keep that from happening. Also they'd be very grateful to whoever tipped them off."

"Bravo. You present an excellent argument."

"Let me add just one thing to it," I said. "It's possible that Sharpe has made a deal with the U.S. Attorney: a lighter sentence in exchange for information about his contacts. If that's true, government investigators already know about Chadler and have started looking into his affairs. Or if they haven't, Chadler may be afraid they're about to. Which is why he was so anxious to shut Ives up. And if Chadler has something to worry about, then so do his clients. Therefore if someone let them know that he's under suspicion and might, under pressure, talk about his dealings with them—

well, I might get some of that what you call magic."

Grendle gazed thoughtfully at the floor. For a long time he didn't speak.

Finally he stood up and said, "Thank you very much, Mr. Bix. It's been nice meeting you."

The move caught me by surprise. "Does that mean you'll help me out?" I asked.

He seemed astonished by the question. "Good Lord! Surely you don't expect me to tell you that. I wouldn't, even if I could—and I can't. All decisions are made by my principals."

"But how will I know?"

"I haven't the slightest idea." He went to the bell pull and gave it two yanks. "I'll have you driven back to your hotel. May I keep the address book and the tape? You say you have copies."

I nodded.

The chauffeur appeared.

Grendle handed me the tape player and my topcoat, and said, "Have a pleasant flight, Mr. Bix."

The chauffeur escorted me down the stairs. He made me put on the dark glasses again before leaving the house.

23

Twisting in the wind, I stayed on in Zurich. I wasn't sure it was a good idea to go home.

Every day I talked to Frank on the telephone. He'd been checking the building where I lived, he said. There was no stakeout, as far as he could tell, but that didn't mean I was in the clear. If those guys in Arizona were really determined, I was still in trouble.

I also called Ramon Aves. He promised to find out what he could. He'd received the body of his son, he reported, and had seen it properly interred. As for the Mountain Mirage, Chili Solana, and William Chadler, there had been nothing about them on television or in the newspapers. He would keep his eyes and ears open, however.

My intuition told me that I'd made the right moves, that it had been smart to work through Bear Mantino and the Cyrano Trust instead of more orthodox channels. The trust, I continued to believe, had closer ties to powerful crime figures than Grendle claimed. People who made you wear glasses you couldn't see through had something to hide.

But alone in my hotel room, or on the snow-covered streets of the city, I admitted to myself that intuition and wishful thinking were often hard to separate.

Something will happen, I thought. Something important. But the days slipped by and nothing did. Thursday, Friday, Saturday, Sunday . . .

Give it a few more days, I thought on Monday morning. Be patient.

But patience was no longer necessary. Something *had* happened. The news jumped at me on Monday afternoon from the counter of the concierge's station, where a dozen copies of the European edition of the *Herald Tribune* were stacked.

The story was in the right-hand column on page one. The headline said: ALLEGED MONEY LAUNDERER SLAIN ON 59TH STREET. And the subhead was: "Frederick Sharpe Shot on Eve of Trial."

What made the story so newsworthy was the sensational manner of the crime. It had been committed in front of Bloomingdale's, on one of the most crowded sidewalks in the world, at one o'clock on a Saturday afternoon in the midst of hundreds of people, and yet the murderer had got away. Sharpe had been walking past the department store on his way home, and someone had fired two bullets into his chest at close range, but not one person had seen or heard anything out of the ordinary. Sharpe had simply collapsed on the sidewalk, and no one realized he'd been shot until blood began to seep through his overcoat. But by then the assailant had escaped into the store or around the corner. Sharpe was pronounced dead on arrival at New York Hospital. It was believed that the assailant had used a small weapon fitted with a silencer, but no one was certain. So far the police had no leads.

I put the newspaper down and went directly to the Swissair office. I was too late for that day's flight, but I was able to get a seat on the one leaving the next day.

Sharpe might have been killed even if I hadn't had my talk with Grendle, I told myself on the way back to the hotel, but that was something I would never know for certain. No doubt some powerful people had been worried about what

Sharpe knew. And often murders that were committed in public like that were intended as warnings: What happened to him could happen to you.

If I were William Chadler, I decided, I'd quit chasing Bix and buy myself a bulletproof vest.

On the day after my return to Chicago I invited Frank for lunch. He was in unusually high spirits. His daughter Maureen had given birth the day before, and everything had gone well. He was enormously relieved. The baby was a boy, to be christened Anthony. Frank and his wife would be leaving for Florida within a week.

I'd asked Frank to find out what he could about Sparrow, and he briefed me. Sparrow's condition had been downgraded from critical to serious, but he would be in the hospital for quite a while.

"How does he stand with the law?" I asked.

"Just traffic violations and illegal possession of firearms," Frank said. "They haven't made up their minds about manslaughter or reckless homicide."

"Does he have a lawyer?"

"Phil doesn't think so." Frank's source of information was Phil Reilly, who had been his partner at one time and was still on the force.

According to Phil, Frank said, Sparrow had had a gun in his pocket when the paramedics examined him. And when the police had fed his name into the computer, the computer had had a lot to say about him. Among the charges he'd faced in the past were assault, assault with a deadly weapon, and attempted murder. Yet he'd never been convicted. The cases had always hinged on the testimony of people who decided at the last minute that they hadn't seen what they'd said they'd seen.

"Mean little prick," Frank mused cheerfully. "Attacked his brother-in-law with a baseball bat. The brother-in-law got away, but Sparrow came back the next day to pick up where he'd left off. Just wouldn't give up."

"What about Horton?" I asked.

"Not clean, either," Frank replied. "Jumped bail back in Ohio. Still wanted there." He paused. "Nobody can figure the accident out, seems like. Too many conflicting stories. Unless you or me clears it up, nobody's gonna know what really happened. And it's too late now for us to do that."

"The accident isn't what they ought to investigate," I said. "What they ought to investigate is the murder of Peter Ives. I tipped off the two detectives, Acer and Rolfe. But maybe what I gave them isn't enough to build a case on."

"So what's the answer?"

"The answer is, the murder of Peter Ives is liable to go unsolved."

"And those guys out in Arizona who you say ordered it?"

I smiled. "That's another story. They, I think, are in big trouble. How about some dessert?"

Frank accepted the suggestion, and as we finished our meal he told me at length about how much Christmas was going to cost him. His wife was buying presents not only for all the children and grandchildren but also for a growing number of grandnieces and nephews and even for people like the old man who lived in the condo next to theirs in Florida.

"That's why," he concluded with a show of embarrassment, "I got to charge you for all the telephone time I've been putting in. Otherwise I wouldn't."

After lunch I went out to do my own Christmas shopping. I hesitated over whether to buy a computer for Eddie, but in the end I bought one. The salesman said it would be of great help to a student. I also bought some software the salesman recommended.

That night I called Ramon Aves again. He had nothing new to report. He and his wife were very much on the alert, though, he assured me, and his wife had made a useful contact—a woman who lived on Eagle Drive and knew the Solanas. So far the woman hadn't been able to supply any information other than the fact that Chili's given names were Charles Lincoln, but Aves believed that sooner or later she would.

It was hard to stop thinking about the Danton case, I found. The man Anita Danton had wanted me to locate was dead and buried. So was she. And a fellow named Sharpe, who was the real cause of her trouble, had been gunned down on a New York sidewalk. There was no reason for me to go on reliving my experiences with the case, but I did—partly because I had no other cases to work on. I'd entered the longest dry spell of my career. I checked with my answering service three times a day, but no lawyers or prospective clients left messages. So I had a lot of time to sit around and brood over the recent past.

I did see quite a bit of Laura, though. Our getting together again was the best thing to come out of the Danton case, it seemed to me. I honest to God liked the woman. How much future there was for us, I didn't know. The fact that she was six or seven years older than I might someday become a problem. So might our careers, which didn't really go together. But we were great in bed, and for the first time in longer than I liked to admit, there was someone I always looked forward to being with.

So I drifted through the last days before Christmas, restless but not unhappy. Then on Christmas Eve, Ramon Aves called. Chili Solana's wife had put their house up for sale, he told me. That very morning a realtor's sign had appeared on the front lawn.

"Christmas Eve is a funny time for something like that," I said. "Know the reason?"

"She's in a hurry," Aves replied. "Her husband's been gone for over a week."

"Gone?"

"That's what my wife's friend said. I don't know where."

He filled in the missing piece a few days later. Chili Solana was in Brazil. According to his wife, he'd had a business offer there that was too good to pass up. She was anxious to join him in Rio with the children as soon as possible.

But by then the Solana move no longer seemed so important. Something more significant had happened. William Chadler had died. A private plane he'd hired to fly him from Tucson to Mexico City had exploded and crashed shortly after takeoff, killing the two people on board, Chadler and the pilot.

That week I got two new jobs, the first I'd had since my return from Switzerland. The pace of my life picked up, and the Danton case drifted to the back of my mind. I'd done my best. Drugs would continue to flow into Arizona, and drug money would continue to change hands there—if not at the Mountain Mirage, then somewhere else. But perhaps I'd made the process a little harder. And perhaps the men with badges who investigated the deaths of Sharpe and Chadler would make it harder yet.

As for Charles Lincoln Solana, with his nice smile and all that magnetism—he'd got off easier than he deserved, in my opinion. But it's an imperfect world, and the bad guys don't always lose. I'd learned that as a kid.

The one question that was still open got answered the last day of January, when I heard from Phil Reilly, Frank's ex-partner. As a favor to Frank, he said, he'd been keeping abreast of the accident case involving Simon Smith. Frank had asked him to let me know of any new developments, and there had been one. The legal angle had been settled. Smith was going to be charged with illegal possession of firearms and reckless driving, but with nothing else.

"What'll he get?" I asked.

"A fine," Reilly speculated. "Suspension of his driver's license. Maybe both. Nothing heavy."

"Despite the fact that a man got killed?" I felt anger rising. "Despite his record?"

"He's never been convicted of anything," Reilly reminded me. "And what I heard is, one of the witnesses who saw the crash said it looked to her like the driver of the camper was trying to defend himself, that the fat man was trying to climb into the vehicle to attack him. Add to that our jails being overcrowded and the courts being backed up, and you can understand."

I thought about how differently things might have turned out if Frank and I had told what we knew. "What about the murder of Peter Ives?" I said. "He won't be charged with that?"

"Ballistics showed the gun found on Smith at the accident scene wasn't the one that killed Ives. And the two people who'd seen Smith said they weren't sure from the pictures that he was the man. Too much time had gone by, I suppose."

"Where is he now?"

"Still in the hospital."

"So he gets out of the hospital, appears at a hearing, is released on bond and skips town, and nobody gives a damn, because the charges aren't serious."

Reilly didn't disagree.

"The guy is a murderer," I said. "As mean and determined as they come."

"So what do you want from me?" Reilly's tone was like a shrug.

I sighed. "Nothing. You've gone out of your way. I'm grateful."

Reilly said he would let me know if anything changed, but I didn't believe it would. The little man with the lisp had got away with murder. It was as simple as that.

But something did change. A week later I received a telephone call from Jill Cranmer.

"I'll bet you never expected to hear from me again," she said.

I thought about the microphone I'd hidden in her living room and wondered whether she'd found it. "I never count my chickens," I said.

The microphone wasn't the problem, however. "I need a favor," Jill said, "and I'd like to talk to you about it."

"What kind of favor?" I asked.

"I need some money. I want to move to Brazil with Andy. I'll tell you the story when I see you."

I smiled. "Well, now." I was tempted to say yes on the spot. The idea of her dropping in on Solana in his new haven appealed to my sense of justice. The man deserved at least that much aggravation.

"It's not as if I won't do anything for you in return," Jill went on. "I'll do you a favor too."

"Oh? And what might that be?"

"I know who killed Peter, and I know where he is. He's been in the hospital, but he's out now and he's planning to kill you. I'll tell you where you can find him."

24

Nearly three months had passed since I'd been to the drab yellow brick building where I'd begun my search for Peter Ives, but little had changed. The decals on the glass front of the vestibule still stated DELIVER ALL GOODS IN REAR and NO PETS. The tailor's business card was still stuck to the wall above the mailboxes. The only difference I could see was that apartment 2-C, which had been occupied by Ives, now had a tenant named Rosehill.

The gun felt heavy in my pocket. I hadn't carried it in years and didn't like having it with me now. Guns were for robbery-in-progress situations, not for visiting unwed mothers and their babies.

Jill had sounded strange, though. Too eager. Too anxious. I could understand her need for money; her source of income had run off to Rio. And I could understand her willingness to sell me Sparrow; he meant nothing to her. But the tremor in her voice had made me wonder.

"Please, Cal," she'd said at the end, "I need the money *now*. Today. And I'm doing you a favor. You're in *danger.*"

Acting was her hobby, I'd reminded myself. The tremor might be for effect. Nevertheless I'd decided to take the gun.

I pushed the button marked "Cranmer."

"Who is it?" Jill asked through the speaking tube.

"Bix," I said.

The buzzer sounded. I went from the vestibule into the lobby and rode the automatic elevator to the second floor.

Outside Jill's apartment I paused to listen. The apartment was silent. No television sounds, no crying baby, nothing.

Too silent?

I took the gun from my pocket.

Jill must have been standing right at the door, for she opened it as soon as I knocked. A Jill I hardly recognized. She was wearing the white terry-cloth robe she'd been wearing the first time I saw her, and her face was whiter than the terry cloth. Her hair was disarranged too, and her eyes were wide with terror.

Clutching herself, she said, pleadingly, in a very low voice, "Cal, help me."

I glanced over her shoulder. There was no one else in the living room. Still holding the gun, I closed the door behind me. "What's wrong?" I asked.

"He's here," she said in the same low voice. "I couldn't warn you."

"Warn me?"

Before Jill could answer, Sparrow came through the doorway from the bedroom. He was holding Andy in the crook of his left arm and a knife in his right hand. A handkerchief was stuffed into the baby's mouth. The knife was less than an inch from the tiny throat.

Smiling as if he was glad to see me, Sparrow said, "Mither Bickth."

Red-faced, the baby squirmed and kicked. Sparrow tightened his grip.

Christ, I thought. Jesus bloody Christ.

"Give me hith gun," Sparrow said to Jill.

She reached out as if to take the child. Sparrow brought the knife blade a fraction of an inch closer to the baby's skin.

"Don't hurt him," she said in a faint voice. "Please."

"Hith gun," Sparrow repeated, no longer smiling.

Jill turned back to me. Her lips were parted, and there was even more fear in her eyes than before.

I handed her the gun. I felt a tremendous regret. There were so many steps I could have taken to avoid walking into a trap, yet all I'd done was arm myself with a weapon that could be used against me.

"Bring it here," Sparrow directed.

Jill just stood there, the gun in her hand, as if unaware that she was holding it.

"Here," Sparrow said.

Andy gave a violent kick. The blade of the knife touched his skin. A bright red line appeared across his throat. Jill gasped.

I willed her to shoot Sparrow, for at that moment she could have done so. He was no more than ten feet away. If she'd aimed at his forehead and fired quickly, he would have fallen and died without seriously injuring the baby. But she didn't do it. I doubted that she even was aware of the possibility.

Like a zombie, she went to Sparrow and held out the gun.

He took it and let the knife fall to the floor. I wondered why he hadn't a gun of his own. Then I realized that the police would have impounded the one he'd had.

Again Jill reached for her child. "He's bleeding," she said in a pebbly little voice.

Sparrow put the muzzle of the gun to the baby's temple. "Thtep back," he said to Jill. "Thtep back or I'll thoot him."

"But he's bleeding."

"Move!"

The sharpness of Sparrow's tone brought Jill out of her trance. "No," she said. "Please."

"Put the baby down," I said to him. "You have the gun."

He paid no attention, however. He merely smiled and said, "Mithter Bickth."

Andy kicked and twisted, as if he knew his life was threatened. Sparrow almost dropped him. Jill reached out.

Sparrow stepped away from her.

The baby wasn't cut badly, I saw. But I was afraid that he would choke. "For God's sake, take that rag out of the kid's mouth," I said.

"Mithter Bickth," Sparrow replied. "My friend Mither Bickth. Itth nithe to meet you."

A sick, sadistic pervert, I thought. A walking plague. "The pleasure's mine," I said. "I've heard so much about you."

He wasn't sure how to take that. His face darkened. It wasn't an ugly face. The features were even, the skin clear, the eyes blue. But the thoughts that churned behind the blue eyes were black. And while the face might not be ugly, the intentions were.

"Take off your belt," he snapped at Jill.

The words didn't penetrate at first. "My . . . ?"

"The belt, you bitth. From your robe."

She glanced at her waist. The robe had a matching terry-cloth belt. She touched the knot.

"Take it off," Sparrow said, "and tie hith writhth."

My insides clenched. I kept fear out of my voice, though. "You're in trouble," I said to Sparrow, expressing the first thought that came to mind. "Chili Solana's in Brazil. Chadler's dead. You have no place to go."

His face darkened again.

"The Mountain Mirage is crawling with federal agents," I went on, mixing what I knew with what I didn't. "Chili barely got away in time, and Chadler was killed in a plane crash, trying to get to Mexico. I'm not lying. Ask Jill. Ask anyone. There'll be no one to help you."

"Tie hith writhth," he said.

"Tell him," I said to Jill with mounting desperation. "Tell him how things are."

She unfastened the belt and pulled it through the loops. The robe fell open. She came toward me.

"He won't let you get away," I said to her. "You're a witness. You're dangerous to him."

She took one of my arms. I pulled it away from her.

"You'll be next," I said with mounting desperation.

Sparrow raised his voice. "Tie them!"

He too was beginning to fray, I thought. If I could stall long enough, he might come apart.

Jill wrapped the belt around my wrist and reached for the other arm. I pushed her aside.

Sparrow lost his temper and fired the gun.

Jill screamed, dropped the belt, and rushed toward her child.

But the child was safe. Sparrow had fired into the floor.

The smile returned to his lips. "Tie the writhth behind him," he said.

Jill picked up the belt, moved in behind me, and under Sparrow's supervision bound my wrists together at the base of my spine.

"Now take *hith* belt," Sparrow directed.

Jill began to fumble with the buttons of my topcoat. Soon she had my topcoat and jacket unbuttoned and was working at my belt. And presently the belt was cinched tightly around my ankles.

Trussed, I watched Sparrow hold the baby out to Jill.

"Here," he said. "Take him, and come with me."

She held out her arms, and he gave her the child. The gun in his right hand, he gripped her arm firmly in his left and led her through the doorway to the bedroom. She went obediently.

I tried to recall what Frank had told me of Sparrow's injuries. Fractured skull? What else? Ruptured spleen? Yes, ruptured spleen and other abdominal traumas.

But I couldn't use my hands or my feet.

Moments later a frightened Jill cried, "No! Please! Not the closet! I'm afraid!"

I couldn't see what was happening, but I heard a thud, as if a body struck a wall.

"Ow!" Jill groaned. "Please! It's dark! I'm afraid! Ow! No!"

There was another thud. Then a door slammed. Muffled cries followed.

Sparrow returned to the living room. He still had the gun in his hand, but he put it in a pocket of his jacket and eyed me with obvious pleasure.

"Nithe," he said. "Very nithe."

I forced myself to smile back at him. The world had shrunk to just the two of us. His intentions were all that mattered. I searched his eyes for a clue to them, but could only see satisfaction. All those weeks in the hospital, in pain and raging within himself, he'd been planning this encounter, and at last it had come about. Bix, the cause of all his troubles, was bound hand and foot, at his mercy.

Without warning he aimed a vicious kick at my left leg. Pain momentarily drove all thoughts from my mind.

"Hurt?" Sparrow inquired.

I clenched my teeth.

He kicked the other leg just as hard. "Hurt?"

"Yes," I said.

"Good."

He drew his leg back like a placekicker. I braced myself for more pain. But the kick didn't come. Grinning, Sparrow said, "Mither Bickth. Want to play thoccer?"

"No," I said.

He shook his head. "Me neither. I want to wrap you up inthtead."

I began to feel a terrible fear. It started somewhere in my chest and radiated out from there.

"Wrap you up like a package," Sparrow said.

Jill was pounding on the closet door. Her future was no brighter than mine, I supposed, but I put her out of my mind. Andy too. With all my being I concentrated on the deadly little man in front of me. The hospital's identification bracelet was still on his wrist, I noted, and his hair was cut very short, like that of someone who had recently had brain surgery. But the scar wasn't visible from the front, and his other scars, whatever they were, weren't visible either. He was pale, though, and I guessed that he hadn't entirely healed.

Unexpectedly, he began to hum. He seemed quite happy. And from the pocket of his jacket he took a small square of clear plastic and a neatly rolled length of string. At first I didn't know what the plastic square was, but then he unfolded it and I experienced a shock of pure horror. What he had in his hand was a transparent plastic bag. The bag was large enough to hold a shirt or sweater, but was empty.

He dangled it before my eyes. "Nithe, huh?"

I was unable to speak.

"Letth try it on," he said. "See how it fitth your head."

I twisted my shoulders left and right. Now I knew what he'd planned, lying there in his hospital bed. For hours at a time he'd enjoyed the vision of me suffocating. He'd imagined my face turning purple as I gasped for breath. Eventually I would lose consciousness, but it would take minutes. Minutes that to me would seem like hours. The last minutes of my life.

Continuing to hum, he put his hand inside the bag to open it. Then he reached up to drop it over my head.

With a violence born of the wildest fear I'd ever known, I jumped in place, bringing my knees up as high as I could. I didn't think, didn't aim, didn't know where the spleen was. I just jumped.

My knees caught Sparrow in the lower abdomen.

"Aich!" he said, doubling up. He dropped the string, but managed to hold on to the bag.

I jumped again, and this time I aimed. My knees hit the same place.

Sparrow's mouth opened, and his face turned chalky. He looked up at me and slid toward the floor at the same time. I stooped and brought my forehead down across the bridge of his nose as hard as possible. I heard the bone crack.

He slumped against me. I jumped sideways and let him fall. He fell on his face. I waited a moment, then took a deep breath and jumped on his neck.

*   *   *

I was unable to turn the doorknob with my teeth. After repeated tries I gave up and began to shout for help.

It was a long time before anyone came. Finally a woman's voice asked, timidly, through the closed door, "Is anything wrong in there?"

"Call the police," I replied. "It's an emergency. Call the police."

The police didn't show up right away, either, and when they did come, it took them a while to enter the apartment. They kept telling me to open the door from the inside, and I kept answering that I couldn't.

"If you don't open the door," one policeman shouted angrily, "we'll break it down."

And in the end that was what they did.

Jill was conscious, but in a state of shock. The baby, despite the cut on his throat, was in better shape than she was.

Sparrow, of course, was dead. He'd died with the plastic bag still in his hand and, I was sure, with murder still on his mind.

25

Jill and Andy left the day after the inquest. I drove them to the airport.

The inquest caused a stir, which pleased my lawyer. The publicity would be good for both of us, he confided to me in an unguarded moment. But he quickly added, "although neither of us needs it."

What the media emphasized were the way in which I'd killed Sparrow and the address at which I'd done it. They were able to say that I stomped him to death, and to remind the public that I'd appeared on television months before in front of the very building in which his death had occurred. By linking my killing of Sparrow with my investigation into the shooting of Peter Ives, reporters were able to create an image of me that was false but that the public seemed to like: I was fierce and I had bulldog determination. They chose to ignore the realities that I'd been off the Ives case since before Christmas and that I'd almost been killed myself. A Rambo was what the media wanted, so that's what they made me into.

According to my lawyer, the outcome of the inquest was a foregone conclusion. Justifiable homicide. But he caused me a fair amount of anxiety by throwing in, "Still, Cal, you did, actually, commit a murder."

"In self-defense," I protested.

"Nevertheless . . ."

Jill was the principal witness and she was a good one. In a quavering voice she told how Sparrow had come to her apartment asking for help and then threatened her and her baby with a knife. Tears came to her eyes as she related how he'd forced her to telephone me and had then described to her how he was planning to watch me suffocate. She sobbed as she gave an account of tying my wrists and ankles and of being locked in the closet. The Cholla Players would have been proud of her.

In the interval between Sparrow's death and the inquest, she and I developed a friendship of sorts. I found that I liked her. She would never be a great role model for growing girls, I thought, and would always be able to deceive herself on demand; but she did love her child and would be a reasonably good mother, and I doubted that she would ever again get involved with anyone as bad as Chili Solana.

I had a hard time talking her out of going to Brazil, but in the end I succeeded. She agreed to settle for Seattle instead. Seattle was where she'd grown up, and she had cousins there. I bought her a plane ticket and gave her enough money to see her through the first couple of months. The money, I said, should be considered a gift from Anita Danton, which in a way it was—I'd received the check from Gordon Lockhart on the first of February.

It was when I handed her the envelope with the money that I told her about the microphone I'd hidden in her living room. She was amazed and embarrassed.

"Did I say anything awful?" she asked when I told her about recording her conversation with Chili.

"No," I said, "but afterwards you cried."

She watched me detach the microphone from the back of the picture and put it in my pocket. Finally she said, "I still cry sometimes."

I didn't expect her to mention the matter again, but on the day I drove her to the airport she did. It was midafternoon, and a light snow was falling. We'd gone most of the way in silence. The back seat of my car was filled with those pieces of luggage that wouldn't fit into the trunk. Andy, unaware that the Chicago phase of his life was about to end, was sound asleep on his mother's lap.

"You know," Jill said unexpectedly, "that day when I said I still cry sometimes—well, it isn't just because of how things turned out with me and Chili. I guess I always expected that, in a way. It's because I'm afraid it's never going to be any different—that I'll always end up with the sort of man who's dangerous. Do you think I will?"

I kept my eyes on the road, because the pavement, like life itself, was slippery. "Maybe," I said. "In my line of work you run across an awful lot of people who've made mistakes. But somehow, for most of them, things get straightened out after a while."

"What you're saying is, silver linings," Jill replied. "Well, I don't believe in them." She looked at me. "Do you?"

I thought of Anita Danton. Then I thought of Allen Mantino. "Sometimes," I said. "The chances are about fifty-fifty."